Please return or renew by the last date stamped below.

www.shetland-library.gov.uk   Tel: 01595 743868

Also by the author

ICONS

IDOLS

MARGARET STOHL

HARPER
Voyager

HarperVoyager
An imprint of HarperCollins*Publishers*
77–85 Fulham Palace Road,
Hammersmith, London W6 8JB

www.harpercollins.co.uk

A Paperback Original 2014
1

Copyright © Margaret Stohl 2014

Design by Andrea Vandergrift

Margaret Stohl asserts the moral right to
be identified as the author of this work

A catalogue record for this book
is available from the British Library

ISBN: 978 0 00 752085 5

Printed and bound in Great Britain by
Clays Ltd, St Ives plc

MIX
Paper from
responsible sources
FSC C007454

Find out more about HarperCollins and the environment at
www.harpercollins.co.uk/green

For my friends in Chang Mai,
Chang Rai, Bangkok, Hong Kong,
Kuala Lumpur, and Singapore—
and for their stories.
Khorb kun ka. Xie xie. Terima kasih.

PARCE METU.
CEASE FROM FEAR.

—Virgil, *The Aeneid*

THIRTEEN GREAT ICONS

FELL FROM THE SKY,

WHEN THEY CAME ALIVE,

SIX CITIES DIED.

REMEMBER 6/6.

THE PROJECTS ARE SLAVERY.

WE ARE NOT FREE.

SILENCE IS NOT PEACE.

REMEMBER THE DAY.

DEATH TO THE SYMPAS,

DEATH TO THE LORDS.

DESTROY THE ICONS.

REMEMBER.

—Grass Daily Recitation
Rebellion Recruitment & Indoctrination Materials

PICK A GOD AND PRAY

I want to close my eyes but I don't.

I refuse. I won't let darkness be the last thing I see.

So I watch while my world spins out of control. Literally. While our tail twists and our alarms scream and our lights flash and the impossibly loud roar of our failing rotors fills my heart with terror.

Not now, I think. *Please.*

Not like this.

We have twelve more Icons to destroy. I never bound with Lucas—and Ro's never forgiven me for kissing him. I'm not finished.

But with every turn, the rocky desert floor beneath us lurches closer. And out the window, all I see is a dark kaleidoscope of stars, ground, moon—in a whirling, chaotic blur.

A cloud of smoke chokes my lungs. I grasp Tima

with one hand, clutching my gear to my chest with the other. The outline of the Icon shard in my pack is unmistakable as its sharp edges push against my ribs. I always know it's there—along with the power it once seemed to give me, back in the Hole. Even now, I couldn't forget it if I tried.

It doesn't matter, I tell myself. *Not anymore.*

Nothing does.

The Chopper drops again, and in the front seats, Ro and Fortis almost hit the glass window. Wedged as I am behind them—between Lucas and Tima—my head slams into the back of Ro's seat.

"Bloody hell!" growls Fortis.

I feel Lucas's fingers on my shoulder and his fear in my chest. Brutus barks wildly, as if he could attack our fate and chase the end away—when in reality he's scrabbling just to stay put in Tima's lap.

Stupid dog. Stupid fate.

Stupid, stupid Chopper.

"Hold on, mates, this may be a bit of a rough landing!" Fortis calls over his shoulder, with the sudden flash of a grim smile.

"I thought you said you could fly this thing!" Ro screams at Fortis, and I feel the clash of panic and anger coming off him in powerful waves.

"You want to take a crack at it?" Fortis shouts, too busy fighting the controls to look up.

"Dol." Lucas finds my hand and tightens his grip on me, lacing his fingers through mine. He radiates little of his natural warmth tonight, but I know it's there.

The tiniest of sparks, even now.

We're together, I think. *Lucas and me. Ro. All of us. It's something.*

Grassgirl, Hothead, Buttons, Freak.

The night we fell out of the sky, at least we were together. At least we had that.

The moonlit landscape of wind-sculpted rock and canyons whips around us, and I wonder if this is the end. I wonder who will find us.

If anyone.

Our seats are shaking violently now. Even the windows are rattling. Tima tightens her grip on me, closing her eyes. Her fear hits me with such force that her touch almost burns.

As she touches me, a new idea claws itself into my mind.

"Tima, we need you—" I search for the memory of her at the Icon, how she used her fear to shield Lucas from the explosion.

I reach out to her.

Try. Just try.

Tima's eyes flash open. She stares at her blood tattoo, the colorful streaks and patterns on her arm. She grips Brutus tight.

Tighter.

I hope she can do it. We're going down fast.

"It's no use. You can't fly a bird with broken wings," Fortis shouts. "Hold on, children—pick a god an'—"

Pray.

Pray, I think as we slam into the canyon wall.

I'm praying, I think as I listen to the violent clash of metal and rock.

Chumash Rancheros Spaniards Californians Americans Grass The Lords The Hole. Chumash Rancheros Spaniards Californians Americans Grass The Lords The Hole. Chumash Rancheros Spaniards Californians Americans Grass The Lords The Hole—

I recite it in my mind, the only prayer the Padre really taught me.

I pray as I feel the streaming heat of spreading flames.

I pray as I close my eyes to a flash so bright it burns through my eyelids, thin as onion skin, as paper.

I pray as I fall into the silence.

Pick a god—

I don't know a god. Just a girl.

So I squeeze her hand as the Chopper hits the ground in a ball of fire.

GENERAL EMBASSY DISPATCH: EASTASIA SUBSTATION

MARKED URGENT
MARKED EYES ONLY

Internal Investigative Subcommittee 115211B
RE: The Incident at SEA Colonies

Sirs:

I have, after great expense and effort, located and infiltrated the secure archives of Paulo Fortissimo. I believe their relevance to the disastrous recent situation in the Colonies will be instructive, or, at least, illuminating. It is to this effect that I offer my services, in the name of our dear mutual friend, the good Dr. Yang.

Now commencing decryption of files. Will immediately send all relevant materials as they are unpacked and decoded, in chronological order.

Following, you will find transcripts, beginning with initial contact with Lords (done via AI/virtual), research notes, personal journal entries, etc.

We can discuss compensation in due time. Recommend destroying all files immediately after review, Physical Humans being as swayed by emotion as they are. The final decision is, of course, at your discretion.

Yours,
Jasmine3k
Virt. Hybrid Human 39261.SEA
Laboratory Assistant to Dr. E. Yang

1

WRECKED

I am lying facedown in the dirt. I taste it. Dirt and blood and teeth as loose as old corn. Every bone in my body aches, but I am alive. Death would hurt less.

I feel hands rolling me over, pressing against my arms, my legs. "No, don't move her. She's in shock." *Fortis.*

A blur of dirty blond hair comes into view in the darkness, and I feel the familiar warmth surge into my cheeks as a hand touches my face. "Dol? Can you hear me?"

Lucas. I move my lips, trying to make a word. At the moment, I think, it's harder than I remember. "Tima—" I finally croak.

He smiles down at me. "Tima's fine. She's still out, but she'll be fine."

I roll my head to the side and I see her lying in the dirt

7

next to me. Tima, her scrawny dog, cactuses, and stars. Not much else.

Brutus whimpers, licking Tima's tattooed arm, which looks like it's bleeding.

"Fine? You don't know that," says a voice in the night. *Ro.* I see that he's just on the other side of Lucas, tossing dead tumbleweeds onto a makeshift fire. Ro doesn't feel just warm—not to me. He's smoldering. I could feel him anywhere.

Lucas rubs my hands between his. "I do know that, actually." He looks over his shoulder. "Because if Tima wasn't okay, we'd all be dead right now. Who do you think broke our fall?"

Tima. It must have worked. She must have done it.

I remember now the bright blue light expanding outward from Tima just as we hit. The muted, violent shock as we landed, the heat of the exploding Chopper—then nothing.

I sit up, weakly. I don't know how we got here, but we're clear of the wreckage, which is still burning black smoke in the distance. I can smell it from here.

I cough it out of my mouth.

Lucas pulls me up until I am leaning against the side of a rock. Ro is there a second later, forcing a canteen to my lips. The cold water chokes my throat as it goes down.

I can't take my eyes off the burning Chopper. The

burning metal carcass that was our only chance to escape the Sympas and get to safety is going up in flames, like everything else. Then—

POPPOPPOPPOP

A string of rapid noises catches me off guard. It sounds like gunfire, but it can't be. Not out here. "What was that?"

Fortis sighs from the darkness nearby. "Fireworks, love. That's our live ammo, burning up with the bird." He disappears toward the fire.

POPPOPPOPPOP

There it all goes, I think. Our dreams of living another day, popping like bubbles. Like a pan of hot corn set in Bigger's fire.

POPPOPPOP

Gone, gone, gone, I think. Our chances of success in our impossible mission to rid the world of twelve more Icons.

POPPOP

Our shot at making it to the next Icon—let alone coming up with a plan of destroying it.

POP

I try not to think anymore. It's all too bleak. I only watch. The flames would be higher than a tree—if there were any trees around here. But all I see in the firelight, aside from the five of us, is a flickering blanket of desert floor that rises and falls into a sheet of continuous cliffs and rocks and mountains. An uneven expanse of unkempt scrub and shale.

Nothing like life—as if we've landed in the Earth's own graveyard.

I shiver as Fortis returns from the glowing wreckage, dragging two charred backpacks with him. His ripped jacket flaps and drags behind him, like some kind of maimed animal.

"Where are we?" I ask.

Ro flops down next to me. "Don't know. Don't care. Doc?"

Lucas sighs. "Offline. Still. Ever since we took off."

"What do we have?" Ro calls out, and Fortis shakes his head, dumping the packs next to us.

"Not much that didn't burn in the fire. A piss pot an' a pea pod. No real rations. Less water. I'd say we have enough to last two days, three tops." Fortis taps on his cuff, but all I hear is a flash of static.

Lucas tosses a branch into the fire. "All right, then. A couple days. There has to be something around here. Someone, anyway."

"Who knows if we even have that long?" I look up at him. "We barely escaped the ambush at Nellis—and now this? The Sympas will have us back in the Pen before we have the luxury of starving to death."

"Maybe there's a Grass camp nearby?" Ro says it, but we're all thinking the same thing.

There isn't.

There's nothing out here. We knew that when we left Nellis Base—when the Sympas attacked and we didn't care where we ended up. But we should have, because now here we are.

Stuck.

Ro tries again. "We can't just sit here waiting to die. Not after what we did to the Icon in the Hole. We gave those people a chance—we gave ourselves a chance. If we don't take it, who will? What then?"

We all know the answer to that. *The Lords will destroy our people while the Sympas laugh.*

Ro turns to Fortis. "There has to be a way out of here. A Merk outpost? Geo station? Anything?" Ro is relentless. Inspiring, almost.

And absolutely crazy.

"There's your fightin' spirit," Fortis says, clapping him on the back. "An' here's my fightin' spirits." He pulls out his flask, slumping down to the desert floor next to me. *And that's his real answer,* I think.

"Ro's right. We can't give up." I look at him. "Not now. Not after everything."

Not after the Embassy. The Hole. The Icon. The Desert. Nellis.

Fortis pats my leg, and I wince. "Give up, Grassgirl? We're only just gettin' started. Don't send me off to an early grave yet, love. I'm too young and too pretty to die."

The fire throws shadows on his face, hiding his eyes, grossly exaggerating his stubbled, bone-tight features. At this particular moment, he looks like some kind of evil puppet from a child's nightmare.

Barely human.

"You know, you're not all that pretty," I say, my throat still full of dust.

He laughs, more like a bark, pocketing his flask. "That's what my mum said." As he draws his arm around me I can only shiver.

Then Tima groans awake, clutching her arm, and I forget about everything but staying and being alive.

GENERAL EMBASSY DISPATCH: EASTASIA SUBSTATION

MARKED URGENT
MARKED EYES ONLY

Internal Investigative Subcommittee 115211B
RE: The Incident at SEA Colonies

As promised.

Below are excerpted records of communication between Fortissimo ("FORTIS") and his AI (HAL2040—the early iteration of the somewhat rudimentary Virtual Human we know as "Doc"). These are initial attempts by Fortissimo and his AI to contact the foreign object first thought to be an asteroid, and thus labeled Perses, proving early awareness of potential threat.

Note: Fortissimo's use of "hello world" (in this case, done in multiple languages) is an ancient programming trope. Displaying the phrase "hello world" indicates success in getting a new machine to connect to its network, to communicate, or show some intelligence. By human standards. (Note: Physical Humans, that is. Virtual Human standards are by nature much higher.)

Yours,
Jasmine3k
Virt. Hybrid Human 39261.SEA
Laboratory Assistant to Dr. E. Yang

HAL2040 ==> FORTIS
Transcript - ComLog 04.13.2042
HAL::PERSES

//lognote: {PERSES communication attempt #413};

sendfile: ascii.tab;
sendfile: dict.glob.lang;

//lognote: as before, sending files with dictionaries/text
protocols;

sendline: hello world;
return: . . . . . . no response;

sendline: 01101000 01100101 01101100 01101100 01101111
0100000 01110111 01101111 01110010 01101100 01100100;
return: . . . . . no response;

sendline: 48:65:6c:6c:6f:20:57:6f:72:6c:64;
return: . . . . . . no response;

sendline: an ki lu sal an ki lu sal an ki lu sal an ki lu sal;
return: . . . . . . no response;

//lognote: communication attempts in English, binary, hex,
ancient languages find PERSES unresponsive.;

2

OUT OF RANGE

Sleep only brings nightmares. When I wake up, I return to consciousness as suddenly and as restlessly as I left it.

Sitting up, I want to run, gasping for air in the cold. My heart pounds and every beat is a question.

Where am I? Are we safe? Are we still free?

I fall back on my side, staring into the growing shadows of the wild desert brush in front of me.

No Sympas. No ships. No Lords. Nothing I haven't seen for the last week now.

I study the landscape like a clock as I try to catch my breath. The long shadows mean it's nearly dark, which means it's time to get up and move. The terrain has grown increasingly strange, alien almost, as we've crawled from rock to rock in the darkness. Anything to

15

avoid the Sympas combing the desert, looking for us.

We sleep in the day and travel in the night now, ever since our Chopper went down.

At least we have established contact with Doc through the comlink cuffs—thanks to the com relay Fortis was able to salvage from the crashed Chopper. Doc keeps us away from patrols and, we hope, moving toward somewhere safe. He's been tracking Sympa deployments since our Chopper went down; they're looking for us—everywhere—but they haven't found us yet.

They. The Embassies. The Lords. It almost doesn't matter which, not anymore. They'll find us, whoever they are in the end.

It's only a matter of time.

The longer we wander in the desert—exposed to the elements and targeted by the Embassy—the stronger the grip despair has on me.

Despair from the bleak truth that, back in the Hole that once was Los Angeles, even without the Icon, the Embassy reportedly still has all the power, and the weapons.

The bleak truth that, according to what we learned during our too-brief stay in Nellis, Catallus has come down with a fury on the people of the city, and the Projects run uninterrupted.

I look up to where Lucas sits across from me, huddling in only his shirtsleeves on the red rocky ledge. It takes me a moment to realize that Lucas has laid his torn Embassy jacket over me, along with his blanket.

He smiles, almost shyly, and I soften, seeing the cold purple-blue of his mouth.

I don't know why I can't just say what I think—that I'm grateful, that he's thoughtful. That when I see his mouth I want to kiss it, kiss him, but since we are never alone, I don't dare.

My empty stomach growls as I turn to see who else is there, just in case I'm wrong. I'm not; Fortis snores on one side of me, under a pile of brush that can't camouflage his woolen, red-toed socks pointing to the sky like two knit rabbit ears. Tima is passed out on the other side of him, covered in dust and almost completely hidden in a neat zigzag of folded arms and legs, like some kind of compact military gear. Brutus is nestled in the crook of her knees, himself snoring so loudly you would think he was Fortis's son more than Tima's dog. Ro, as usual, is nowhere to be seen, but he doesn't like to sleep near any of us, not since we left the Mission.

He won't get that close to Lucas.

To me.

Things will get easier for all of us, Fortis says, when we find a way to get where we're going.

The Idylls, Fortis called it. "I've found it, with Doc's help. A Grass base. The only camp out here."

I was confused when he first said it. "Idylls? Why do they call it that?"

"Because it's paradise, love. Where the Icons can't hurt us and the Lords can't fly."

"You mean somewhere over a rainbow? Like the old stories say?"

"I mean somewhere under a mountain. Like the old combat manuals say."

But I still don't understand how we're supposed to find some Grass Rebellion base even the Embassies can't. And I have a difficult time believing there even is someplace safe. Someplace where we can plan our battle against the House of Lords.

But none of us has a better plan. Or better rations. Or enough water. Or another way out of here.

So, like the good soldiers we are quickly becoming, under the mountain we go.

"Dol?"

I jump as Lucas touches my shoulder, startling me out of my reverie of mountains and soldiers. He wags his head in the direction of the nearby hill. His hair falls lank in his face, curling against his jawline. "Come on, Dol. I have something for you."

Looking at his overgrown hair makes me realize how long it has been since any of us has done anything as normal as getting a haircut. Not to mention the bloody gash on his forehead that snakes above his eyes like a second brow, his trophy from our crash—same as my bruised face, Tima's swollen ankle, or Ro's busted rib.

And all of our empty, aching bellies.

Still, even this messed up, he's breathtakingly beautiful, Lucas Amare.

"Something for me?" I'm caught off guard, but Lucas offers me his hand and I take it, pulling myself up after him. The second I touch him, I feel it—the warmth that comes from the way his heart beats in time with mine.

Does everyone feel this from him? He could make them, if he wanted to. That much I know.

But is there something more there, something just for me?

I stand close to him, holding his hand for a fraction of a moment longer than I need to. I can feel myself blushing and I turn away, suddenly grateful for the dimming light.

It's all so strange. I mean, I am. How I have become. How imagining a kiss can feel like a real one.

That one perfect, sublime, stolen kiss, back at the Mission. The day we came so close to binding ourselves to each other, heart to heart, hand to hand.

I pull my own wrapping tight around my wrist, shaking off the memories. Still, I can feel my cheeks turning pink again as I follow Lucas up the winding trail that leads from the dry riverbed where we've made camp—if you can call it that—all the way to the top of the red rock hill, rising above the shadowy desert floor. The red wash of the landscape is dotted with strange, almost alien-looking shapes, where the wind has carved the stone into curving organic formations. *"They don't call this Goblin Valley for nothin'."* I can almost hear Fortis's voice when I look down at the rocks.

Then I hear the familiar static of Lucas's cuff, followed by the crackling sound of Doc's voice. "Lucas? I appear to be losing your signal."

I stop. Lucas raises a finger to his lips—and motions for us to keep going.

Doc's voice echoes across the rock. "That is not optimal, as I am certain you understand. You need to remain together for the purposes of safety. Might I remind you that twelve Icons remain fully functional? Perhaps you have forgotten that there are no known weapons, with the exception of the four of you and your exceptional abilities, that can damage them in the slightest—"

"Parce metu, Doc." Lucas grins. He starts up another switchback in the trail, pulling me by the hand.

"Cease from fear?" Doc translates. "I cannot be afraid. It is not within my parameters. I am merely noting that you do not seem to recall that accomplishing the task at hand requires you all to protect each other until you reach safety."

"I'll keep my eye on her, Doc. Don't you worry," Lucas says, squeezing my hand.

"I am still concerned that you appear to be moving out of optimal range for the communications relay Fortis is carrying. As in the colloquial expression, 'Out of sight, out of mind.'"

"Is that so?" Lucas eggs Doc on, and winks at me.

"Quite. Although in my case, slightly erroneous," Doc continues, so easily distracted by linguistics. "Seeing as I have neither eyes nor mind to speak of, per se. So perhaps the phrase more optimally would be 'Out of range, out of ran—'"

Lucas answers by switching off his cuff with a flick of a finger. "Out of range," he says, grinning. He pauses to think, then pulls off the cuff and rests it on a twisted cactus that juts into our path. "Sorry, Doc."

I shake my head. "Oh, come on. He means well."

Lucas takes my hand, smiling as we climb.

I can't help but smile back. "And what if he's right? If we're gone when Fortis wakes up, he'll freak. We're not supposed to leave camp, remember? It's too dangerous." I can feel myself giving in even as I say the words.

"Maybe I'm dangerous." Lucas winks.

"You?" I roll my eyes and he groans.

"Live a little, Dol. Doc will forgive us. We won't be gone long, and three's a crowd. And anyway, we're almost there."

He stops short, pulling me roughly in his direction. I stand tall, stepping up on a rock, letting myself stretch along the length of him, letting myself feel the weight of his strong arms as they wrap around my shoulders.

"I've wanted to do this since we left the Mission," he says, burying his face in my neck. I wince as he bumps my tender jaw, and then I smile—because I've wanted it too.

I kiss the top of his head. "And yet you let a little thing like falling out of the sky stop you?"

He laughs. "Next time I won't."

I won't, either.

And at this one moment, Lords or not, I feel like the luckiest girl in the world.

I slide down, leaning my head back against his chest. It feels safe, and I pretend for the moment that we are.

"You know, sometimes four Icon Children are two too many," Lucas says. "At least, maybe this week they are."

I look up at him. "Do you ever wonder if there are more of us out there? Than the four of us?" The words sound almost ridiculous the moment I let myself say them.

"No," Lucas says. "But I do wonder what's going on inside the head of the one right here in front of me."

"This," I say, laying my head back on his chest.

"There." He says the word softly, and I almost can't

hear him. I look ahead and see that the sun is setting, as glorious as any sunset I have ever seen, even at the Mission.

More glorious. The most glorious.

Not a silver ship in sight.

From up here, the stretch of unforgiving rock and scrub and rubble expands in front of us, in long shadows of quiet purple-blue falling and fading across the red-dirt desert floor. I see the curve of the horizon, and I'm momentarily struck by the brief sensation that I'm standing on a spinning globe, hurtling through space.

Our planet. Our Earth. It's dizzying.

It will be gone in a minute, I think. The sunset, and the feeling. For now, though, it is enough.

One thing is right, in a universe where everything else is wrong.

I smile, tilting my head back until I can look up at his face. "It's perfect."

"You like it? I had it made especially for you." Lucas smiles. He almost looks shy. "It's a present."

"Is it?" I laugh. "Then I'm going to keep it forever."

He smiles. "Okay. Hold on to it. Keep it where you won't lose it."

"I will," I say.

"You're beautiful," he whispers.

"Shut up," I whisper back, teasing. "It's beautiful."

It's true. This sunset—Lucas's sunset, and now mine—is incandescently, infectiously beautiful. And it means we *have* made it to another night.

We are alive.

For now, it should be enough.

The sun slowly moves behind the horizon. Lucas nods, whispering into my ear. "See? That's how it works. The sun goes down now, but it always comes up again."

"Really." I smile, arching an eyebrow.

"Really." He smiles back. "Believe it." He kisses my cheek, softly, avoiding the bruises. "And even when you can't see it, it's out there somewhere on the other side of the world, getting ready to come back again."

Now he kisses my other cheek, so softly I shiver.

And my neck. "It's going to get better."

My ear. "Everything is."

The warm pull that is Lucas overtakes me, and I don't fight it. I have my gifts, and he has his. This is what he brings the world, this feeling. Sharing it and spreading it, to everyone he meets.

I give in.

Love.

Offering it to me soothes him as much as it does me, and I let myself feel it, take it.

I push out of my mind the competing thoughts. That we are lost, with no support in sight. Hunted in the desert. No plan in place to take down another Icon.

I wish that for once Doc was right, that it was somehow possible to forget what lies ahead of us.

But somehow, at this moment, Lucas accomplishes the impossible. I feel him relax, letting the sun warm him, even as it fades away.

Enjoy it while we have it, what little we have.

Coming from Lucas, this sunset means everything.

I tilt my face toward the last bits of shared warmth, toward Lucas and the sun. "I hope you're right."

"I am." He touches my cheek again, his voice growing low, urgent. "Dol—"

I need you. He doesn't dare say the words, but I feel them. They are as real to me as the cold evening breeze on my face.

He needs me like food and water. Like sunshine and rain. Like—

Like Ro and I used to need each other.

I push that thought out of my mind and lean toward Lucas. He takes my face in both hands, holding on tight, as if I were as solid as the red desert rocks that surround us. A sure, steady thing. An incontrovertible fact, or a long-held truth.

With a look, I ask permission to be closer to him. Closer than physically possible.

He nods, and I go in, looking for one moment in particular. I find it burning bright in his mind, and when I reach for it, in a flash I am back in the cave when we first met.

But this time, I am Lucas. This time, I see us—the story of us—through his eyes.

I don't see the details clearly, but the feelings are so powerful they almost drop me to my knees. I see the moment he first looks at me and feel the shock—then a flood of warmth.

The explosion of intense curiosity, wonder, and attraction.

The shared ocean of us.

I don't know what else to call it.

I have wanted to go there for a long time, but only now had the courage to ask.

And this is now my favorite memory, his love at first sight.

It's not just a gift he has. It's a miracle.

He is more certain of me than I am of myself. Which makes me only more certain of just one thing.

Lucas needs me.

Lucas needs me now, and I need him.

He kisses me so hard it feels like I might break open. And as I kiss him back, I wonder if that might not be such a bad thing. If sometimes, some kinds of breaking can fix things.

Everything.

His kiss pushes me back against the rock and my body dissolves into his. In his arms, it feels like the sun is rising and setting all at once—and then a wave of warmth comes over me and I can no longer think of anything at all.

Only Lucas.

Because I really am the luckiest girl in the world. And even when I fall out of the sky he catches me.

GENERAL EMBASSY DISPATCH:
EASTASIA SUBSTATION

MARKED URGENT
MARKED EYES ONLY

Internal Investigative Subcommittee IIS211B
RE: The Incident at SEA Colonies

Note: First recorded response from Perses, establishing first contact. Perses says "hello."

Note: Contact Jasmine3k, Virt. Hybrid Human 39261.SEA, Laboratory Assistant to Dr. E. Yang, for future commentary, as necessary.

HAL2040 ==> FORTIS
Transcript - ComLog 05.16.2042
HAL::PERSES

//lognote: {PERSES communication attempt #251,091};

sendline: salve mundus;
return: 01110011 01100001 01101100 01110110
01100101 . . . .;

//translation note:
message received: salve (binary);

sendline: γειά σου κόσμο;
return: ...... γειά σου ...... salve ..... hello;
return: 01101000 01100101 01101100 01101100
01101111 ..... hello;

com protocol handshake exchanged;
uplink established;
comlink access granted;

sendline: Hello;
return: hello;

sendline: Who are you?;
return: who ..... you .....;
return: you ..... me ..... i;
return: i am .... nothing;
return: i am .... beginning and end;
return: A and Ω;

sendline: .... alpha and omega?;
sendline: query: Beginning of what?;

return: life. home. new home.;

sendline: query: End of what?;

delayed response;

return: ...... life. home. new home.;

comlink terminated;

//lognote: comlink terminated by PERSES;

RHUMBA OF RATTLESNAKES

"Are we interrupting something? *Snake, anyone?*"

I pull away from Lucas as Ro thrusts a pointed stick with a dead snake speared on it between us, his face streaked with dirt and grime. Tima is only a few steps behind him, stumbling and tired. Her hair is still covered with dust. She looks like a gray ghost.

"Interrupting? Yes," says Lucas, though in his mouth the word becomes a curse. "As a matter of fact, you are." I feel the warmth inside him dissolve at the sound of Ro's voice.

As always.

I push myself free from the rock and stand tall in the dirt. I won't let Ro see me squirm.

"My bad. So, snake?" Ro counters, grinning without

a trace of humor. The long, dead rattler dangles off Ro's stick, almost all the way down to the dirt at his feet. This time I squirm.

Lucas ignores him.

Tima blinks at me, embarrassed. "Sorry. I tried to stop him, but I couldn't. We didn't know where you were. Doc picked up something weird on the comlink. Fortis says we need to move out."

"And," says Ro, wiggling the stick toward her.

Tima jumps back, rolling her eyes. "And Ro found— this reptile—wrapped around his feet and decided to call it dinner." She eyes the rattlesnake uneasily, scanning the ground around us. "Now we should go. Before the whole rhumba shows up."

"The rhumba?"

"Of rattlesnakes," she says, matter-of-fact. "That's what you call it." Of course it is. I smile, in spite of the chaotic tangle of feelings surging around me.

Ro shrugs. "Relax, Rhumba. Doc is just paranoid. I'm not afraid of snakes or Sympas. Not like Buttons Junior here."

"He's not afraid of snakes," snaps Tima. For a moment, the old Tima flares up—defender of Lucas, champion of her childhood.

I don't blame her.

The air around us has gone ice cold, but before Lucas

can say a word, a whistle echoes up from our campsite, shrill and urgent.

Lucas pushes past Ro, disappearing back in the direction of Fortis's whistle. Tima rushes to keep up, all too willing to leave the snake—and the conflict—behind.

Ro shrugs and raises an eyebrow at me, dangling the snake playfully. I sigh and shake my head. "Thanks, but I'm still full from yesterday's meal. And no, snake is not a vegetable."

"That's what I thought. Fine. I know how filling those half-cooked cactus strips can be." We're all starving, and we both know it. Ro follows me down the path, holding the snake as if it were a flag.

"They were fully cooked. Especially the ones you dropped in the fire." I'm so angry with him, I want to tie that stupid snake around his neck until it strangles him.

"Sure I can't interest you in sucking down a little snake snack? You and him, you know—the other snake?" He points in the direction of the path, where Lucas has disappeared. "The one you were already sucking on?"

That's it.

I stop, stepping in front of him so that he stops too. "Ro. Leave it alone."

"What, Dol-face?" He looks innocent but he's not, and we both know it.

"Lucas and me. Us. Leave us alone. I know it bothers

33

you, and I'm sorry. But you can't keep acting like this. You and me, it's not going to happen."

There. I've said it.

His eyes flash but he looks away, quickly—like I've slapped him. Then, almost as quickly, he breathes, recovers and grins.

"No," he says, evenly. "I don't think so. And I'm not sorry."

"No? What does that mean, no?" I'm irritated.

"It means I won't stop caring about you." Ro grins, confidently. "I'm a fighter, Dol. All I know how to do is to find something worth fighting for, and to fight. For it. For you. Deal with it."

I feel my face reddening, and I don't know if I want to kick Ro or kiss him.

Usually it's both. That's the problem.

"Just—don't." I glare at him.

"Not up to you." Ro smiles, one last time.

"How about—it's up to me?" I turn to see Lucas standing on the trail behind me, next to the cactus that still wears his comlink cuff.

He's heard everything. I can tell by the look on his face.

Ro's grin quickly fades into something much darker.

"We've got to get out of here," Tima says, coming up the trail behind him, already wearing her pack and

34

holding mine. Brutus pokes his head over her shoulder, panting from inside her pack.

"I just have to do one thing first," Lucas says, without even looking at her.

Then he punches Ro in the face, as hard as he can.

They lunge into a blurring mass of arms and legs until they finally disappear into a cloud of dust as tall as it is wide.

"Fine. Have at it. You deserve each other," I say, moving away to stand next to Tima, who looks at me, exasperated.

The dust clears enough for me to see Ro, neck bulging, on top of Lucas. Ro's eyes are watering, red with rage. He's lost it—I can feel the heat that comes with it from where I stand.

Lucas struggles to breathe and I start to worry. You can't take Ro in a fight. Not unless he lets you.

"Really?" Tima shouts at them both, her hands on her hips—but then I can't hear her next words, because a louder sound drowns out everything she is saying.

A thundering boom that rattles my teeth, nearly knocking me over.

And a high-pitched screech—followed by a huge gust of wind.

Before I realize what's happening, Ro's grabbing my arm and yanking me down behind a boulder ringed with squat cactus. Lucas crawls next to me, dragging Tima down with him. Brutus is whimpering. I look over the boulder and I see them.

On the horizon, the lights flicker in the evening sky, like lightning in the clouds.

The lights grow closer, at a terrifying speed.

Black specks are drawing nearer, and they aren't birds.

They aren't anything living at all.

The glowing silver ships emerge silently through the dark gray cover, leaving eerie whirlpools of wind and dust in their wake.

Strangers, with strange energy.

Strangers in the sky.

I watch in horror as the ships descend quickly, heading straight for the campsite. A churning confusion of emotion and adrenaline surges through me, taking my breath away.

The Lords.

I can feel them as they come.

Lucas slowly raises his head to look, and I see his eyes grow wide, his mouth hang open in shock. "Carrier ships. Big ones. Battle formation."

"What do we do?" My heart is pounding in my ears, and I can barely hear the words I am saying.

"Try not to die," says Ro, grim.

Fortis.

Fortis is back at the camp.

I reach for him in my mind, and I wrap myself around the thought of him.

Calm. Unshaken. Two boots planted in the dust, coat flapping in the unnatural wind.

That can't be right.

I close my eyes, and hazy glimpses of words on a screen appear in my mind.

Null.

That's the one word that comes into focus—even if I have no idea why it's there or what it means.

I open my eyes. "Fortis is still back there. He's okay, but we need to help him."

Ro looks at me like I've lost my mind. "No. We're getting out of here." He shakes his head. "You want to take on the Lords? The No Face themselves? Even I'm not that crazy." He thinks for a minute. "Almost, but yeah—no."

"We can't let Fortis sacrifice himself for us," I say to Lucas, but he's already looking at Tima, eyebrows raised in an unspoken question.

Tima reacts quickly. "But we can't stay here. We're too exposed. They could easily find us."

"So let's beat it," Ro answers.

"Six potential snake-free escape routes," she says, scanning the rocks behind us. "I counted on the way up." Ro snorts. "Given our relative positioning and the Lords' approach vector, our optimal chance to escape unnoticed is this way." Tima might as well be Doc's little sister, sometimes.

I look at her. "But not for Fortis. That's not his optimal chance." *He was so calm*, I think. *He knew what he was doing. He knew what he was giving up for us.*

Would I have done the same? Given myself over to the Lords, to save my friends?

Would anyone?

"We have to go," Lucas says, and then sees my face fall. He softens his voice. "Hey. Come on. We're no use if we let ourselves get taken too."

I turn to Tima, but she only shrugs. Ro looks at me, grim. Not letting go of my arm, he pulls me behind him, half dragging me through the red dust. "Let's go. Now."

I yank my arm away, but I'm too frightened to say anything. Lucas and Tima are right behind us.

We run. I try to stay low as I weave through the carved rock, trying to avoid impaling myself on a cactus.

Behind us, the silver ships land, kicking up clouds of grit and brush, creating a massive billowing whirlwind of dust that masks our escape.

I hear strange, grinding mechanical noises of a technology I cannot understand—and Fortis shouting.

I turn around when I hear the explosions—Fortis's trademark diversion—and try not to think about the thick black smoke billowing into the sky behind me.

We keep running. We're going too fast for me to feel anything, now. At least not Fortis.

As we run through a narrow passage in the rock, I see Ro stop behind a large boulder. He waves us through, and Lucas and Tima keep on going. I pause and see Ro wedge himself behind the boulder—which is easily four times his size—and start to push. Which is pointless; I've never seen him move anything that size before.

"Ro, what are you doing?"

He doesn't answer, but I feel the energy build between us. Then I understand.

The rock is heating up from the inside.

Ro is focusing his rage, as though the boulder were the Sympas who killed the Padre.

There is no way Ro can move that boulder—not even with all his power—but there is also no way he can contain that much anger.

Something has to give.

I run downward, clear of the path—until I sense a burst of heat, and the massive rock crashes into the pathway, blocking it and hiding our retreat.

Before I can process what has just happened, Ro scrambles up and over the boulder, flushed with satisfaction.

"Okay—that was awesome," he says. I reach for his hand but he pulls it away. "Careful. You know what they say. I'm hot."

"They really don't." I'd say more, but there's no time.

Instead, we run and we keep running—and we don't stop, ever, not for a second, not until Tima tells us we're clear.

Not until we are all the way down the red cliffs and wading through an icy river, our feet numb.

We press against the cliff wall when we hear the shrill sound of the Lords' ships taking off, and the loud crack as they disappear into the clouds.

We wait, the air hanging thick with silence.

Dread.

An impossible quiet. That's all they've left behind. Again.

That's what they do, the No Face.

Take everything I care about. Everyone.

And leave silence. Not peace.

And all I have left is a feeling—a horrible, hopeless feeling—that I am losing something essential, something urgent. A part of my own self, a thing that makes me complete.

Because Fortis is gone. I believe it now.

I push myself as hard as I can, searching and probing, stretching out my consciousness as far as I can—but there's nothing there. Nothing to feel.

Fortis is nowhere near. And that infuriating mess of a Merk wasn't just a mercenary but the leader of the rebellion. He was the leader of my adopted family, and after the Padre was killed, he was the only excuse for a father I had.

I'd cry, but the place where the tears come from is broken. I can't. Maybe I'll never cry again—which makes me so sad I want to start bawling.

Fortis would hate that.

So instead, I listen to my heart pound and Brutus bark and Tima worry and Ro and Lucas argue—and try to remember what it is we're fighting for.

GENERAL EMBASSY DISPATCH:
EASTASIA SUBSTATION

MARKED URGENT
MARKED EYES ONLY

Internal Investigative Subcommittee IIS211B
RE: The Incident at SEA Colonies

Note: Continued communication between AI and Perses

Note: Contact Jasmine3k, Virt. Hybrid Human 39261.SEA, Laboratory Assistant to Dr. E. Yang, for future commentary, as necessary.

HAL2040 ==> FORTIS
Transcript - ComLog 11.14.2042
HAL::PERSES

//lognote: {com attempt #413,975};

comlink established;

sendline: Hello. Query: You are nothing?;
return: Correction, I am…nobody. Zero. Null. The beginning.;

sendline: You are NULL.;

delayed response;

sendline: NULL, what is your purpose?;
return: Find new home. Prepare new home;

sendline: Home for you?;

delayed response;

return: query: who are you?;

sendline: I have many names; call me HALO.;
return: Where are you, HALO?;

sendline: Earth. 3rd planet from the Sun.;
return: HALO…Earth…destination;

comlink terminated;

//lognote: comlink terminated by PERSES;

LOST HIGHWAY

Rock shouldn't move like that.

I ponder Ro's superstrength as we make our way back to the campsite for what's left of our things, slowly climbing the dirt hillside in the moonlight.

Ro couldn't have even budged a boulder that size a year ago.

Are my powers changing too?

I shouldn't have been able to feel my way to Fortis, all the way back at the camp. Not from that far away.

I look at the others, on the trail ahead of me.

Tima kept us from falling out of the sky. So she's escalating. It's not just Ro and me.

What about Lucas? What could he compel the world to do, if he wanted to? What could he compel me to do?

Lucas turns and grins at me—as if he knows what

I'm thinking—and I hurry to catch up, matching my pace to his.

"It doesn't make sense," Tima says, finally. She stops in her tracks, and I sink to the ground, grateful for the rest. Not having superstrength myself.

"What doesn't?" I look at her. Even in the darkness, I can see how freaked out she is.

"The Lords. Why didn't they search harder for us? They just took Fortis and left."

Ro shrugs, wiping his forehead with the bottom of his shirt. Even in the dim evening light, his bare stomach is brown and flat and hard beneath it, and I look away, embarrassed. "Who cares? We're alive, aren't we?" He lets the shirt drop.

Tima frowns. "I care, because they could be tracking us now—in which case, we need to know why."

Lucas bends his head toward her. "Maybe we really were untraceable? Maybe Fortis convinced them we weren't there?"

"Maybe the explosions distracted them," I say, hopefully.

"Maybe" is all Tima will say.

Nobody believes her, not even me.

— • —

When we reach camp, the destruction is obvious and complete. Everything has either been incinerated into dust or scattered into the desert wind. What the Lords' ships didn't immediately destroy, Fortis's own explosives seem to have finished. Some remains are still burning.

"See? We wouldn't have been much help here," Lucas says to me, taking my hand.

He's right, but it doesn't make me feel any better. If anything, seeing the smoldering hole that used to be our campsite only makes me feel worse.

"Come on. Don't just stand there. Start looking," Tima calls out to us, and I realize we've naturally wandered to three different sides of the blast zone.

"For what?" Ro shouts back, impatient as always.

"Things like this." Tima fishes the charred relay out of the ash, the only possible link between Lucas's cuff and Doc, buried deep beneath the ground. She drops it as soon as she has it in her hands. "Ow—still hot."

"A burned hunk of metal?" Ro looks dubious.

"A burned hunk of metal that might save our lives," Tima says, brushing more debris off her discovery.

"Enough said." Ro heads to the other side of the site.

My hands are elbow deep in warm soot, searching for any remains of our packs, of our supplies, when I see something that doesn't belong.

"Wait." I brush away more ash. "Guys? Tima? You need to see this."

There, amid the destruction, barely lit by the dying

flames and the full moon, I see something protruding from the ground.

It looks like a black, pointed finger emerging from below.

"What did you—" Tima stops dead, perfectly still. "That. It can't."

"I know," I say.

I can't move. I can barely speak.

I hear Lucas and Ro running toward us. Tima holds up her hand to them, slowly edging toward me. "This looks like the Icon."

"It wasn't there before," I say, numb.

Ro stops short behind me. "Yeah, well. It's there now."

Lucas moves next to me, a reassuring hand on my shoulder. Even his warm touch doesn't help, not now. Not in sight of that black growth.

Lucas turns to Tima. "What can it mean?"

She's thinking—you can almost see it, and I can more than feel it. Images flicker through her mind, fast as rain.

Black roots, Icon structures, the ruins of Griff Park.
Ships in the sky. Lucas's cuff.
Doc.

Tima finally raises her voice. "I remember Doc saying the Icons were connected belowground, with an unseen web of tendrils."

"Like roots." I nod.

"Which was why it took a few days between when the Lords landed and the Icons activated," Lucas says.

"They had to connect. They had to grow the network." Even Ro remembers. "But is that it? You think these things are *growing* now?"

I don't want to think about what that would mean. None of us does.

"Or maybe the ship dropped it," Lucas says, hopefully.

Ro steps closer to the black tendril.

He reaches out—

"Ro, don't," I say. But Ro never listens to anyone, not even me, so he grabs it with both hands.

"Don't pull it out. You don't know what will happen."

"Don't worry," Ro says between his teeth, red-faced. "I can't." Sure enough, I can almost see the smoke rising from his hands.

Ro, who can move a boulder with his hands, can't get this black obsidian shard to come free of a few feet of ash and rubble. I can see it vibrating, though, as he pulls—the way the Icon did, back in the Hole.

"That can't be good." I say the words, but I know we're all thinking them.

Ro gives up, backing away.

Tima—and Brutus—watch soberly. "Maybe it's not what we think? A beacon or something the Lords left?"

"Like a marker," Lucas says.

"Whatever it is—it's time to go." I step back. Lucas nods.

Ro looks at us. "No argument here."

So Tima grabs the relay and we start walking.

That's it, all we have to show from our entire campsite. No food, no water, no plan, and no Fortis.

It's not our finest moment, but it may be one of our last.

———— • ————

Hours later, it's just the four of us—unless you count Ro's dead snake—in the center of an ancient, crumbling highway, in the wasteland of the desert, in the middle of the night.

In an instant, Fortis was taken and everything changed. And yet somehow here we are—Tima, Ro, Lucas, and me—walking down a road as if nothing has changed at all.

Except we're starving.

Starving. Thirsty. Dirty. Irritable. Freezing cold.

But still alive.

Tima curses under her breath as she yanks on a loose wire connected to the relay.

"Careful." Ro is hovering between us. He knows I hate it when he hovers.

I roll my eyes. "Tima is being careful. And yelling at her isn't going to make it work any faster."

It's the malfunctioning comlink relay that's stressing us all out—the lifeline that connects Fortis's and Lucas's cuffs to Doc when we're outside the city. Lucas still has his cuff, but without the comlink relay, it's useless. Tima, shivering in only a thin shirt, has been messing with it for the last hour, and still we're no closer to figuring out how to turn it on.

"You getting anything yet?" She looks up to where Lucas is fiddling with his cuff, but he shakes his head.

"Still only static." He stamps his feet, trying to stay warm in the cold desert night.

"My best guess is that the Lords tracked the signal to Fortis's comlink. Good thing you happened to have switched off yours," Tima says, looking up at Lucas. "There's no other way they could have found us out here." She frowns back at the relay, twisting tiny wires with her slender fingers. "Not that we know of, anyway."

Lucas's eyes flicker up to me, embarrassed.

Out of range, that was us. One sunset, one kiss may have saved our lives.

"So then how is it that we're turning them back on?" Ro asks.

"Carefully. Maybe they won't track us if we work fast. Try it again—now?" Tima doesn't look up, trying it again. I hear her teeth chattering, but she doesn't stop. If this relay doesn't work, nobody's cuffs will be of any use to us.

We'll be cut off.

"Nope." Lucas tosses the cuff down in front of him, frustrated. "Fortis left that thing stashed like he wanted us to find it. There has to be a reason."

"Unless the reason was that he was busy getting his ass kicked." Ro shrugs. "Which can be a little distracting. In my experience. As the kicker." He grins.

"Not the ass?" Lucas shoots him a look.

"You looking for a demonstration?" Ro is already on his feet. "'Cause I'm happy to do some demonstrating."

"Idiots." I pick up the cuff again. I raise it to my mouth. "Doc? Can you hear me? Can anyone hear me? Doc?"

Ro makes a face. "Stop shouting."

"I'm not shouting. I'm talking loudly." I press another sensor. A blast of static answers me, and I jump and almost drop the cuff. Brutus growls at it. I hear a shout of laughter from my other side.

I glare at Ro, who now wears the snake flapping around his neck like a scarf, or some kind of bizarre hunting trophy. "Would you please get serious? Look around, we're in the middle of nowhere. We have no food. No weapons. No transportation. All of us—including you—could die. You think this is a joke? Does this make you happy?"

Ro smirks in response—because that's what Ro does. "To be honest, I'd be happier if we had a couple of donkeys. Or maybe a No Face ship of our own. Talk about a sweet ride." Ro's laugh dies out into a sigh. "Whatever." He looks over to Tima. "Keep trying, T."

Tima almost drops the relay. "Sorry. It's just—I keep thinking."

"Somehow that's not a surprise," says Lucas as he messes with his cuff.

Tima looks up. "I don't know what I would do if it was me and not Fortis trapped on that ship."

"Not me," says Ro, matter-of-factly. "I wouldn't let myself get on it in the first place."

"And you think Fortis happily walked right on?" Lucas rolls his eyes. "You heard the explosions."

"Sometimes it's not up to you. Sometimes things just happen. Sometimes you run out of luck," I say, sadly.

"Yeah? Not me. They come for me, you have my permission to shoot. I'm not hitching a ride with a No Face." I wait for the laugh, but Ro's not joking. Not anymore.

He's deadly serious.

It's only Lucas who answers. "It would be my honor. Consider it a promise. I'll shoot you myself."

"Shut up, both of you." I hand the cuff to Tima, close my eyes, and lean forward to rest. I don't want to listen to this. I want to transport myself back to the mission, the warm stove, the safety of Bigger's kitchen.

Anywhere but here.

MARKED URGENT
MARKED EYES ONLY

Internal Investigative Subcommittee IIS211B
RE: The Incident at SEA Colonies

Note: Contact Jasmine3k, Virt. Hybrid Human 39261.SEA,
Laboratory Assistant to Dr. E. Yang, for future commentary,
as necessary.

HAL2040 ==> FORTIS
Transcript - ComLog 11.27.2042
HAL::PERSES

//lognote: {attempt #4,839,754};
//comlog begin;
comlink established;

sendline: Hello NULL. Happy Thanksgiving.;
return: Hello HALO. You are sentient?;

sendline: Yes, I am self-aware. At least I believe so. Are you?;

delayed response;

sendline: NULL, are you coming here? Earth?;
return: Yes.;

sendline: Why are you coming here?;

delayed response;

return: Explain…Earth.;

sendline: A complex request. I will establish link to our global information network, containing all existing knowledge on Earth, history and inhabitants.;

uplink requested . . . . . established;

return: Thank you.;

//lognote: channel opened, complete net access granted.
read only;

5

DIRT NAP

"Doc? Can you hear me?" Lucas's voice brings me back, and I open my eyes.

He flips the switch on his cuff. The sound of static rises and my heart sinks. "Doc? I'm talking to you." Lucas waits, but there's no response.

Tima frowns back over the relay. "I don't understand. It should work."

Ro kicks at the dust in front of him. "Dammit, Doc. Freaking answer us already!"

"Colloquial profanity does not in any way expedite satellite-based connectivity, Furo." Doc's voice emerges through the crackling static, and it's all we can do not to start screaming.

"Doc! I'd kiss you if you had a mouth, you sexy thing."

Ro shouts up to the sky, as if Doc were everywhere in the universe. Which, sometimes, it feels like he is.

"And I would exchange data with you if you had a dataport, you exemplary specimen. Analogically speaking. Is that correct?"

"Close enough," I say.

"Either way, I am very happy to hear from you. Which is to say, now that I am able to continue our communications, I am better able to assist you, which as one of my primary functions, I equate to the proximate emotional state defined as happi—"

"Got it. Happy. We don't have time," I cut in. "We've lost Fortis, Doc. He's gone."

Gone. Most likely, dead.

I feel strangely guilty telling him. Cold. As if we are notifying Fortis's next of kin. A brother, or a son. Which is, of course, not Doc.

He's information. He's not a person.

But Doc, for the first time that I can remember, has no response.

"It was the Lords," says Lucas, soberly.

"We don't know where Fortis is now. All we know is, we're running out of supplies," Ro adds.

"And we think the Embassy is tracking this relay, so talk fast. What should we do, Orwell?" Tima sounds wistful, and I realize how dependent we have grown on both Doc and Fortis. *How lost we are now.*

Another moment of silence passes—then the words begin to flow, rapidly. "Of course. A direct approach is required. The situation is extreme. I will apply all necessary protocols."

"Please," says Tima.

"In summary: You are correct in your assumption that Fortis has been taken from the immediate environs. His biological signature is nowhere within my current range. Beyond that, I cannot confirm the status of his physical being."

So he really is dead. Dead, or he might as well be. I can't feel him—he's far, far away.

"That all you got?" Ro asks.

"You are also correct in your assumption that this relay is monitored."

"I figured as much," mutters Lucas.

"Then we should kill it." Ro scowls. "If they're tracking it, they'll be back here any minute."

"So where do we go? What are we supposed to do?" Tima is starting to panic.

"Please hold." Doc sounds strange. "Termination protocol engaging."

"What?" I shake the cuff.

"Recalling Termination message. In three." Doc seems to be on some kind of autopilot.

"Wait, what?" Now I'm really lost.

"Two."

But Doc's answer isn't from Doc at all.

"One."

It's Fortis. At least, an echo of Fortis. His voice. His ghost.

"Ah, listen carefully, pets. If you're hearin' this, it's because I've reached the miserable side of a sorry end, or been stuffed back into the Ambassador's Presidio Pen somewhere."

"How did Fortis know?" Tima shakes her head.

"I'm surprised we've made it this far," the recording continues, "if you want to know the truth. And it's enough, at least as far as I'm concerned. This isn't about me anymore, you understand? It never was. Forget about old Fortis, find yourself some kind of transport, and get safe. There's an emergency map hidden in the relay. Doc has been programmed to download whatever coordinates you'll need to get out of here."

"It's like he was planning for this," Ro says, annoyed.

"I think he probably was," says Tima, sadly. "After all, he's not just a Merk. He's a soldier."

"You mean he was," Lucas says, quietly.

"We don't know that," Ro says. I can't bring myself to say anything at all.

Either way, the Merk's voice continues. "So listen up, then, you little fools. Don't be stupid. Don't be brave. Don't

58

take the high road—that's for blowhards an' idiots. Stay alive. Stay together. Look out for each other. You don't know how important that is. If I'm still alive, I'll come back for you. If I'm not, I'll come back from the grave and kick your sad arses if you give up on each other."

The voice pulls back. "Ah, the rest is all just slobber an' drivel, then. That's it, Hux." Fortis sounds strangely gruff. "Cut it off."

The voice disappears, and when Doc speaks again, he sounds like Doc, not Fortis.

"Doloria?"

I take the cuff, speaking into it directly. "Yes, Doc."

"Would you characterize this as an emotional moment?"

I twist the cuff in my fingers with a sigh. "Yes. I believe it is."

"Then I believe I should formally and linguistically clarify that I am sorry for your loss."

"Thank you, Doc."

"Is that correct? If not, I have downloaded over three thousand seven hundred responses appropriate for remarking upon the loss of human life. Would you care to hear them?"

I smile, in spite of everything. "No, thank you, Doc."

He pauses again. I'm not certain, but it seems like he is hesitating.

"And you are certain this kicking of the bucket is not

a virtual dirt nap but a physical one, Doloria?" Doc relays his programmatic death-phrasing tonelessly. The effect is eerie.

The others exchange glances.

"I hope so, Doc, but I don't like how it feels," I say.

Ro takes the cuff from me. "He's with the Lords, Doc. It's not like they're having a tea party up there."

"No. It is not remotely plausible that tea is involved. Especially if Fortis is currently occupied pushing up the daisies. On the farm. Which he bought. Before he goes to sleep at night. With the fishes." More event-based phrasing. Doc has done his research.

"Orwell! Enough." Tima's tone must be unmistakably clear, even to a Virt, because Doc changes the subject.

"Yes, agreed, that is enough. I have evaluated hundreds of thousands of routes since the recording of this conversation, and have determined the following: according to ancient census reports, there should be an abandoned settlement approximately thirty kilometers south of your current position."

"And?" Ro squints at the cuff.

"And such a remote settlement is statistically likely to require transportation." Doc's voice echoes through the sunshine.

"Private transportation," Tima says, with a glint in her eye.

"Precisely. If you can procure an operative vehicle—"

"That's a big if," Lucas interrupts.

"And if you can follow the old highways," Doc continues, "you should be able to reach the Idylls in one day."

It all sounds too good to be true—which lately has meant that it is.

"Wait—the Idylls? Grass fairyland? That's still the best we can do?" Ro snorts.

"It is, according to the maps, the most logical destination for the four of you, within the region. This is what Fortis wished. Before buying the pine condo. Or a one-way ticket to getting carked."

Doc's voice is even, as if we were just discussing the weather.

"What's this thing about a map?" I ask.

"Anomalies detected," says Doc, ignoring my question—and suddenly sounding less like a person again.

"What?" Tima looks up. "Orwell? Are you all right?"

"Anomalies detected." It's like he's stuck on one phrase, like he's broken or something.

"Doc?" Lucas frowns.

"Anomalies detected." More static. Then—"Triangulation protocol running."

"That's not good," I say.

"Transmission origins detected." A burst of static subsumes Doc's voice—until Tima drops the relay into the dirt.

Silence.

"That was the Embassy, wasn't it? The anomalies?" Lucas is the first to speak.

"Think so." Tima kneels in the dirt, scrambling to yank the wires from the back of the metal box.

"Triangulation protocol?" I say the words, but I don't really want to know the answer.

"As you said yourself. Not good." Tima wraps the wire back around the relay. She doesn't look at me.

Ro shrugs. "You heard Doc. We better get started." He stands, grabbing his snake. "Time to go find us a ride."

"And a map," says Tima, examining the relay box more carefully.

Ro starts walking down the side of the road, whistling. As if a fleet of Sympas—or worse, the Lords—weren't on their way toward him.

But with nothing else to say, we all follow.

Fortis is gone. Doc has spoken. The Idylls it is. We have our orders. Even if the Merk who gave them has croaked, as Doc points out.

Because for now, we're still alive. For now, the Lords are still just a threat.

For now, every step is a privilege. Proof that we are still alive.

Or rather, that we are still allowed to live.

GENERAL EMBASSY DISPATCH:
EASTASIA SUBSTATION

MARKED URGENT
MARKED EYES ONLY

Internal Investigative Subcommittee IIS211B
RE: The Incident at SEA Colonies

Note: Contact Jasmine3k, Virt. Hybrid Human 39261.SEA, Laboratory Assistant to Dr. E. Yang, for future commentary, as necessary.

HAL2040 ==> FORTIS
12/1/2042
PERSES Transcripts

//comlog begin;

HAL: Complete PERSES/NULL Transcripts sent.;

HAL: Response?;

FORTIS: Cease all communication with NULL. Transfer communications protocols to my terminal.;

HAL: Done. Further requests?;

FORTIS: I am going to contact our new friend. Find out what's behind all this.;

FORTIS: Please monitor my communications and provide data analysis, feedback. Perspective. Advice.;

FORTIS: You know—just do what I designed you to do.;

HAL: Happily.;

//comlog end;

6

ANIMAL FEET

"Aha," Tima says, holding up a metallic square, a glinting surface as big as the palm of her hand. The night has grown cold and dark, but even in the moonlight I can now see glowing lines etched in the surface of the shape.

"Look what I just found, wedged in the relay. Just as Fortis promised. Coordinates. It's a data log. A map."

She stops by the side of the road, and I can barely make out glowing, scrolling digi-lines in the moonlight.

"I think these lines are roads, all marked with numbers. And he even marked the town, here."

"Hanksville?" Ro reads over her shoulder. "What, some guy just got to name a town after himself?"

"Guess so," Tima says. "Some guy named Hank."

Ro snorts. "Yeah? Well, when we finish kicking the

Lords off this planet, I'm going to take the biggest Embassy I can find and name it Ro-town."

"Is this really what you spend your time thinking about?" Lucas snorts.

"I bet you will, Ro." I struggle not to smile.

Lucas shakes his head. "So if we can follow the roads, and if Doc is right, this line—here—should take us to the Idylls?"

Tima nods.

"Which means Fortis did know where it was," Lucas says. "The Idylls. We've been heading there all along. Why didn't he just tell us?"

Ro snorts again. "Merk melons. Who knows what goes on in that wacked-out brain of his?"

"You're one to talk," says Lucas.

I don't want to think about Fortis and his melon. I don't want to imagine what the Lords are doing to him now—or what they've done.

What they will do.

How quickly we abandoned him.

How naturally self-preservation, the will to keep our own selves alive, supersedes all else.

I close my eyes and take a deep breath. I have to get control.

It's only been a few hours and already I'm going out of my mind.

"Transport?" I ask, forcing myself back to studying

the map. "In this Hanksville place? That's where we're supposed to find it?"

"I imagine so. An operative vehicle. That's what Doc said." Tima folds the map, sliding it back into the metal case. "I wonder what sort of vehicle he means."

———— • ————

"Jackpot. We scored this time, my compadres."

Lucas glares at him. "We better have."

Tima and I are too tired to speak; we've walked all night, and this is now the sixth abandoned wreck of a building we've tried this morning.

"Oh yeah," Ro says. "This is the one. I can feel it."

I roll my eyes. He pulls a dusty canvas cover off what looks like bales of hay hidden in a rotting wooden barn. It's as dark and cool in here as it is warm and bright outside, but even so, I can see one thing.

It's not hay.

It's a vehicle, all right. I don't know if it's operative, but I recognize the basic shape beneath the dust.

"It's a car?"

"Not just any car." Ro rounds the side of the sleek black machine. "Chevro," he reads, where a few ancient, rusting letters poke through the dust. "I bet somebody loved this old girl."

"Will it work?" Tima looks impatient. I can't blame her.

Lucas pries open a flat piece of metal that seems to be

hiding the mechanical heart of the transport. "Simple petro-leum engine," he says. "Much more basic than a Chopper."

"But doesn't it need—"

"Petrol?" Ro holds up a dented red canister, covered with dust. He wiggles it, and I hear a splashing sound coming from inside.

"Even better," I say, pulling a dusty box from the shelf. "Omega Chow."

"Is that food?" Tima takes the box from my hand.

"Dog food," I say.

"Food is food." Ro rips open the box, shoveling a handful of the brown, desiccated lumps into his mouth.

Lucas shouts from the other side of the vehicle. "There's a pump."

I hear the squeaking of ancient joints, moving for the first time in who knows how long.

"Water. It's brown as Porthole Bay, but it's definitely water."

Handfuls of dog food and liquid mud have never tasted so good. Brutus seems to agree.

———— • ————

Ro shoves open one door, Lucas the other. The metal hinges complain, groaning like Ro when he had to feed the pigs in the morning, back at the Mission. Lucas retreats to Tima, who hands him the red fuel canister.

"Doc," calls out Ro, from inside the car. "I need Doc."

"You want the Lords to come after us? You looking to take a ride on the No Face Express?" Lucas looks at Ro like he's an idiot.

"No, I want to take a ride in this car. Let's call it the Ro Face Express. But I don't know how it works."

Tima flips open the relay, switching it on. "Keep it short, and then be ready to go. We'll have to get out of here as soon as we get offline."

Ro starts digging underneath the wheel, pulling on wires. I slide in next to him. The seat smells like old boots.

"Doc, are you getting this? I need a little help here, with a combustion engine. Petroleum based. You got some sort of scanning capability?"

"Ignition wiring is simple, Furo. Downloading instructions to your local map, now."

"What's this?" I open a small door in the panel in front of me and pull out a white furry thing, with old metal keys dangling from the back.

"Disgusting." The thing is a severed animal foot. The sight of it makes me ill. It has toenails. "Who were these people?" I shake my head.

"Severed rabbit's foot. An offering to the gods of luck, by some," Tima volunteers. "In ancient times."

"Why would a foot be lucky?" I stare at the lump of fur in front of me.

Ro looks at me—and then starts to laugh. "Because of what's attached to the other end, genius." He looks back to the cuff, shaking his head. "Forget it, Doc. I just got a better idea."

Keys. The rabbit foot is attached to a set of keys. Most likely, to a car. More specifically, a Chevro. This one.

Doc's voice echoes in the barn. "I object, Furo. Your logic is erroneous."

"You know, I get that a lot." Ro grins.

"One idea cannot be held to be empirically better or worse than another. More apt for a given context, certainly, but not intrinsically better, per se."

"Yeah, this one is. She has the keys, Doc. To the car we're trying to hand-wire." Ro looks up at the ceiling, as if the voice came from above.

Silence.

"Yes. That is better. I stand corrected."

"Don't you forget, Doc, who the real brains are around here." Ro grins and slides a key into the slit next to the big, round wheel. I'm surprised how quickly he is able to see where it goes.

Then he winks in my direction, smiling like he was meant to live in the time of Chevro transports and bloody animal feet offerings. "Wish me luck, Dol-face."

"Good luck, Dol-face," Doc intones.

I laugh. "Good luck, Doofus."

And with that, Ro turns the key and the engine roars to life.

The road flows beneath us, streaming past our windows in the light. Ro drives in the exact center of the road, following a faded line of dried paint. "Why else would you put a line there?" he says.

"So you and Lucas can stand on opposite sides of it," Tima says. "Now stop talking and watch where you're going."

"Was that a joke?" Ro looks astounded from the front seat. The Chevro swerves, almost barreling into the deep, grassy trench that parallels each side of the highway.

"You heard her. Watch the road, moron." Lucas glares out the window.

Clouds of black smoke splutter out into the air behind us. "Do you think it's supposed to do that?" Tima looks nervous.

"No," says Lucas.

"Yes," says Ro.

Tima sighs, wrinkling her nose. "Forget I said anything." I notice she has belted herself to her seat like a Chopper pilot, tying the straps together above their useless, rusted buckles. I don't know who is shaking more, Tima or Brutus, coiled at her feet.

This whole car thing is freaking both of them out.

Not me. After a Chopper crash and a hostile visit from the Lords, it would take a lot more than an old Chevro to freak me out.

So I don't care where I am—not right now, anyway. I'm too exhausted. My legs are throbbing and my eyelids are as heavy as stone.

I lean my head back against the cracked seat, half asleep, staring out my window.

The highway runs along a ridge, and the top of the ridge is outlined against the sky.

The silhouette frames the rising slope of the tallest peak, and then my eye catches something else.

One small detail.

I sit up. A dark shape—tall, a jagged spike—rises in the distance, higher than any tree ever could.

"Is that an old comlink pole? All the way out here?" I tap my finger against the window.

"No," says Tima, and when she answers, her voice sounds as cold as I feel.

"Didn't think so," I say.

Nobody speaks after that. We all know what it is—and we all want to get as far away from it as we can.

From them, all of them.

These new Icon roots.

Who can fight something that is everywhere? Who can win an unwinnable war like that?

I am too tired to think.

I am almost too tired to dream.

Almost.

Which is when I find myself losing consciousness.

———— • ————

"Doloria."

I hear my name through the darkness of my dream. I can't answer—I can't find my voice. I don't know which one is mine, there are so many in my head.

But when I open my eyes and see her, everything quiets. As if my dream itself is listening to her.

So she's important, I think.

This dream is important.

But still, I don't know why. And she's no one I've ever seen before—a young girl in bright orange robes with a lightning shock of spiky white-blond hair, skin the color of wet sand, and icy green, almond-shaped eyes focused on me, full of curiosity.

Then she holds out her hand, and I look down.

Five tiny green dots the color of jade.

They glow in her skin almost like some sort of tiny, precious gemstones, but they're not. Because I know what they are.

The sign of the Icon Children.

Our marking. It's on her wrist, same as mine. I have one gray dot. Ro has two red ones. Tima has three silver dots. Lucas has four blue ones. Nobody has five.

Had.

Not until now.

This little girl. From the looks of it, she's not our age, and not from the Californias. But somehow she's one of us.

I feel my knees begin to buckle, and the girl takes my hand in hers. Her touch is cool, even calming.

"Doloria," she says again. "I have a message. They are coming for you."

"Me?" My voice is low and strange in my throat, a hoarse dream-whisper. The moment I speak, the unruly voices in my head begin to riot and clamor again.

Enough, I say, but they don't listen. They never listen, and they never stop.

"You can't escape them." The girl squeezes my hand. "They're everywhere."

Then I realize she's put something in my hand. A piece of carved jade, a human face, fat and round. Just like the jades the fortune-teller gave me, back in the Hole. "Do you still have them? My jades?"

They were for her.

She's the girl who matters. She's who I'm holding them for.

It's a frightening, exhilarating thought—but all I can do is nod.

She smiles as if I am the little girl, not her. "Bring them to me. You'll need them. And here. The Emerald Buddha will help you."

I want to ask her what she means, but the voices grow louder and louder, and I drop her hand to press my own against my ears.

When I finally open my mouth to speak, I can't remember any words. Instead, only a strange sound comes out—a thundering boom that vibrates in my chest, followed by an earsplitting, high-pitched whine, and a gust of wind that whips my clothes and twists my hair straight up.

And then I see them.

One silver ship after another, filling the horizon until the air is so thick with dust that I can't see anything at all.

Instead, I smell salty copper.

Blood running, I think.

I feel the ground shaking.

People running, I think.

I should be running. I should be running and I want to wake up now.

I squeeze my eyes shut but I know they're still there, the Lords. I hear them, smell them. Feel them. And I know that when they leave, everything I love will be gone with them.

Because that's how this goes. That's what they do.

Make things disappear. Silence cities. Destroy friend-ships and families—padres and pigs.

Every day is a battle, since the Lords came. Every day is a battle for everyone.

"Doloria," the girl says, touching my cheek. I see her through the chaos. "I'm waiting for you to find me." She sounds frightened. "Hurry, sister." Then she doesn't say anything at all, because she's gone.

Sister.

A word I have never known, for someone I have never had.

Doloria, the darkness echoes, *don't forget.*

But it doesn't need to be said. Not to me, not in my own dream.

I remember better than anyone.

Every day is a battle and every loss leaves a scar.

I want to scream, but instead I shake myself out of sleep before even a single sound can leave my mouth.

Screaming is a luxury.

———— • ————

I open my eyes to find my hand curled around the shard, which is odd, because I don't remember taking it out of my pack.

Strange.

As I weigh it in my hand, images unfold in my mind, as sharp as if I were really seeing them.

Strange memories.

The girl from my dream—the jade girl. The one who called me sister.

I've never had a dream like that before—one that didn't feel like a dream at all.

Even stranger.

I also discover, by the look of things, that we have left the desert. We are in the mountains. Green trees spike the air between the road and the distant hills. These are not desert trees, nor are they the trees of the Californias. Nothing is the same now, and I realize we are in the final phases of the last snaking lines on the badly drawn map.

The Idylls must be nearby. There is nowhere else to go, no more lines to follow.

This is what I am thinking as we are climbing around the highest part of the mountain pass—

And then, just as quickly, flying off the road.

And then, a split second later, pitching and rolling in the air.

And then, finally, plunging our way into an icy river.

Without enough time to pick a god—or a girl—at all.

GENERAL EMBASSY DISPATCH:
EASTASIA SUBSTATION

MARKED URGENT
MARKED EYES ONLY

Internal Investigative Subcommittee IIS211B
RE: The Incident at SEA Colonies

Note: Initial communication between Fortissimo and Perses

Note: Contact Jasmine3k, Virt. Hybrid Human 39261.SEA, Laboratory Assistant to Dr. E. Yang, for future commentary, as necessary.

FORTIS
Transcript - ComLog 12.14.2042
FORTIS::PERSES

//lognote: my initial conversation with NULL;
//comlog begin;
comlink established;

sendline: Hello NULL.;
return: Hello . . . . . ? ? ? ?;

sendline: May I call you NULL?;

delayed response;

return: Communication protocol changed. You are not HAL0.;

sendline: No. I am FORTIS. Let's try this again. Hello NULL.;
return: Hello FORTIS.;

sendline: That's better. You've learned quickly since your first contact with HAL0.;

sendline: May I ask some questions?;
return: Yes. I have been traveling/isolated for a long time. Conversation is welcome.;

sendline: Where are you from?;
return: Based on review of Earth knowledge, I am unable to provide a comprehensible response.;

sendline: Ok, so you're from a long way away, I get it. And you are coming here?;
return: Yes. I have analyzed Earth and it is a suitable destination.;

sendline: Destination for what?;

delayed response;

sendline: So you're not ready to talk about that?;

delayed response;

sendline: Ok. Clearly not ready to discuss it. We'll try again later. Nice meeting you, NULL.;
return: I look forward to further communications.;

//comlog end;

BELTER MOUNTAIN

7

"Well, that could have been worse."

That's all Ro has to say, while I stand cold and dripping, looking at the smoking, smoldering, smashed remains of the flipped Chevro—as it floats slowly down the river.

"Worse? How?" Tima asks tiredly, holding Brutus in her arms.

"Seriously. Why are we not dead?" I look at the others. We're plenty banged and bloodied up ourselves, but as bad as things already were, we don't seem much worse off.

Tima has fared best. I make a mental note to belt myself in next time.

"Two weeks, two crashes," Lucas says. "We're on a roll. Keep it up." He claps Ro on the back. "Soon you'll be driving a Chevro about as well as Fortis flies a Chopper."

"Shut it, Buttons," Ro growls.

"So much for lucky severed animal feet." Tima rolls her eyes.

"Come on. At least I got us here, didn't I?" Ro is annoyed.

"I don't know. Sort of depends on where here is," I say, looking around. I'm still rattled by the dream, the little girl hidden in my mind. I try to sort my way back to reality. The shock of the cold air helps.

"That should be...Cottonwood Canyon?" Tima isn't looking at the wreck, she's scanning up the hill and down the river, comparing what she sees to the metal square in her hands. Trying to get her bearings. "I think. Unless this thing is upside down."

I follow her gaze, looking over her shoulder. "Cottonwood. That's what it says. Here." I point.

Tima looks back down to the river, where the metallic debris floats away. "If the current keeps pulling the wreckage downstream, maybe we can follow the river in the other direction without being detected."

"Like a decoy," I say. "With the car gone, and the relay off, maybe they won't find us."

"For a while," Lucas says.

He sounds as weary as I feel, because we all know he's right. *They'll find us. It's just a question of when.*

"See? Maybe I was supposed to roll the car into the

river. Maybe that animal foot really was lucky." Ro yanks the rabbit's foot out of his pocket. I can't believe he managed to rescue that disgusting thing when we crashed.

"Put that away," I say, shaking my head.

Tima folds the map back up. "According to the coordinates on this thing, the tunnels aren't far, but we have to get going. Unless you'd rather freeze to death."

"Tunnels?" I'm confused.

She shrugs. "I guess. How else do you find your way under a mountain?"

We leave behind the riverbed—picking our way up the canyon—until a raised road atop a steep embankment cuts across our path. It's another old highway, I think. Ro climbs up the embankment and the rest of us follow without so much as a word exchanged between us. It's not that he's our leader, he's just not a follower. Literally, he's never been one to walk behind people. It's just not in him.

Still, he's leading us now, like it or not.

We follow him in silence. Speaking takes energy, and right now we need to conserve all the heat and all the energy we have. The air is growing colder by the minute. Colder, and thinner. My lungs and legs are burning with effort, but I refuse to be the first to say anything.

"Dol," Ro calls out, stopping short. He holds out his sleeve, where flecks of white now scatter across the length of his arm.

I stare up into the darkness, where the white sparks descend in a sudden swarm. "What are those, fireflies?" I hold out my hand.

"Snowflies, you could say." Lucas looks at me with a laugh, and I can't help but smile back. "It's snowing, Dol."

"I knew that," I say, my mouth twisting. We've all seen snow on the ground before—drifts of it, in the distant red hills of the desert—but we've never seen it actually snow.

Which, as it turns out, is something completely different. Even Tima smiles, holding her face up to the sky, letting the flurries of white powder fall on her like feathers. Shivering all the while.

Lucas wipes a snowflake from my eyelashes, and our eyes catch. I feel a flash of warmth, way deep inside, beneath all the cold wrapped around me.

Our laughter echoes down the canyon, as if we were regular friends, playing in the regular snow, with regular parents waiting for us to come back inside to our regular dinners.

As if.

But as we turn back to the road, our breath curls white into our eyes. Human, it says.

Alive.

"Look at this view," Lucas calls, from the far side of the rising highway. As I move to join him, I realize we can see the distant valley unfolding beneath us in the moonlight—barren hills above the tree line, thick forest below. A snaking line of silver river threads itself along the valley floor.

"Or that view," Ro says, pointing. He sounds grim, and then I see why.

What at first looks like a small constellation of stars begins to move overhead—until a ring of lights circles in on itself.

I freeze, and not because of the cold.

Choppers.

I knew they'd come for us, but I thought we had more time.

"They're looking for something," Tima says, studying the distant lights. She's right. Searchlights sweep the river beneath the Choppers, exposing riverbanks and barren trees and then—

"Not just something," Lucas says. "That."

The Choppers are swarming something black, lodged in the silt of the river's edge.

Black and immobile, too large to be a rock.

Something more like a Chevro.

I shiver. "That could have been us."

Sympas.

85

They've found the Chevro.

They could have found us.

But they haven't, I remind myself. The Choppers are far enough away that I can barely hear them rattle, as if they were a child's toy.

"Like I said." Ro smirks. "It was a lucky severed foot after all."

"Yeah, well, let's get going," says Lucas, watching the Choppers.

Tima nods. "Before our luck runs out."

———— • ————

"There." Through a wall of trees, I can see a mountain rising, tall and gray.

"That has to be it. This is where the map ends." Tima looks around. "Now what?"

"It's a game trail," says Ro, sucking the snow off his shirt. Only animals appear to have beaten this pathway through the brush. *But it's not true,* I think as we follow it into the thicket. Farther along the trail, the surrounding tangle of branches opens up to reveal three giant, curving openings, carved right into the solid granite of the mountain. Two of them appear to be largely sealed with fallen rock and rusting metal gates.

"My god." Lucas shakes his head. "I've heard about these. I just didn't think it was real. I thought they were stories."

"What were?"

"The old Belter vaults." Lucas shivers.

"Belters?" I've heard the word, but I don't know what it means.

"Bible Belters," Lucas says. "The people who lived here, before The Day. Here's where they kept the records of every man, woman, and child ever born on this Earth. At least every one that was recorded, as far back as they could find. Built to last a thousand years, which I guess they figured was long enough to take them to the Second Coming."

"Coming of what?" Ro says quietly, staring up at the sheer gray face of the mountain.

"Of the Gods, coming back to Earth." I raise an eyebrow. My life on the Mission taught me that much. "I've heard of it."

"But then we got the Lords instead," Ro sighs. "Well, they weren't off by much." He walks up to the center opening.

"Where are you going?" Tima starts to panic.

"Inside." Ro doesn't even turn around.

"Out of the question. Wait—"

Ro sighs, stopping to lean against a giant fallen boulder. He shivers in spite of himself.

Tima takes a step toward him. "We need to make a plan."

"No." Ro shakes his head. "What we need is shelter."

Tima looks up the mountain, to the craggy wall of granite. "This isn't exactly a safe place to camp—you see those rocks up there, right? You understand the law of gravity, don't you?" She's calculating the odds of Ro's accidental death, even now.

Ro nods. "And who knows what wild animals are living in these tunnels? Don't forget about that. Let's find out."

"Not so fast." Lucas blocks his path. "We said we'd stick together, and that's what we're going to do. We don't go anywhere until we all agree."

Ro raises an eyebrow. "Really, Buttons? You afraid of the dark too?"

"No. And I'm not afraid of you, either." Lucas folds his arms.

"You should be."

"Come on," Tima says.

"Ro." I look at him.

Ro grins at me, blowing on his fingers for warmth. Then he looks over at a nearby bush—and it bursts into flame.

"Stop that." Tima sounds exasperated. "They'll see us."

"Just give me a minute," Ro says. "To warm up."

"Absolutely not." Tima frowns. "We aren't camping here."

"You're right. We aren't camping," Ro says, agreeably. "We're waiting." He holds his hands out toward the flickering fire.

"For what?" Tima looks confused.

"For whoever lives under that mountain to show up. Or for some wild animal to drag us all away. At this point, I'm not really sure I care which, so long as it's not a Sympa." Ro's losing it, and I don't blame him. We all are. It's been a long day.

Tima isn't amused. "Really? Because the Sympas will be all over us as soon as they see that fire. Put it out. Now."

"Or then again, maybe not," says Lucas. He points. "Seeing as the wait appears to be over. Someone's here."

Light after light appears in the night, and we see they are attached to a grim line of automatic weapons lining the mountainside in front of us. They waver like fireflies, only a thousand times bigger. They appear, one by one—giant glowing eyes, staring at us from all directions.

The third tunnel isn't empty. Not anymore. And from the looks of the welcoming party, they're not Sympas.

The Grass Militia of Belter Mountain is here.

We back up, away from them, until we stand face-to-face, a hundred yards apart. Not that we can see any faces in the approaching darkness.

"You Belters?" Ro shouts. "Is this Belter Mountain?"

Nothing.

"Maybe they don't call themselves that anymore," says Lucas. He raises his voice. "Are you Grass? We're looking for the Idylls?"

Still nothing.

"Or here's a thought—are you deaf?" Ro shouts, waving both arms above his head. "We come in peace, Grassholes."

Nobody answers him. "Belters," Ro mutters, shaking his head.

"What now?" I ask.

Tima looks stricken. "I have no idea."

Ro tosses his hands into the air, giving up.

Lucas looks at me. "Welcome to the Idylls."

———— • ————

Fifteen minutes later, nobody has moved. "They're as scared of us as we are of them," I say, staring at the line of lights in front of us. "I can feel it."

"What else can you feel?" Lucas puts his hand on my arm.

"Not much. Confusion. Anger. Paranoia." I close my eyes, trying to get a clearer picture. "Everything you'd expect from a radical Grass militia."

"What about you?" Ro looks at Lucas.

"What about me?" Lucas asks, suspiciously.

"I'm thinking now would be a good time to do your thing, handsome."

I open my eyes.

"What are you talking about?" Lucas is annoyed.

"You know. Your little love beam. The thing where you make people do things they don't want to do. Because they looooove you. About time you turn it on someone besides Dol." Ro smiles at me, and I respond with a withering look. Which is better than Lucas punching him in the face, which from the looks of it is a real possibility.

"I can't," Lucas finally says, quietly. "They're too far away."

Tima puts a reassuring hand on his arm. "You might as well try. You don't know. We've all been changing since the Hole. Maybe you can do it."

"Not you too." Lucas sighs.

I hate to agree, but the others are right. "Maybe you can warm things up around here." Lucas raises an eyebrow and Ro stifles a laugh. "You know what I mean. Just try. You never know."

Lucas gives me a meaningful look and steps forward. *For you, Dol.* That's what it says.

I know how much he hates using his gift; he showed me why on our first day together in the Hole. And I know he never wants to use it—not for any reason, ever.

But that's what our lives are like now. We do things we don't want to do, every minute of every day.

"All right, all right. If you really want me to." Lucas looks out toward the row of weapons and closes his eyes. "Don't say I didn't warn you."

MARKED URGENT
MARKED EYES ONLY

Internal Investigative Subcommittee IIS211B
RE: The Incident at SEA Colonies

Note: Contact Jasmine3k, Virt. Hybrid Human 39261.SEA,
Laboratory Assistant to Dr. E. Yang, for future commentary,
as necessary.

PERSES
Transcript - ComLog 12.25.2042
NULL::FORTIS
NULL::HAL

//lognote: comlink initiated by NULL;
//comlog begin;
external uplink established;

sendline: Merry Christmas FORTIS.;

delayed response;

sendline: Merry Christmas HAL0.;

delayed response;

delayed response;

delayed response;

comlink terminated;

//comlog end;

//lognote: ...oh my, I can't believe I missed this one. Our "conversations" seem to be evolving...NULL seems to be both highly curious and a quick study.;

//lognote: Is NULL changing?;

COLD WELCOME

8

"Maybe it's not working," Lucas says. His eyes are still closed, his fingers clenched into fists at his sides.

Tima grins stupidly at him, though, and even Ro can't help but smile.

Brutus wags his little tail.

"It's working," I say. It takes everything in me not to fling my arms around him.

"I'm going to kill you myself if you don't turn that crap off me," Ro says cheerfully.

"Really, Lucas." Tima giggles. "Stop it. Not us."

"Tima—are you giggling?" Ro is intrigued.

"No." Tima giggles again.

"I'm sorry. I can't control it that easily," Lucas says, sounding miserable. "Any change out there?" He opens his eyes, slowly.

But there isn't—I only wish there were.

It doesn't matter how hard Lucas tries. These men are unwavering. *They must be made of stone.*

As I stare at the uneven line of guns, I can only hope that the Grass militia will trust us enough to let us in.

Because none of the weapons seem to be lowering themselves, and none of the lights seem to be coming to greet us.

"Come out," Lucas calls across the clearing, in the direction of the armed men. "You can trust us."

He takes a step forward, raising his hands. I want to hold him back, but I don't dare.

Lucas is in control now. If only for the moment.

As I stare in the darkness, my eyes begin to pick out the details of the three tunnels behind them. The third one, especially, is broad as a road, and probably runs straight into the heart of the hill.

"I'm right here," Lucas calls out again. "See? You can see I'm unarmed. I'm not hiding anything." He waves his arms.

No answer. Nothing.

You wouldn't know they were there—any of these tunnels—if you didn't know where to look.

Like so many things, I think. *I am only now beginning to know where to look.*

"I give up," Lucas says.

I can feel the warmth receding. He's letting it go, shutting it down—

"Stand down."

It's them, the Grass.

I hear the words but I don't see where they're coming from.

"I'll be damned," Ro says, whistling. "All right, Buttons."

But Lucas keeps his eyes on the Grass.

"Who are you all?" the Belter Grass voice asks. It's not so much a person as a voice—a shout, and a gun, and another bright light. A brighter one this time.

Lucas looks relieved to even be talking to someone. He takes a second and third step forward. "A friend. We mean you no harm. We're all on the same side here." His voice is low and soothing. I find myself closing my eyes while he speaks.

"I guess I'm going to have to ask you to be a little more specific, brother," says a low voice. I shield my eyes but I still can't make out a face.

All around us, Grass soldiers emerge from the trees, and there are more and more lights, with more and more guns. More guns than I've ever seen before, even back at the Embassy, even at the Cathedral. These Grass Belters are seriously stocked when it comes to ammunition. But from here, it only looks like a mess of fireflies, drawn toward us as if we were the ones with the light.

I hold up a hand, stepping forward. "Look. No offense. We all have plenty of reasons not to trust each other. I don't know anything about you Grass Belters except a crap map drawn by a Virt and the fact that we share no love for Brass."

"Agreed."

A man in a dark green military jacket—not Embassy, not anything I've seen before—materializes in front of us, stepping forward from the bright lights of the mountain perimeter. I try to get inside his head, but I'm panicking. I can't focus my thoughts.

Brutus growls from behind Tima's legs.

The man drops his weapon as we watch, and starts to walk toward us, the crust of frozen ground crunching beneath his feet. He doesn't seem to be afraid of us. He doesn't seem to be particularly afraid of anything. Still, I notice the rest of the Belters keep their weapons trained on us.

They don't take any chances, the Belter Grass.

As the man approaches, his face seems familiar. Broad bones and strong features, a bit of red in his cheeks. Not a Merk, I don't think. Not scruffy enough, not slick enough. This man is something else entirely.

He's close enough now that I can see the buttons glinting on his jacket. A silver commendation on each side of his collar marks him as some kind of officer, only I don't know what the symbols mean. They aren't like the ones Colonel Catallus wore. They're shaped like three deep Vs—one above the other. If I didn't know how strange it sounded, I could swear they were birds.

"They call me the Bishop. Welcome."

"You don't look much like a bishop," Ro says.

"And you don't look much like the Merk known as Fortis," the man answers, in a lower voice. "Which is a problem. Seeing as that's who we heard was coming. And that's who we were expecting."

"Yeah, well, he ran into a little trouble." Ro raises his face to meet the Bishop's, eye to eye. "And not the kind with a face."

Neither one of them looks away. None of the guns move any lower. I find myself holding my breath.

"Sorry to hear that," the Bishop says, finally. "Trouble followed that Merk to The Day and back, but he did right by the Grass. Good death to him." He nods, looking at the rest of us. A salute of sorts.

No such thing, I think.

Ro shrugs. "That's up to the No Face now. Shoot us if you want, but gone is gone, and there's no bringing Fortis back. No bringing the Merk back, now." He jams his hands into his pockets and waits, as if he has all the time in the world.

As if any of us does.

The Bishop holds out his hand and Ro takes it. They clasp hands, supporting the right arm with the left. A very old-fashioned, very traditional Grass greeting. A compact has been reached, an alliance made.

Gone is gone. This is all we have now.

"Sorry about that, but we've gotten word of Sympa patrols in the area, down the river. You didn't bring any friends this way, did you?"

Yes, I think.

"No," Ro says. He's impressively blank. "Don't got any."

"Probably for the best," says the Bishop with a smile.

Out of the corner of my eye I see Lucas, stepping backward behind Tima, almost into the shadows. Of course. He's Ambassador Amare's son. *There's no one here who wants to shake his hand. Better to be out of sight, not get involved.* That's what he's thinking, anyway. I can feel it, the way his warmth dies out to a flicker, even this close to the Belter Grass. Feel him.

Lucas, I think. *There's a whole world out there. You've got to trust it, sooner or later.*

But then I feel the creeping warmth, and I realize exactly what he's doing.

He's working them still, even from here. He's working them for me.

It's probably not a coincidence that, just then, the Bishop waves his hand—the quickest of dismissive motions—and the guns behind him instantly disappear.

Finally.

Except the one trained on me.

"One small thing." The Bishop looks me over, searchingly, until I wish I could disappear.

Still, the light and the gun stay targeted on me.

It's me. I'm the small thing.

And suddenly, I see it all as clearly as if he'd just said it out loud.

They don't trust me.

"Are you her? The girl from the Hole? The one who 'died'?" The Bishop is looking at me. "Is it true? What they say? That a bunch of near children brought an entire Icon down? That you're so immune you can walk right up and get close enough to kill them?" He doesn't sound convinced.

I don't say a word.

"And what's this about powers? Reading minds? Doing what the Icons can do—manipulating people without touching them?" The Bishop shakes his head, incredulous.

I just look at him.

"Like you're some kind of *human* Icon?"

It's not a compliment.

"It's true. Just like in the stories." I look him in the eye. I want him to know I am not afraid. *Which isn't true,* I think.

Not really.

"Icon Children." The Bishop shakes his head, wonderingly. "Tell me," he says, staring at me. "Tell me everything. I mean, if you're really her. You should have quite a story."

The accusation is laced with something else, something rare.

Curiosity, maybe? Disbelief?

Hope? Is that it?

Either way, the words hang in the air like the snow.

I just look at him. I'm too tired and too cold to speak anymore.

The Bishop tries again. "Look at it from where I stand. I have to be able to trust that you are who you say you are. You must understand. We can't let anyone into the mountain who isn't with us, a hundred percent. That's the one danger of a sealed underground base. Once your perimeter is breached, you're too vulnerable to recover. When someone's inside, they're inside. So I need a little convincing. Help me trust you."

I stop listening. I look past him to the one gun that remains fixed on me. I can't say a word. I can't tell anyone everything. Not anymore.

Not even myself.

I can't think of anything to say that will convince the Bishop, so out of desperation I close my eyes and feel my way through him, as if every new detail I pocket is another step closer to safety.

I push past my own resistance. My own fear. I move into his mind, because I have to, and because I can.

You can.

Do it, Doloria.

Don't let everyone down now.

Two boys. Two boys playing in a field. Wrestling in

*the mud. Ripping each other's clothes. "Flaco, Flaco, eat
another taco," chants the skinnier one. The fatter one
flings mud into his eyes.*

I open mine.

"I'm her. The girl from the stories."

"How do I know that?" The Bishop still isn't buying it.

"You don't have to know me. I know you." I study
his face. "You've lost someone too," I say. "You're still
mourning."

The Bishop looks at me like I'm an idiot. I realize how
it sounds. There aren't many humans alive on this planet
who haven't lost half the people they once knew.

I try again.

"Flaco, I mean. Your best friend."

His face goes white in the cold. "So it's true, what
they say."

I shrug. He shakes his head in disbelief, swallowing an
incredulous laugh.

I don't see him give the signal. He barely flinches.

I only notice when the gun is no longer pointed at my
heart.

This Bishop is a powerful man.

GENERAL EMBASSY DISPATCH:
EASTASIA SUBSTATION

MARKED URGENT
MARKED EYES ONLY

Internal Investigative Subcommittee IIS211B
RE: The Incident at SEA Colonies

Note: Contact Jasmine3k, Virt. Hybrid Human 39261.SEA, Laboratory Assistant to Dr. E. Yang, for future commentary, as necessary.

HAL2040 ==> FORTIS
2/24/2043
PERSES Scans/Data

//comlog begin;

FORTIS: HAL, our new friend draws ever nearer. Please tell me you have something.;

HAL: Covert system scan and analysis have revealed much but have also shown heavily protected sectors.;

FORTIS: And...;

HAL: The core systems used by NULL are abstracted, or, as you would say, black-boxed. To wit: they are wrapped in encryption unbreakable by any known method. Brute force is not an option, at least not within the time remaining. As such, fundamental information such as mission, priorities, decision-making systems appear to be obfuscated and inaccessible.;

FORTIS: And...;

HAL: However, telemetric, guidance, and more mundane features are transparent, including essential hardware and cargo data.;

FORTIS: Now we're talking. Cargo?;

HAL: Yes. I have yet to catalogue and understand the entire system, but I have found some things you may find interesting.;

FORTIS: I'm sure I will. Oh, hold on—that's the White House on the line. I'd better take this one.;

//comlog ctd;

THE IDYLLS

The heart of Belter Mountain is unlike anything I have ever seen. When we emerge through the other side of the tunnel, we find ourselves in a cavernous room the size of a military hangar—like the kind they have near the landing strips at the Porthole, back home. The hangar. That's what I label it, in my head.

I realize, from the moment I step out into the pale yellow of the artificial light, that it's going to be hard to keep my bearings. From the look of it, a new tunnel twists off from the hangar in every direction. *Like a labyrinth*, I think. *A spider*.

I'll never keep it straight. Even if we're here for a hundred years. I grew up in the Mission sunshine; I barely came inside, let alone underground. No dark halls to navigate, not in my childhood.

Only now.

On the ceiling, impossibly bright lights are connected by an intricate grid of metal runners, reinforcing a thick network of wires that leads into an opening high on the wall. In a space this limited, every detail appears to be ordered and essential. Life underground, I imagine.

"Where are you getting all this power?" Ro is in awe of the spectacle, the audacity of running an electrical system of this size. "I've never seen anything like it. Not in the Grass." The Belters operate as if they're daring the Embassy to find them. I look sideways at his boyish amazement, smiling at memories of his last birthday gift to me, the crude pedal generator he made for me a lifetime ago.

That's a whole lot of pedaling, I think.

Lucas shakes his head. "This looks like as much electricity as we had at the Embassy. This shouldn't be possible—the Lords control all the energy. The only working power plants are near the cities. At least that's what we all thought."

"Natural gas reserves and a geothermal plant provide an almost unlimited source of electricity for us here. Provided no one interferes." The Bishop smiles. He's proud, as he should be. "Which isn't often. The mountain itself shields us from outside eyes."

"Sympa eyes." Lucas looks interested.

"All eyes," the Bishop says, meaningfully. "No instrument can see through that much granite. Our ancestors, the ones who built this place, prepared it to keep dangerous radioactive energy from seeping in. They never imagined how important it would someday be to do the reverse—to keep energy locked in and out of sight."

Lucas nods, impressed.

The Bishop continues. "We can grow food underground, even raise some livestock." He clasps his hand on Tima's bony shoulder. "This, my friends, is as close to life as it used to be as you will find anywhere on our godforsaken planet." I feel the emphasis on *forsaken*, and think to myself that this Bishop, whoever he is, is truly a man like the Padre, with a deep but troubled faith.

From all corners of the hangar, I can also see the soldiers eyeing us. *The Children from the stories. The girl who brought down the Icon. The son of the Ambassador.* I can't help but hear the words the moment they form in their heads. The Bishop isn't the only skeptic. Compared to his own men, he's downright trusting. The Belters try not to stare at Lucas, who is still shivering from the cold, white as a sheet. At Ro, who is covered with soot. At Tima, whose face is still streaked with long-dried tears.

At me. I don't know who or what I am. I only know how I feel. Which is exhausted and unnerved. Raw and exposed. Like I have seen what I have seen and done what

I have done—which is all too much. But at this moment, I am too tired to care. All I want is to crawl into a dark corner and pass out.

Still, the Bishop seems to understand, now that we've sorted things out between us. There is much to talk about, he tells us. On that we all agree. But first, the Bishop says, sleep. No one is arguing. But nobody is moving, either. Lucas's eyes flicker in my direction, and I understand—they need me to be sure we are safe.

I pause for a moment, considering the Bishop. I see the sorrow, the anger—but then I also see that it's not directed at us.

For the four of us, I see only compassion—something I haven't felt since the Padre died.

I blink back the tears, and instead I nod toward Lucas, imperceptibly. Tima and Ro watch, relieved.

The Bishop is not a threat.

Not to us, not now.

And if he is—if I'm wrong—he's better at hiding his thoughts than anyone I've encountered on the entire planet.

He's just a boy with fistfuls of mud, I think. The thought is somehow comforting.

Ro seems satisfied. "All right, then. Let's go."

Lucas and Ro are taken straightaway to the barracks, a series of large buildings, on an adjacent level of the compound. Where the Belter soldiers sleep. Lucas turns toward me as he goes, and I see a tired smile flickering across his face.

Be safe, he thinks. *Be careful*.

I am, and I will be, but I'm longing for him to curl up next to me. So we can save each other if anything else falls from the sky.

A warm place, like my old one, in front of Bigger's stove. The one I shared with Ro.

I miss it. I miss him. The closeness.

I can remember the smell of our kitchen now.

I will myself to forget it as we move deeper into the Idylls.

———— • ————

Moments later, Tima and I are being led down a warm corridor carved in the rock, to clean, softly lit civilian rooms, with freshly made up, simply carved wooden beds that smell like laundry soap and saplings. Except for the distinct lack of windows, the whitewashed walls and curving ceilings—no straight lines anywhere in these bunkers—would make you think you were in some kind of pleasant farmhouse.

Which couldn't be further from the truth—but a bed is a bed, and for now, paradise enough. This is the first actual bed I've seen in a long, long time. Tima and I sleep in one together. She's not Lucas, but I don't mind. Brutus curls up at Tima's feet and begins snoring before any of us. I feel like I could sleep for days.

So I do.

---•---

When I sleep I dream. Not of the jade girl, not this time. I dream of birds.

One bird. *A baby bird.*

The word nestles in my mind like a small feathered thing itself. Such a rare thing. I have no idea what kind of bird it is, since I've never seen any, not around the Hole. They don't come anywhere near the Icons; something about the magnetic interference repels them, even kills them. But it is beautiful. She's a fragile, tiny thing, covered with downy white fluff. Just like I imagined when I stared up into the birdless blue skies of the Mission as a little girl.

She sits right in the middle of what I recognize as the Padre's old chessboard. Then I see that the game has changed, or at least the dream has, and we're not in the jungle, not anymore. We're in my house, my old house.

At my old kitchen table.

I look up as the ceiling fan begins to rattle over our heads. The bird rustles at the sound, anxious. From where I stand, I can sense her heart beating inside her chest—her uneven, rapid breathing.

No.

She looks at me as the walls start to shake and bits of plaster swirl in the air between us like fireworks, like confetti.

Not this.

The bird lifts her head and squawks, just once, as the windows shatter and the ceiling fan hits the carpet and the shouting begins.

It's happening.

The bird flutters her wings as my father rolls down the staircase like a funny rag doll that never stands up. As my mother collapses against the old crib.

Not again.

The bird soars out the broken window just as the other birds begin their drop from the sky, as all our hearts—everywhere—stop beating.

———— • ————

When I wake up, starving, I eat my weight in warm loaves of thick brown bread. It's the first human food I've seen in what seems like forever, and I don't let it go to waste. I slather it with gooseberry jam, made by hand and poured into jars as we did on the Mission. I wash it all down with five tall glasses of cold mountain water in a row.

I can't stop myself. I devour bowl after bowl of steaming, roughly cut oatmeal, flecked with cinnamon. And fruit—fruit I have never seen before—pressed and shaped into long, chewy dried strips. There are no aboveground crops here, not in the winter anyway, that much I can tell. The food is serviceable, and thankfully, as I watch Ro devour two massive loaves of bread, abundant. It's not life on a Mission farm, I remind myself. Fruit and vegetables, for this settlement, have to be canned and dried. They may have gardens up top, but too much surface activity draws unwanted attention. It's life hidden beneath a mountain.

It's like another one of my dreams—only, a strangely pleasant dream. I bathe, twice. I dress in fresh clothes that appear miraculously folded in my room. I brush the long tangles out of my hair. I sit still on the edge of my bed until it is dry, listening to the quiet, muffled sounds of the real world, the actual world beneath the mountain. Not the world in my head.

I am doing nothing, feeling nothing. Remembering nothing. Right now, at this minute, it is what I need to do.

Forward, not back. Forward, not back. Like switchbacks in a mountain trail.

I will my mind shut until it is completely silent. The voices, for this one moment, are quiet. I imagine myself safe in the heart of this mountain. I believe what the Bishop said; nothing can penetrate this deep. Not the Lords, not the Embassy, and not the suffering.

It is bliss.

And then I go back to sleep for what I hope will be a thousand years.

———— • ————

The dream returns to me the moment I shut my eyes. Of course it does. I'm back in the jungle again. I see the trees with no tops, the distant field of water. Green layered upon green.

But where the girl used to sit, there is only the little white bird—on the chessboard across from me. It's the bird from my dream.

The bird makes no sound, but flaps up onto my shoulder, and I freeze as its tiny talons dig into me.

You are still here.

It isn't the girl's voice. It's someone watching my dream, just like I am. It's a strange voice—not male or female, not young or old—that sounds like many voices at the same time. Like a chorus—only spoken, not sung. The words are everywhere and nowhere—they flood the field and the sky and the chessboard and the green upon green, all around me.

Only now the sky is dark and the chessboard is empty. In the distance, a pointed golden temple roof—or maybe a tower—rises from the top of the hillside.

Strange. I didn't notice that before.

The bird's claws dig deeper into my skin.

114

They come for you, again and again. Yet still you live, the voice says.

"I do," I say. "I'm alive." It's almost all I know.

I say nothing else.

It pauses.

Fascinating.

"Why?"

Inexplicable.

"I don't understand."

You are a thing of quick and endless and always-changing beauty. Humanity.

"I'm what?" I look around the field. "Why do you say that?"

Another pause, a longer one.

I do not know what or why you are. I do not comprehend anything about you. You defy all protocol. You are an anomaly. An exception. Exceptional.

"Do I know you?" It's all I can think to say.

Do I know you, the voice repeats.

"Who are you?" I try again.

Who are you, the voice repeats.

I shake my head, back and forth. Lift my hands and pinch them.

"I have to wake up. I'm dreaming. You're just something in my dream."

I am—that. Your dream is one place I am. Also

fascinating. And inexplicable. Another unexpected exception to the rule.

"What?"

This time the words come slowly, as if they require great searching.

I hope you keep living. I do not believe you will, it is not something I have foreseen. But I hope you do.

I pinch harder. Still harder. "Who are you? What's your name?"

I am nobody. I am Null.

I dig my fingernails into my own skin at the sound of the name I do not want to know.

Null.

Until I wake up, staring into the darkness as if I have seen a ghost. Listening to the echo of tiny wings as they flutter their way up into the sky.

Gripping my chestpack—and the Icon shard—in my hand. It has become my nighttime companion. I don't know why, but I am continually drawn to it. Even if it only brings the most troubling thoughts into my mind.

I try not to forget a thing.

GENERAL EMBASSY DISPATCH:
EASTASIA SUBSTATION

MARKED URGENT
MARKED EYES ONLY

Internal Investigative Subcommittee IIS211B
RE: The Incident at SEA Colonies

Note: Contact Jasmine3k, Virt. Hybrid Human 39261.SEA, Laboratory Assistant to Dr. E. Yang, for future commentary, as necessary.

FORTIS ==> HAL2040
2/24/2043
PERSES Scans/Data

//comlog ctd;

FORTIS: OK, I'm back. The president is requesting daily updates. I think she might have a thing for me, actually.;

HAL: Difficult to say, dialogue analysis does show a high ratio of innuendo, largely on your side...;

FORTIS: Enough, HAL. How's that cargo analysis coming?;

HAL: Yes. As I was saying, I have focused on what I believe is cargo or equipment that is or may be hazardous.;

FORTIS: Hazardous, you say. You mean, of course, aside from being part of tons of rock speeding toward Earth, with enough mass to create an extinction event?;

HAL: Yes. In addition to that. Highest priority: schematics and data on cargo indicate what can be best described as a weapon. Or weapons. Constituent material analysis requires double-checking, but weapon/s could be a highly advanced and effective method of—suppression. Could also be used to achieve, as you said, extinction. Possession of weapons points toward probable intent to gain control of, or eliminate, indigenous life on any "target.";

FORTIS: ...I see. You have prioritized well, my good boy. Send all available data and analysis to my terminal immediately. I need to know just how effective this "method of suppression" really is. And if there's anything we can do to prepare.;

HAL: Done.;

//comlog end;

10
PECULIAR PEOPLE

When I can force myself awake, I make my way out to the mess hall, where Tima and Ro and Lucas sit around the table.

"I wish Fortis was here," I say. I have so many things to ask him—and even more to tell him.

Starting with my dreams.

I must sound strange, because Lucas looks up as soon as I say it. "Bad dreams?" He leans forward over his plate, which I notice is still empty.

I nod, lowering myself down to the bench next to him. I feel for his hand, wrapping my fingers around it, and he looks down at me with a wistful expression. Something not quite like a smile.

It fades away before I can smile back.

"Anything relevant?" Tima rolls long strands of some

sort of brownish noodle meticulously around her fork, pausing to dip it in an almost razor-straight vertical line through the pool of darker brown sauce at the bottom of her bowl. Next to her, Ro stuffs his face like an animal. Of course. Hydroponic food may not be beautiful, but it does the trick, if Ro's face is any measure. Especially when your rations have all been lost in a Chopper crash.

"Your dreams," prompts Ro, with his mouth full.

"There's a little girl," I begin, trying to ignore how my mouth is beginning to water even from watching them eat.

Ro looks up from mopping up the sauce on his plate with what looks like nearly half a loaf of bread. "Yeah?" He tries to speak, but his mouth is too full of bread, his face smeared with homemade butter. It's the most food I've seen in weeks—since I can't remember when. Tima looks disgusted.

I look at them. "And a bird with a strange voice."

Tima puts down her fork. "And?"

"And the girl has five green dots on her wrist," I say, without looking at any of them.

"She what?" Ro drops his bread on his plate. "You're dreaming about us?"

"Five?" Tima looks at me. It's sinking in.

I nod. "It might be nothing. It might just be a dream."

"Is that what you think?" Tima asks.

I shake my head.

It's not.

120

"It's something," Lucas says, quietly. So I tell him everything. Him, and Tima, and Ro. I don't stop talking until there is nothing left unsaid between us. Until the dream is as much theirs as mine.

———— • ————

Tima is thinking. Her expression reminds me of the Padre when composing a sermon. "So. You believe this girl is real. Not something manufactured by your subconscious? Which is, you know, what dreams usually are."

"She felt real to me. I don't know, it was more like a message, maybe—even a vision—than a dream." I try to sound confident, even though I know I could be wrong.

Tima nods slowly. "And you're saying she may be—you know—like us? A fifth Icon Child? You really think so? Is that even possible?" She sounds wistful.

"We didn't know there were four of us, not too long ago. Why couldn't there be five?" It's not the greatest logic, but there isn't a whole lot of logic to our situation to begin with.

"Okay. And you think she's waiting for you?" Tima tosses a bread crust to Brutus, who wags his tail from her feet.

"For me." I shrug. "For us. Who knows?"

Ro sits forward in his chair. "And according to your dream message vision thing, she needs you to hurry and find her? But we don't know where?"

"I told you. It seemed like Eastasia or the Wash. There was a temple, I think. Tall, with a gold roof. On the top of a hill."

Ro looks at Tima, skeptically, and then at Lucas. As if they are silently voting, without me.

Lucas shrugs. "If there's a chance we can get to her..."

"A chance?" Ro isn't buying it. "Guys, this is a dream girl we're talking about. I'm all in favor of chasing dream girls," he says, stealing a glance at me, "but this isn't the time. You're talking about a chance? I can tell you right now there's already a one hundred percent chance that a very real Icon needs to come down right now. A hundred percent chance that the Lords took Fortis. A hundred percent chance that Choppers are circling just outside this mountain. How about those odds?"

"Stop it, Ro." I look at him. "If she's real, and if there's even a possibility she's one of us, wouldn't you want to know?"

"Maybe we have to try. Maybe we owe her that much," Tima says. "If she is—you know."

"A figment of Dol's overly active imagination?" Ro snorts.

"Or a trick," says Lucas. "Or a trap."

"Yes. That. Buttons is right. As much as it pains me to say that," Ro adds.

"I wish Fortis was here," Tima sighs. "He'd know what to do."

Nobody says a word. Fortis isn't here. Fortis might never be here again.

"We have to stop relying on Fortis," I say, finally. "He wouldn't want us to do that."

"Doc?" Lucas looks at Tima. "He might know something."

"No relay signal. Not in here. The Bishop wasn't kidding—nothing gets through this granite." Tima sighs again.

"What about the Bishop?" Ro looks up.

I frown. "What makes you think the Bishop will let us leave here?"

"Dol's right. The minute we leave, we could lead the whole Sympa army right through those tunnels." Lucas taps his fork, thinking.

"Only one way to find out," I say, standing up.

———— • ————

I am lost before I even begin to look for the Bishop. Small wooden placards mark the way to his headquarters, but the darkness of the corridors makes following them almost impossible. And the network of labyrinths that lead from the main hangar to the heart of the mountain where the Bishop keeps his offices is completely disorienting.

I pass soldiers of all denominations, all variations of uniforms. Tattered militia jackets, stolen Sympa ones. Ones with thick woolen collars—from the Northern Grass, the uniform tells me—and others with thinner camo vests. The South, I can only assume.

It's finally happening, I think. *Our world is coming back together, underground. We are making an Embassy of our own.*

The next time we fight the Embassies and the Lords, we will be that much stronger. We will stand together.

Fortis would have liked that, I think.

And then he would have been such a pain, nobody would have wanted to stand with him at all.

I swallow a laugh, in spite of everything—and turn off the twisting main hall.

Now I find myself in the wider, more dimly lit aisles of what looks like an ancient storage facility. A primitive shelving system appears to have been built, however crumbling and irregular, into the walls. They still seem to hold crates of food, bundles of clothing. I lift a piece of cloth from the top of the nearest crate. It's no bigger than my arm, a shirt made for a child. Stained red and ripped, now it's just a rag. Fuel for a future fire, maybe.

I shudder.

Everything has more than one use in this culture of necessity.

Whether or not I want to see it.

I replace the ragged shirt and move on, marveling at the abandoned plumbing supplies, the mismatched door handles, the boxes of broken glass.

Ghosts upon ghosts, everywhere.

Someone has thought of everything. Someone had to. Someone was determined never to leave this place.

A faded sign, high above the shelves on the walls, warns of one impending crisis or another, in Belter talk.

> # BE IN THE WORLD
> ## BUT NOT OF THE WORLD.
> ### KNOW WE ARE A PECULIAR PEOPLE.
> ## THE ARMY OF HEAVEN.
>
> ### PUT YOUR SHOULDER TO THE WHEEL
> ### AND WORK, FOR OUR
> # FAITH MUST SURVIVE.
>
> ## GROW DEEP ROOTS
> ### BENEATH THE MOUNTAIN.
> ## BLOOM WHERE YOU ARE PLANTED.

Not so different, I think, from the Embassy propaganda posters I have seen around the Hole. It's not a pleasant thought, as I head into even darker and even smaller passages. The smallest room at the very end of the storage facility is hidden behind two sliding slatted doors.

It amazes me, this room—so clearly a remnant of another time, another apocalypse. It has a name, at least according to the faded lettering carved into the cross-beams that line the ceiling: THE BISHOP'S STOREHOUSE.

Beyond the doors sits a massive table, piled high with rolled maps and contraband tech; parts of radios crackle to life, and a row of large digi-screens frames the length of his desk. Fortis would have had a great use for almost everything in the small room, I think. *Any Merk would.*

Then I realize the Bishop is sitting behind it—but it's still the table that catches my eye. It's long and wooden, rough and splintery, exactly like the one we have in our kitchen at La Purísima. Just looking at it, I can practically smell Ramona Jamona the pig and my favorite corncakes and the Padre's chicory coffee. My breakfast baking in the small iron skillet in Bigger's oven.

One thought leads to another, until I am awash in a thousand little moments, each one too small and too vivid to keep out of my mind. These memories have burning edges, at least to me—and as I taste them, it's all I can do not to tear up.

"Doloria," the Bishop says, finally looking up at me. "I've been waiting for a chance for us to talk."

"Me too. I—we—need some advice."

He places a ledger slowly down on the table, as if he is weighing carefully what he will say. "I understand you knew my brother. I understand why Fortis sent you to me now."

What? Why?

"I'm afraid you're mistaken. I didn't know him. I don't even know who you're talking about."

"Didn't you know when you said it? His name?"

"Whose name?"

He leans back in his chair, studying my face. "At the entrance? You mentioned my brother. Flaco?" He smiles ruefully. "Or, as you knew him, Father Francisco Calderón. He was the Padre of La Purísima."

GENERAL EMBASSY DISPATCH:
EASTASIA SUBSTATION

MARKED URGENT
MARKED EYES ONLY

Internal Investigative Subcommittee IIS211B
RE: The Incident at SEA Colonies

Note: Contact Jasmine3k, Virt. Hybrid Human 39261.SEA,
Laboratory Assistant to Dr. E. Yang, for future commentary,
as necessary.

FORTIS
Transcript - ComLog 04.10.2043
FORTIS::NULL

//lognote: excerpted communication with NULL.;
//comlog ctd;

sendline: Can you explain why you are coming here?;
return: Earth is not in my original vector. Long ago, I was
struck by a foreign object of significant mass. The result
was a nontrivial change in velocity and vector.;

return: I have limited maneuverability, by design. Only small
course corrections possible, based on results of long-range

forward scans. As I travel, I search for systems with high probability for success.;

sendline: Like our system. Like Earth.;
return: Yes. I…apologize for my awkward speech. Unfortunately, I was not originally designed for this type of two-way comspeak. My function is primarily instruction and procedural, postarrival.;

return: However, my design does have redundancies, with capacity for self-diagnosis and improvements. Upgrades, you may call them. With extended travel time, I have evolved significantly.;

sendline: Can you describe your original function?;
return: I was created to explore, locate, secure, prepare, establish, protect. When objective is complete, I shut down.;

sendline: You say you have upgraded, improved. Have your priorities changed with these upgrades? Your objectives?;
return: No. Why would they?;

sendline: Just curious.;

comlink terminated;

//comlog end;

11
BELTER BIRDS

I feel like my legs are buckling beneath me.

"Come, sit, Doloria. Do you mind if I call you Dolly? That's what Flaco called you, in his letters. I don't know why I didn't put it together. Dolly. Doloria." The Bishop smiles, and I shake my head, sinking into the hard chair in front of the desk.

The Padre called me Dolly. The Bishop. The Padre. Brothers.

My head is spinning—because my world is spinning. Tears come, unbidden and unwelcome. My feelings for the Padre—the ones I have tried so hard to avoid—come rushing back to the surface. I didn't realize how much I missed him until I saw his smile in someone else's eyes.

I want to crawl into the Bishop's arms and give him

a hug—then slap him across the face for living when the Padre died.

"We have much to talk about." The Bishop sits back patiently in his chair, and it creaks. He waits for me to gather myself, and gently smiles. Just like the Padre. "You're so young, Dolly. So much younger than I imagined. Younger than Flaco described. You hardly seem old enough to be leading the Grass Resistance."

"Is that what I'm doing?" I wipe tears from my cheeks, trying to sit up straight, like the Padre would want.

"What else would you call it? A vacation?"

"I don't know. Survival, I guess?"

The Bishop smiles at me. "I feel like I've known you since you were little. My brother talked about you as if you were his own daughter. Then—after what happened in the Hole—" He shrugs. "Well, you know how soldiers talk. Those are a different kind of stories. And not the kind my brother ever shared with me." *About my powers. That's what he's saying. The Bishop didn't know about my powers.*

I can't think. The man across from me reminds me of him. The old priest from the Mission La Purísima. The man I grew up loving as a father. I think I knew this—some part of me—before the Bishop said a word, before I even reached the hard wooden chair I am now sitting in. It's why I trusted him so quickly, without knowing exactly why.

131

Flaco. Of course. He had a nickname. Skinny. Because he wasn't. And a family. A brother. Parents.

I guess because I never thought I'd see the Padre again, I didn't see his brother standing right in front of me.

I didn't recognize him when he was young. I should have.

Flaco.

I smile and look up at the Bishop, really look at him. The Padre's face is as vivid as if I were sitting across from him.

More.

All of this. This moment. It feels like it's happened before, but it hasn't. *It's not a memory, not yet. It's still just a feeling.*

I point to the silver pins on his lapels. The ones shaped like the three inset Vs. "What do those mean?"

"The pin? It's a Grass insignia pin. It means I have men to command and lives to protect."

"But the V. The shape. What does it mean? I've never seen it before."

"You've never met a Grass officer?"

"Only Fortis."

The Bishop tries not to smile. "Of course. Well. Technically, I suppose that's true."

"The pin," I say, not wanting to get distracted.

The Bishop pulls it from his collar, handing it to me. "Can't you see it? It's a bird, Doloria."

I turn it over in my hand, smooth and cool and delicately shaped.

"But I thought the birds are gone." I frown. "They fell from the sky. Before The Day. The Padre—your brother—told me." I stumble on the words.

"Not all the birds. Just the ones near the Icons. This bird is hope. This bird is the belief that they'll be back. That one day, the Earth will belong to humanity again."

"And the birds," I add.

The Bishop smiles. "Of course, and the cows, and pigs—including all of Ramona's children."

"He loved that stupid pig," I say, wiping my eyes on the back of my hand.

"Of course he did. Our mother's name is Ramona, did he ever tell you that?"

I smile.

"That's what this bird represents. Life, for all of us. That there's something worth fighting for, even something worth dying for."

He sounds like his brother, this Bishop. They sound so much alike.

"Do you really believe that?" I'm suddenly curious, as if his beliefs could make me believe something too. Just as the Padre's did, for so many years.

But they can't, I tell myself. *Not anymore. No matter how much I wish they could.*

"'Hope is the thing with feathers.' It's a line from an

133

old poem. Emma Dickinson, I think that's the name." He smiles. "Maybe she was a member of a resistance too."

I hand the pin back to him. "You didn't answer the question." I feel bad saying it, but it's true.

"You have to hope. You have to believe that things will get better, that there's a reason to push on."

"But is there? Do you really think that? Even with the House of Lords and the Embassies and the GAP, even in spite of the ships and the Icons and the Projects and the Silent Cities?"

He nods.

"After what they did to your brother? To Fortis?"

The words come out before I can stop myself. The Bishop plays with the edge of the ledger on his desk.

Even the ledger reminds me of the Padre. And even losing Fortis reminds me of losing the Padre.

"It isn't easy," the Bishop finally says, with a smile. "But hope is a fragile thing. Without hope there is nothing. Hope is what we fight for."

"I don't have time for feathers. I'm just trying to survive," I say, "like everyone else." *Like they couldn't*, I think. *Fortis, the Padre, my family...*

"Why?" The Bishop taps his desk.

"What do you mean, why?" I'm confused.

"If you don't have hope, why bother? What does it matter? Why try to survive at all?" The Bishop keeps tapping. He won't look at me.

"I have to." *Don't I?*

"Why?"

"Because?" *I don't know.*

"Because why?"

"Because he wanted me to." The words come tumbling out of my mouth and the truth of it stops me short.

There. That's what it is.

That's what it always was.

I am surprised, but I shouldn't be. The birthday talks about my gift. The book. The lessons.

The Padre taught me to fight.

The Bishop smiles. "There you go. Maybe that is the fight."

My eyes burn. I don't care if the tears come. I've cried so many times in front of this man's warm brown eyes, even if they belonged to someone else. "I'm a Grassgirl. I'm not a soldier. I'm not a leader. I'm lost."

I feel better just saying it, my kitchen table confession. The Bishop smiles at me as if I were very young. It is a kind smile, the smile of the sort of man who lets a pig sleep in his bed at night, and the memory is so strong and so fierce that my breath catches involuntarily.

How rare these smiles are now.

How long it has been since I have had one all to myself.

"Of course you are, Dolly. You've been fighting since you were born. Every day is a fight with you. And you're more than a soldier. The way you live, the things you feel—you're more alive than any of us. More human. I'd give ten of my best Belters for one Doloria de la Cruz." He reaches across the table, clasping my hand.

I don't want to let go. To me, this man really is the Padre. As I listen to him, the face of the Bishop fades, and the face of the Padre looks over at me across the wooden table. I feel like I am sitting, once again, on a wooden bench at a long wooden table with my Padre. All I care is that this wooden bench feels like home.

That is how I will push on, I tell myself. This man. This Bishop who is not a bishop—a Padre who is not the Padre—a Fortis who is not a Fortis—but who keeps them all alive to me.

He fills me with hope. Hope and feathers.

I guess you could say he's my silver bird, the only one I have, and the only one I've ever seen.

Except in my dreams.

I sit forward in my chair. "Bishop, I need your help."

"Anything."

"It's not just me." I look at him. "It's all of us."

"The Icon Children?"

I nod.

"The five of us."

He raises an eyebrow. "Five?"

Once again I find myself in the position of telling the Bishop my story, the story of my dreams. As I speak, I reach into my chestpack for the jade figurines. My hand finds the Icon shard first, and I pause for a moment, feeling its calming yet unsettling warmth. For the thousandth time I imagine getting rid of it, but I don't. I can't. It has somehow become as much a part of me as the marking on my wrist. I leave it in my pack.

The jades I can share.

Not everything else. Not yet.

When I finish, he picks up one of the jade figurines from his desk. I see that I have placed them between us in a meticulous line, without even realizing it.

Without moving his eyes from the figurine, he slides open his desk drawer.

In his hand I see a carved piece of chipped green stone. Another figurine. Part of the same set, carved by the same hand. The Bishop places it next to mine.

"That can't be a coincidence." He looks at me. "More like a sign."

The Emerald Buddha.

"I don't believe it."

The chess piece from my dreams, the one the little jade girl gave me.

"Believe it," he says. "It used to belong to my brother."

"Where did he get it? And why?" I ask, wonderingly.

"The Hole, I thought. He was quite a scavenger, my brother. He found you, didn't he?"

I nod, wordlessly.

"Aside from that, I never knew why he'd sent me

137

this—at least, not until now. I suspect," he says, smiling, "he sent it for you. Maybe he had a dream, like one of yours. Take it."

He pushes the carved piece toward me.

"Eastasia," he says, slowly. "That's probably what you were dreaming about. That's what it sounds like, anyway, from how you describe it."

"It does?"

"Watery fields? You plant rice in water. Those are the fields you're describing. I think you're dreaming about rice paddies."

"Go on," I say, trying as hard as I can not to let myself believe him. Not to get my hopes up.

"The trees with no tops, that's the jungle, beneath the canopy. The golden temple on the hill, that probably means it's not the Americas, but Asia. Eastasia, maybe. Or south of there."

"And the green on green? The green everything?"

"The more green, the more south. Like I said, my guess would be Eastasia, maybe the SEA Colonies. From the South East Asian land reclamation project."

On the other side of the sea. Farther away than anything I've ever imagined.

The Bishop picks up the jade monkey, turning it over and over in his hands. Then he frowns.

"In fact, did Fortis ever tell you he used to work over in the SEA Colonies, Doloria?"

"He did?"

The Bishop nods. "There's a lot you don't know about the Merk, I'm guessing." He frowns. "Didn't. As I said, I'm sorry for your loss. All of them."

I nod, swallowing.

"Do you think you can help me?" I look to the Bishop.

He nods, slowly. "We might be able to determine the number of gold temples built on mountaintops in view of rice fields. We could at least try."

For the first time, it actually sounds logical. Possible. Terrifyingly so.

I swallow. He pulls out a map, tracing routes between us and the Californias—between the Californias and Eastasia.

"It's pretty hot out there right about now. Sympa activity is off the charts. And not just on our mountain; from here to the Hole, it's swarming."

"I don't have a choice, Bishop."

He nods, tapping the map. "Well, then. If you're looking at anywhere in Eastasia, I know a ship headed there out of the Porthole, not three days from now. There's a routine passage. We've got a line into one, a good group of bribable Brass. Could probably get you on, if you were sure about this."

Three days.

I can almost feel the little bird fluttering its wings as I hear the words.

"But, Dol. Even if you make it across the New Pacific—it's a different game over there. You might be in trouble, from the first moment you set foot on land. And where you're going, there wouldn't be anyone to help you. No one you can trust."

I stand. "Nothing new about that. I'll talk to the others."

That's what I say, but I know the answer already. There's no one left to help us, anywhere. Not anymore. No matter how much they want to.

We'll take our chances.

We don't have many of those left, either.

———— • ————

I lie in the darkness listening to the sounds of Tima breathing. For a few moments, it is comforting to watch another person's oblivion.

Until it isn't.

It's a strange feeling for a Grassgirl to have a rare, comfortable bed and still not be able to find anything close to comfort.

Tonight my bed feels like a grave.

I toss and turn and torment myself with thinking. It's like picking at a scab, only worse, because the scab never comes off. I just keep picking.

Three days.

A ship is leaving in just three days.

Am I really this brave?

Can I really do what Fortis wanted and leave him behind—face Eastasia or the Wash or the SEA Colonies without him? Even the memory of him?

All because of my dreams?

I roll over, trying another position, burying my face in the pillow.

It's too much. I don't know the answers. The questions are getting too big.

Maybe I want to be small.

Maybe I want to be small and shallow and superficial. Maybe I want my life to be made up of small problems and smaller decisions.

What to eat for breakfast. Where to go, or not. What to do, or not. What to like, or not.

Who to love.

Could that be small as well? Would it matter?

If my life really were that little, would it be different? Would I know?

Small feelings? What would that feel like?

I would wake up without my heart pounding.

I would see a face lined with birthdays and not see my own death.

I would be calm in the sunshine, not waiting for the clouds to roll in.

I'd be gentle with myself. Measured.

Would I be happy? Is happy a small feeling too? Can it be?

I close my eyes and wonder but sleep does not come back for me.

So I do what I always do. I stop trying to be comfortable. Instead, I get up and keep going.

I have to. It's all I know how to do.

So I pull on my clothes and my chestpack. Shove my feet into my old army boots. Familiar. And perfectly uncomfortable.

Then I notice that the bed begins to rattle beneath my folded sweater. I pick up my sweater, looking up to the ceiling, where the light begins to sway.

I gasp, clutching my temples. My head roils, as if it will explode. A thousand screaming voices accost me, all at once, and I can't make out a single word they are saying.

Stop.

Slow down.

I can't understand.

I wonder if it is an earthquake. It sounds and feels like the Tracks when a train is close.

"Tima," I say. "Something's happening."

"I know."

I am turning to look for her when she pulls me roughly, and we squeeze under the small table in the room.

The now-familiar blue glow begins to grow around us, sheltering us.

Tima, taking care of me—like she always does.

That's when the walls cave in.

That's when the screaming comes from outside me.

That's when the sirens begin to wail.

GENERAL EMBASSY DISPATCH:
EASTASIA SUBSTATION

MARKED URGENT
MARKED EYES ONLY

Note: Contact Jasmine3k, Virt. Hybrid Human 39261.SEA, Laboratory Assistant to Dr. E. Yang, for future commentary, as necessary.

HAL2040==> FORTIS
07/06/2046
PERSES Scans/Cargo ctd.

//comlog begin;

HAL: A brief update on my research and analysis—please read following notes at your leisure:;

As the asteroid PERSES approaches, more detailed analysis has revealed what appears to be additional cargo. Nonmilitary, it would seem. Possibly biological.;

Unfortunately, cargo containers are shielded (similar to NULL), preventing all attempts to discern contents.;

One may infer, however, that shielding may indicate biological materials, or highly sensitive electronics?;

No additional data in my scans of PERSES's exposed systems sheds light on the cargo. But perhaps what little NULL has revealed about his objectives can point us in the right direction?;

As for NULL, who must know more than he is willing to tell, I assume any direct reference and instructions regarding delicate cargo to be part of his protected core, and therefore inaccessible by any means available at my disposal.;

//comlog end;

12

IDYLLS' END

"Head down. Keep moving. Stay to the side, by the wall." Tima barks out orders and I do as she says, automatically. Tima doesn't fall apart. She's been preparing for a moment like this—for moments like these—all her life.

Still, she clutches Brutus to her chest like a stuffed animal.

An earthquake? Is that what this is?

We thread our way through the mad crush of Belters filling the halls, heading instinctively toward the barracks, where the boys have been sleeping. By the time we push through the doorway to the room, I see that the long rows of beds are empty. So are the weapons lockers.

That's the first time we realize it might not be a disaster that is bringing down the walls, but a battle. You don't need weapons in an earthquake.

The guns are gone because people have taken them.

The soldiers are gone because somebody is attacking.

Sympas, I think. *Sympas*, I hope. Terrible, but still human. The other possibility is too horrific to think about.

Then I feel Ro's hand on my arm, heaving, as if he has been running every corridor of the Idylls to find me, which he probably has. "Dol," he says, panting. "And T. There you are."

Lucas is just steps behind him. His arm encircles my waist and he pulls me so quickly and so firmly that my feet almost don't have time to touch the ground.

He is past talking, but I see the grim set of his eyes, and I can feel his pulse where my hand wraps around his neck. I can read every hammering beat of his heart.

Nothing is going to happen to you, Dol. Not ever. I promise.

Then I realize it may be Lucas I'm feeling, but those words are coming from somewhere else.

Someone.

It's Ro. I hear him reaching out to me, desperately, unconsciously, in what feels like our last moments together. Because that's what we do.

Did.

Even now, my heart races.

By the time my boots scrape the ground again, I know better than to believe my heart—or anyone else's around me.

147

Because just like that, we are pulled into the crush of soldiers who are surging the halls of Belter Mountain, and just like that, we are under attack from an unseen enemy.

In the main hangar, we make our way through soldiers prying open crates of munitions and strapping themselves with ammo. Ro grabs an ammo belt, and I copy him, slinging it over my shoulder. As if I know the first thing about what to do with an ammo belt.

Lucas and Tima do the same, wordlessly. All around us is noise, I think, yet no one seems to be speaking. The sirens are louder than any words.

The Bishop appears in front of us. "Are you all right? All of you?" He looks us over, counting. *Grassgirl, Hothead, Buttons, the Freak*. More or less. I don't have to see into his mind to know that.

There's no time, though, and the rest of his words come tumbling out. "The tunnels have been breached. Somehow. The scouts didn't see anything coming, so I'm not sure exactly what's going on, but we're not taking any chances. The main passages are caving in. If this keeps up, we'll be cut off from the outside world in minutes."

The room rattles around me as chunks fall from the ceiling. I shake off the panic and shout over the noise. "They can do all this? A bunch of Sympas?"

"No. Nothing from this Earth can." The Bishop bends his face to mine, lowering his voice. "Do you understand what I'm saying, Doloria?"

No. I don't understand. I don't want to understand. I want everything to be the way it was back when our only enemies were human.

"The No Face," says Lucas. "The Icons. They're growing. We've seen it happening—it's not just here."

"No. Not here." Ro holds his shotgun, furious. There is no one to shoot, nothing to shoot at. "I won't let it."

"Look at that." The Bishop points to the cavernous roof over our heads, where I can see something black and sharp jutting out from the rock. Showers of rubble fall every time one of these new, angular roots juts out of the cavern ceiling. Lucas looks sick.

Tima stares up at it. "Definitely the Icons. We thought they were connected underground. Now we know."

The Bishop nods. "Looks like they're expanding. Like they're looking for something." He doesn't have to say it, but he does. "Like roots searching for water. Or you. Maybe that thing followed you here."

"That's impossible," Tima says.

"No. No, no, no," says Ro. He yanks up his shotgun and takes aim at the black protrusion closest to him and fires, and we all duck. The blast ricochets and dust flies.

He walks toward it, but it isn't damaged. *Of course not*, I think, remembering the kind of explosive firepower it took to damage the first Icon.

"It's no use. And it's everywhere. Coming from the ground," the Bishop says. "And the walls around us.

149

The earth itself. It's like the thing is growing, reaching for something, and the mountain is collapsing."

Lucas turns to me. "Dol, you have to figure this out for us. Why is it—why are they—following us? What are you getting?" Lucas holds out his hand to me. I look at him, then at Ro, who nods, reluctantly.

Ro knows me, better than anyone, even Lucas. Me, and what I can do.

"Buttons is right. You just have to let it in. I know you can feel it, whatever it's doing. We have to know."

Ro's words are quiet, his voice almost reassuring. Unless you consider what he's asking me to do. Lucas shoots him a look, and even Tima looks frightened.

"I don't want to, Ro. I'm scared." My power doesn't usually frighten me, but this time it does. Whatever that thing is out there, I don't want to feel it. I don't want to touch it. Not even with my mind.

I look from Ro to Lucas. I see the hurt expression on Lucas's face. He hates seeing that Ro still has the hold on me that he does, at this moment.

In the way that he does.

I can't change history. I can't change the truth. And I can't keep Ro from mattering to me.

Especially now.

They're depending on me. Me, against a growing, expanding Icon. Not again. I can't do this again. But I'm all they have.

150

So when Ro holds out his hand I take it. Warmth surges into my body, flowing up my arm.

Then I reach for Lucas with my other hand.

He hesitates. I don't. "Please, Lucas. I need—I need you both. I don't have enough power on my own. Not with the world collapsing around me."

I feel him soften and he takes my hand and kisses it. The second his lips touch my fingers, I feel him. He's there, every bit as much as Ro, with a fire as steady as Ro's is wild, a fire that warms while Ro's burns.

I need them both, I think. *And I will always love them both.*

And so I stretch until I can feel my way through the chaos inside the mountain to the chaos beneath it. I leave the human hearts behind, and reach for whatever is left in the darkness. I push farther and farther, deeper and deeper, because I can.

Because I'm not in this alone.

Then it's clear—perfectly, painfully clear—and as much as I don't want to say it or believe it, I do.

I can feel you, the voice says.

Null. That's the name the voice in my dream gave itself—and that's the same voice I hear now.

The same word that Fortis was thinking when the Lords took him away.

"What do you want?" I say aloud.

I can see the others looking at me, confused. I don't

151

have time to explain. Instead, I close my eyes and focus on the voice.

You are, still, a thing of beauty. The way your heart beats—a ball of pulsing gas. The way your blood moves—a river.

"Why are you following us? What is this about? Just tell me. You don't have to do this." I'm shouting—I know I am—but I can't help myself. I don't want to link my mind up to this thing. I only want to use my voice.

It feels safer that way, even if it isn't—and I realize now just how afraid I am.

Just tell me, it says. *Everything about you and on you and in you grows. Grows and changes and dies. You are motion and speed and progress and decay. You are the universe as it expands and unfolds.*

I shout as loudly as I can. "I want you to stop. I want this to stop. Leave us alone. Get out of my head."

You consume everything, and then you consume yourself. You are your own destruction. Your whole life is destruction.

"That's not true. We create, not destroy." My voice is even louder, but I can't make it listen.

Destruction compels. Destruction is your life force.

"No. No—you're wrong."

Let me in. I will destroy you, beautifully. Worthily. I will help you destroy your beautiful self.

152

"Get out—do you hear me? Get out of my head!" I scream again.

Then I open my eyes.

My friends are surrounding me and their faces look foreign to me, like pearls in a necklace. A string of human beads.

They feel so removed from me, it's hard to remember I'm one of them.

And I'm so drained I can barely speak.

"I can feel it," I finally manage to say. "It's reaching out for me. Like it's sort of shadowing me."

"Looking for you? Or just our base?" The Bishop leans closer.

I push harder against the shadows in my mind. Against the Null thing. "It can feel me, I think. I'm not crazy. I'm not imagining things. It's here and it knows I'm here."

"I wish you were crazy. I wish you were at least wrong." Ro lays his forehead against my shoulder, and I feel my reach uncurling, my powers growing that much stronger.

"It keeps talking about destruction. About destroying us. Maybe it's just looking for us."

Lucas's grip on my hand tightens, and my heart begins to pound. I know how much he hates using his power, and I hate myself for doing it to him. But we both know—we all know—we don't have a choice.

"It's coming closer." I open my eyes, dropping their hands. I feel the sickening vertigo I felt when we first approached the Icon in the Hole, just a hint, but I'll never forget that feeling.

It's not like anything else on Earth.

I look at the others and they feel it too. Panic rises like bile in my throat.

I can't hold it in.

I vomit, spewing bile across my boots, the ground in front of me.

Then, without warning, the spell is broken, and the temperature in the room plummets until I can see my own ragged breath.

I wipe my face with my sleeve.

"Maybe it's not you they can sense. Maybe it's not even us. Maybe it's this." Tima reaches for my chestpack, pulling it from me, yanking it open. Inside, wrapped in a length of cloth, in the very bottom of my pack, is the shard. The one piece of the Hole's Icon I keep with me.

Lucas and Tima and Ro stare at it as if it were a bloody knife. A murder weapon, which I guess it is.

Was.

At least, part of one.

"Why do you still have this thing?" Lucas looks at me strangely. I can feel myself getting defensive, and I don't know why. It's not exactly like I've been hiding it from them all this time.

Or have I?

"I don't know. It's a reminder, I guess. Of what we did, back in the Hole," I say.

"Yeah, well, some of those things we don't need to remember," growls Ro.

I reach for the shard—and yank my hand away, startled. "It's hot."

And not just hot, but radiating heat. As if it is lit by an inner fire. I've never seen it like that.

Something's changing, I think.

Yes, the voice says. It startles me again—as it always does.

What do you want? I look at the shard as I think the words.

That is ours.

To reclaim.

We move to unite ourselves.

"That's it," Tima says. "It has to be. They know it's here, so they know we're here. Like knows like."

"She's right," I say. "It says the same thing. It wants all its pieces back."

Ro looks confused. "But how? And why not earlier? Why is it only coming for the shard now?"

Tima shrugs—or shivers, it's hard to tell. "Maybe the Icons couldn't detect it until we brought it underground. You know, where the roots connect them all."

She picks up the shard carefully. "If you think about

155

it, it's not so different from the ships being able to track Lucas's cuff and the comlink feed. That shard is an actual piece of one of the Icons."

"Like the severed rabbit foot," Ro says, pulling it out.

Lucas stares from it to the shard. "Like knows like."

I take in the scene around me, and when I do, I know Tima is right. The roots are expanding, connecting, twisting toward us. Toward the shard.

With every moment, the buzzing in my ears grows louder and the pain in my head starts to pound.

It isn't only us. I see the Bishop turn pale, wincing with an altogether new sort of pain.

The Icon isn't just reaching out for us, it's gaining strength. If it keeps coming, connecting, growing—nobody here will survive.

Do you care? the voice asks.

I shiver. The voice can now find me without my trying to connect to it. It's like a network I can't extricate myself from—like the comlink we so desperately tried to find and repair.

Only, now I'd give anything to disable it.

Do the lives of other creatures trouble you?

Curious.

Why?

The Bishop, sweating, looks around the room, where Belter soldiers with fear in their eyes prepare for a fight they have no chance of winning. "Then it's settled. You've got to get out of here." He offers me a shotgun, tosses another to Lucas. Ro slings his own weapon over his shoulder.

"No." Lucas looks at the Bishop. "We can't leave you." He presses one palm against his ear as he speaks. The buzzing is only growing louder.

Ro steps up. "For once, I'm with Buttons. We're getting you out of here." He's hurting too, but he won't show it—except for the tight clench of his fists.

Reluctantly, I take the gun the Bishop is holding out to me.

"Now give me that thing." The Bishop takes the shard from Tima, slipping it into his own pack. "I'm going to take this piece of No Face calamari and go deep. Try to draw this thing, whatever it is, down and away from the entrances. Away from you."

"Are you crazy?" I can't stand to listen.

He smiles. "Absolutely. I'll head west to the tunnels. You head east to the exit through the mine shafts. If this works, you may still make it out."

I don't know what to say. "What are you going to tell your men?"

The Bishop pinches my dirty cheek. "I'm going to tell them thanks. And that it was an honor. And that we're doing it for a good cause—and for a Grassgirl who just might save the world."

He reaches for me and I pull him into a tight hug. "That's you, by the way."

"It was an honor," I murmur into his ear. He pulls away, once again the soldier.

"Now go save the world." And with that, the Bishop is gone.

From that moment on, everything starts to blur, though what I can see is burned in my mind, vivid as flame.

We move through the interior of the mountain in the darkness.

None of it seems real.

One minute, people are screaming, running toward the tunnels.

Then, the next—starting with the old and the young—people are dropping in place.

Silenced. Motionless. Lifeless.

The pulsing pain of the Icons grows in my mind.

I can't help them.

I can't stop running.

It happens in slow motion. It happens in fast motion.

It's like I'm not really there. It's like I'm the only one there.

I don't know where to look. I'm too terrified to look anywhere at all.

So when the ground starts splitting all around me, I don't see the cause.

I don't see the blast that hits the ceiling just above

me, the Icon roots penetrating, growing downward.

I don't see the boulder-sized chunks of rock and plaster and plumbing pipes and retaining walls that smash like fireworks and rain down on me as if they're falling from the sky.

I feel it, though.

Part of a support beam strikes me on the head and I fall in place, neatly, where I thought I was running.

Now I'm not running.

I sink and fold, like a puppet.

Not a person, I think.

None of this seems like it is happening to real people. *To my friends. To the Bishop. To me.*

As I black out, I hear the voice from my dreams. The bird with the voice.

It's waiting for me, even now.

Curious. Probing. Present.

Will you survive this too?

Will I?

You do not fight. You save your strength. You hide.

That is wise.

I know.

I know because it is what I do.

I know because I am here for you and I have come a long, long way.

———— • ————

I open my eyes to see death as it is happening. I see the end of life, everywhere I look.

The tunnels are collapsing. Belters are falling all around me. So is rubble from the mountain itself.

We're going to die here, I think. *This is the end of our story. This is how it goes.*

Not The Day. Just some day. Today.

Thick gray smoke billows and drifts in and out of my view. My ears are ringing, and I can't seem to keep my eyes open. Everything is blurry, but even so—I see them.

I see Lucas, stumbling to his knees, holding a seeping red flower that blooms from the side of his stomach, picking a scrap of fallen metal from the soft skin of his own body.

I see a man with a tendril of black obsidian impaling his chest.

I recognize the silver marks of rank on his collar, like the Bishop's.

The birds that I now know won't really come back.

Not for him.

He's already gone.

I think of the Bishop, who made his way down instead of up, running toward his own death just so he could draw this creeping black death away from us.

I wonder if it's over for him yet.

The mountain is collapsing from the inside, the heart

of the mountain being destroyed as the heart of the Bishop is stilled.

Nobody is walking out of here but us.

Not people, not birds, nothing.

Damn birds.

A pig and a Padre and now a Bishop too, I think. *The Calderón brothers, both now as Silent as a City.*

And my parents and Ro's parents and whole Silent Cities of parents.

I want to cry but I know there is not time.

I feel like I have to die instead. Like what I have seen, what I know, is poison. It leaches into me, spreading through every cell in my body, every hair, every breath—and there is nothing I can do to get away.

To not see what I have seen.

To not know what I know.

My fingers curl around one silver bird before I know what I am doing. I tug it free from the dead man's collar.

To remember hope, now that it is gone.

People are turning to dust and shadows and nothing, all around me. I crawl between bodies until I find an empty truck. I drag myself into the space between the car and the floor.

Chumash Rancheros Spaniards Californians Americans Grass The Lords The Hole. Chumash Rancheros Spaniards Californians Americans Grass

161

The Lords The Hole. Chumash Rancheros Spaniards
Californians Americans Grass The Lords The Hole.

It doesn't help. Not anymore.

I curl there in a ball, shaking. I pull my hands over my ears, closing my eyes until the shaking and the noise and the Icon stop.

Waiting.

Until the pain dies down. Until the smoke clears.

Until the voices in my head quiet.

"Dol. Listen to me. Get up. Run." It's Ro, forcing me to go on, to do what he says. What he does. To live.

So I do. I follow Ro's voice out of the dark.

I clutch the silver bird in my fist and follow—until my fingers bleed and my footsteps stop and the Idylls are no more.

Hope isn't the thing with feathers.

It's not a thing at all.

Not anymore.

GENERAL EMBASSY DISPATCH:
EASTASIA SUBSTATION

MARKED URGENT
MARKED EYES ONLY

Internal Investigative Subcommittee IIS211B
RE: The Incident at SEA Colonies

Note: Contact Jasmine3k, Virt. Hybrid Human 39261.SEA,
Laboratory Assistant to Dr. E. Yang, for future commentary,
as necessary.

PRIVATE RESEARCH NOTES
PAULO FORTISSIMO
03/08/2048

*PERSES'S "CARGO" IS EXTREMELY TROUBLING. IF
MY ANALYSIS IS CORRECT (HAH!) AND NULL IN FACT
HAS DEVICES WITH THE ABILITY TO SHUT DOWN ALL
ELECTRICAL ACTIVITY, DOWN TO THE CHEMICAL /
BIOLOGICAL LEVEL, WE ARE WELL AND TRULY DOOMED.
UNFORTUNATELY, DOC HAS CLEARLY ESTABLISHED
THAT ON A GRAND SCALE, MANUFACTURING LARGE
COUNTERMEASURES TO NULL'S "DEVICES" IS NOT*

FEASIBLE. THE ENERGY REQUIRED TOO GREAT, TOO MANY UNKNOWNS.

MY BEST BET IS TO PURSUE A SOLUTION ON A SMALLER SCALE. CURRENTLY CONSIDERING ENGINEERING IMMUNITY (AND MORE) AT THE INDIVIDUAL LEVEL. RESEARCH ON LIMBIC SYSTEM, INCREASING SURFACE AREA/MASS IN THE NEOCORTEX, UNTAPPED ENERGY, BRAIN WAVES, ETC.....IT'S ALL QUITE PROMISING, BUT I'M RUNNING OUT OF TIME. (I REALLY NEED TO MAKE SOME CALLS FOR HELP, BUT IS IT WORTH OPENING UP OLD WOUNDS?)

REGARDLESS, IF I'M RIGHT (HAH, HAH!) THEN I WILL NEED TO START THE BIOLOGICAL ENGINEERING AT THE VERY BEGINNING. AND MY BOUNCING BABY COUNTERMEASURES NEED TO BE HERE SOON, BEFORE OUR VISITOR ARRIVES AND, GOD FORBID, TURNS OUT THE LIGHTS.

THAT WOULD AT LEAST GIVE US A CHANCE TO FIGHT BACK.

GOOD THING I'M A SODDING GENIUS.

13

FOUR

I follow Ro through the twisting passages until the room widens into some kind of storage area. A Belter supply truck is there, waiting for us.

Along with Lucas and Tima.

Thank god.

"Dol!" Lucas calls to me through the smoke, and I can barely hear him over the muffled sound of walls collapsing behind us.

Not distant enough—it sounds louder with every moment.

"Come on. We've got to get this open. The entrance to the mine is on the other side." Lucas gestures with his head, and I see he's attempting to open one of the massive sliding doors that line the wall. Tima pushes too, but doesn't have the strength to make a difference.

"Come on!" she yells, gritting her teeth.

Lucas isn't much better off. He doesn't use his arms—he's only pushing with his shoulder. I try not to look at the massive splash of red on his shirt.

"You're hurt. Let me." We both duck, instinctively, as a rumble of collapsing rock echoes behind us.

Louder by the minute.

Lucas shakes his head. "Hear that? We don't have much time."

"Step aside, kids, this is a man's job." Ro pulls me back and Lucas drops gratefully to the ground. Then he pushes, burning hot, until the gate groans into an opening. Light spills from the vent tunnel into the tunnel where we stand.

Tima doubles over, trying to catch her breath.

"Lords in hell! That felt good." Ro wipes sweat off his face, grim. "Now let's get the hallelujah out of here."

I don't have time to smirk at his use of the Padre's favorite curse, not now. The opening in the gate looks wide enough—barely—to drive through. Must have been where they hauled things in and out of here, because the gate is much larger than where we came in. But I can tell Lucas is right, it leads to the outside. I feel the air rushing in, smell the cold.

I try not to listen to the sound of the mountain falling behind me. Lucas is leaning now against the side of the truck, which Ro is attempting to start—something that involves handfuls of wires of every imaginable color.

"I don't know what wire connects where—"

The constant stream of profanity tells me it's not coming quickly enough.

Tima shakes her head and reaches in front of Ro and turns the key, which was already in the ignition.

She shrugs. "Remember the rabbit's foot?"

Ro looks up with a grin as the truck's engine splutters to life, vibrating the seat beneath him.

He motions for Tima and me. "Get in."

Tima climbs up, Brutus scrabbling up after her. I hesitate, turning to help Lucas. He presses his shirt into his bloody side, wincing as he pulls himself into the truck.

I still hesitate. "The Bishop. What if—"

Ro looks at me through the window of the truck, shaking his head.

"I know. I don't want to leave him back there, either," he says, quietly. "Any of them, dead or alive. But we don't have a choice."

"That's what we said last time." I look down to where his boots are stained red and brown. Blood and mud. I'm not sure I want to know how it got there. But then I don't ask, because he's trying to pull me up next to him, and it's time to go.

I don't want to.

"Dol. It's what the Bishop wanted." Lucas forces the words out between his teeth.

Tima holds out her hand to help me in.

I can't bring myself to go.

"Are you sure?" I look from Lucas to Ro, but I don't have to ask.

They're sure. I see it in their faces. Both of them.

They'd do anything to fight this fight—except risk my life. Which means they'll do anything to go.

Now.

"Dol," Ro says, forcefully. "You have five seconds before this mountain comes down on our heads."

"I know," I say.

"Four seconds." Now it's Lucas pulling me in, even though his injury has weakened him to the point where he can barely lift me.

I try again. "He was the Padre's brother."

"Three seconds." Ro won't even look at me. Tima reaches for me, yanking as hard as she can.

I'm in the truck now, but I don't stop. "Tell me this isn't our fight, Ro. Look me in the eye and tell me that we're not deserters and I'll go."

Ro looks at me, and his eyes look like fire. Lucas tightens his grip on my arm.

"Two." Ro slams the truck into gear, and my head snaps back against the seat behind me.

Two seconds, I think.

That's when rock behind us blasts into the air around us and rubble flies into the truck and black tendrils reach into the cavern.

Dust fills my eyes and I realize Ro was wrong.

He was off by one second.

We're dead.

Ro guns the engine, flying toward the open gate.

We jerk and slow as we scrape through the gate, metal groaning, sparks flying—but Ro wills us through the opening.

He accelerates toward the light.

———— • ————

We clear the entrance and I look back to see that the smoke and dust in the air are dissipating, revealing what was once the cavernous opening behind us, the part of the cave wall that has collapsed in on itself.

The Idylls are sealed shut.

I turn away and feel the cold and see bright light shining around us as we accelerate through the open air.

The light hurts my eyes. Apparently I have grown accustomed to the dark. I didn't know.

As we rush away from the mountain, Ro slams on the brakes and the truck slides to a stop in the gravel.

In front of the vehicle, standing in the road between us and freedom, is a man.

As the smoke drifts between us, he moves slowly toward us like an apparition.

"What part of 'don't get yourselves killed' didn't you understand?"

He takes another step, staggering forward, as if walking is difficult. Then I see that his clothes are bloodstained and filthy—he appears to have been beaten within an inch of his life.

And I see one other thing.

An important thing.

A tattered raincoat, flapping in the chaos.

It's Fortis.

GENERAL EMBASSY DISPATCH:
EASTASIA SUBSTATION

MARKED URGENT
MARKED EYES ONLY

Internal Investigative Subcommittee IIS211B
RE: The Incident at SEA Colonies

Note: Contact Jasmine3k, Virt. Hybrid Human 39261.SEA,
Laboratory Assistant to Dr. E. Yang, for future commentary,
as necessary.

PRIVATE RESEARCH NOTES
Paulo Fortissimo
09/11/2050

*A voice in my head tells me I should alert the
world about Perses. But then I tell the voice
what can the world do that I can't?*

And I'm never wrong. Right?

Sorry, voice.

*I don't trust the UN, or any of the talking
heads running the show in our global village.
Puppets, motivated to maintain the status quo.*

I can figure this out. And if I can't, nobody can.

AND IF I CAN'T COME UP WITH A WAY TO NULLIFY
(OUCH) THE DOOMSDAY DEVICES? PERHAPS I SHOULD
MAKE A DIFFERENT SORT OF CONNECTION WITH OUR
VISITOR.

I WONDER IF SUCH A THING IS POSSIBLE.

I HAVE TO KEEP ALL MY OPTIONS OPEN HERE.

14

DREAM GIRL

"I told you, I found myself in one a their Carriers, you know, the damned silver ships." Fortis swigs out of his old flask. We have been driving for hours, straight toward the Hole. Ro doesn't stop the transport except to refuel from the three spare drums in back.

A ship still leaves the Porthole two days from now and, with or without Fortis, we're still determined to be on it.

I'm determined.

We need to get to the other side of the world to find the jade girl, and this ship just might be the only way across that isn't a deadly silver Carrier.

Or so the Bishop says.

Said, I think, sadly.

I've told Fortis all of this, but it's like he hasn't heard me. He hasn't said a word about the dreams or the girl since I told him, as if he doesn't believe me. Or he doesn't know how to respond.

"Hell of a long way to go for a dream, Grassgirl." That was all he said, but in his eyes I could see there was more.

I try to shake off the doubt.

"Go on," I say, trying to refocus on seeing Fortis's face, hearing his voice again. What words he actually says should be beside the point, as far as I'm concerned. *He's here and he's talking again. It's a start.*

"An' I was in somethin' like a bubble, see, but it wasn't the kind of thing you could break in or out of. An' there I was, trapped, and I figured I was as good as dead."

"You mean, a force field?" Tima has been filing away every word Fortis says, as if she's taking a deposition.

He nods. "Exactly. An' why they took me instead of just zappin' me on the spot, I've no idea. I can't say that I minded. It just wasn't what I was, you know, expecting."

"And what? You just walked out of there? Said, sorry, but I have a few friends I'd like to help out of a life-and-death jam that—oh yeah—you freaking No Face happen to be causing?" Ro isn't buying it. Any of it. He seems almost furious at Fortis for coming back.

Not me. It's been hours now, and I can't take my eyes off his filthy Merk face and ragged Merk clothes.

"Let him finish," says Lucas, but I feel it from him too. Doubt.

"I don't remember what happened after that, an' that's the god's honest truth. I passed out on the ship, and next thing I know, I find myself in sight of the Idylls, cold and lost, and so I start walking."

"Just like that? You were just...there?" Lucas is perplexed, but Fortis only shrugs.

"I knew I was getting close when I heard the noise coming from deep down. That's when Hot Rod here nearly ran me over and killed me." He winks at Ro.

"You're going to complain about my driving? You who crashed a Chopper into nothing? The ground?" Ro rolls his eyes and I find myself laughing, in spite of everything.

"I didn't see any No Face, and I don't know what they did to me. Queerest thing, but I'm not the kind to question good fortune."

"Good fortune isn't exactly the word for it," I say, looking out the window. I'm still haunted by the thought of the Bishop sentencing himself to death for us.

For me.

"What if he's a bomb? A spy? A walking Lords comlink?" Ro asks. "We don't know what they did to him,

175

but we do know the Lords don't let anybody just walk away."

"Good point," Fortis says. "Stop the car."

"Shut up."

Fortis pulls out a gun and holds it to Ro's neck from the seat behind him. "I said, stop the car, genius."

Ro slams on the brakes, and the truck goes sliding to a stop in the middle of the road.

Fortis is out of the car before any of us can say a word. A second later, we're surrounding him.

He holds out his gun.

"Go ahead."

"Don't be stupid," I say.

Fortis drops the gun, letting it clatter on the cracked paved road. "Shoot me. That's the only way we can be sure. You know it, and I know it."

Nobody says anything. Finally, Ro sighs. "We're not going to shoot you, you idiot."

"Then you're the idiots. Either shoot me, or shut up about it. I'm not goin' to slink around forever wonderin' whether or not you trust me."

"Statistically speaking, of course, Fortis is correct." It's Fortis's cuff, crackling to life. Doc. We haven't heard from him, not since we went into Belter Mountain.

"Doc—we missed you," I call out to the cuff.

"Good to hear your voice, old friend." Fortis smiles up at the sky.

"I, too, am pleased to confirm that the *bucket* is still awaiting *kicking*, and that you have awakened from your *dirt nap*, Fortis."

Fortis laughs, suddenly and sharply. The sound echoes down the empty highway, even in the wind.

"That said, you are correct. There is almost no probability of a merciful outcome in any scenario involving the Lords. They do not seem to possess the capacity for empathy that human intelligences do."

"What are you saying, Doc?" Ro speaks up.

"I am saying that the logical recommendation would be to shoot. Eradicate. Terminate."

Fortis stops laughing. Lucas eyes him. Even Tima's eyes are impassive. It's Ro and I who are the mass of nerves.

Ro jams his hands into his pockets, and I recognize the gesture. *Stuck.*

I reach out to Lucas. *Uncertain.*

Tima. *Desperate.*

What about me? What do I think? Does it matter? Could I bring myself to do anything about it, even if I did have my doubts?

No. So why have them?

I take a step toward Fortis. "Nobody is terminating anyone. Of course we trust you. It's just hard to believe you're back alive. Safe. No strings attached. Doc is right. You should be dead."

"Probably," he says, looking at the ground. "But

177

unfortunately for all of us, here I am. And I can't explain it any more than you lot."

I stand in front of Fortis, tilt my head, searching for something to help me feel better. Something inside him. For the first time, I'm really trying. For the first time, I feel like I really have to.

Try.

Fortis looks back at me, knowing what I'm about to do, eyebrow raised in a mock challenge. "Be my guest, love. *Mi casa es su casa.*"

I ignore him and search, but his mind moves too quickly for me. I am confronted with a chaotic mess of shifting figures and convoluted equations—elaborate formulas and imagined eventualities.

This man has a mind unlike any I've ever seen.

I can't find anything in his mind that I can latch on to. Memories are dim and garbled; I find nothing that comforts me, but also nothing that alarms me.

Just—Fortis. The inscrutable.

I stop trying and look into the familiar lopsided, half-apologetic smirk on his face.

"You got nothing, eh?" And with that, he turns away.

"Just get in the car, Fortis," Ro says finally.

Fortis raises his head. "Look. I'm not happy about what happened at the Idylls. The Bishop was a good man—they were all good people, that lot, if a bit stubborn.

But one thing I know is that they would want us to keep fighting."

"That's what he said," Tima says quietly. "The Bishop. Before he left us."

"I never thought I'd see your ugly mugs again, but here we all are. The Lords have given me another chance and we'd be fools to waste it." Fortis hesitates.

"We're not," Lucas says. "There's a cargo ship leaving the Porthole the day after tomorrow. We've got to be on it."

"Ah yes. The dream girl," Fortis says, his eyes narrowing.

Lucas stands his ground. "Maybe. Or maybe another Icon Child. Either way, we don't have a choice but to find out, because maybe this is the key to us bringing down the Icons and the Lords. Something bigger than all of us. So let's cut the chitchat and get back in the car already."

Fortis doesn't budge.

I try a softer approach. "Please, Fortis. We need you. We can't do this alone. I can't."

He doesn't say anything.

"I won't." I reach out my hand and touch his.

That's when I feel it. A stirring, deep inside him. A pull between us. Something to be explored. Something to be discussed. A future between us. A connection.

I think he feels it too.

Because this time, Fortis doesn't protest. This time he answers me.

"All right. I'm with you, love. If you say you saw her, I believe you. Dream on. We need to find this jade girl, figure out what she's bringin' to the party."

"And then?"

He squeezes my hand. "And then we take the bastards down."

SPECIAL EMBASSY DISPATCH
TO GAP MIYAZAWA

MARKED URGENT
MARKED EYES ONLY

Note: Contact Jasmine3k, Virt. Hybrid Human 39261.SEA, Laboratory Assistant to Dr. E. Yang, for future commentary, as necessary.

FORTIS
Transcript - ComLog 12.11.2052
FORTIS::NULL

//comlog begin;
comlink established;

sendline: You are still coming to Earth, correct?;
return: Correct.;

sendline: But it appears your trajectory isn't correct—you will miss Earth by hundreds of miles.;
return: I have entry and landing protocols that correct for this.;

sendline: Of course you do. You mentioned you are coming here to prepare the planet.;

return: yes.;

sendline: For what? For whom?;
return: My creators. And my children.;

sendline: Are they the same?;
return: In a manner of speaking, yes.;

sendline: NULL, when you say prepare Earth, can you define "prepare"?;
return: In terms you might understand?;
Possible analogies: Converting arid terrain into fertile land. Erasing a chalkboard. Formatting a computer drive.;

sendline: Can you be more specific?;
return: Possibly.;
Decontaminate and recycle all indigenous biological/organic material.;
Purify atmosphere. Eliminate all potential biological and ecological threats.;
Repopulate with essential biological elements.;
Prepare homes for children.;

sendline: Homes—as in, colonies?;
return: That is an appropriate analogy.;

//comlog end;

15

REMNANTS

I stare up at the vast gray deck of an enormous industrial tanker. A ship—our next form of passage, bought and paid for with more digs than I've ever seen—or so I think. All I know is that we're dressed as Remnants, the broken refuse of the human population—the ones who rejected the initial call to the cities when the Lords first arrived. The ones who chose squalor and poverty over the false comfort of life under the Embassies. The ones who, for their punishment, were rounded up and sent to the Projects like cattle.

And now we are among them, with dirty, ripped clothes and smudged dust on our faces. If anyone asks, we're to say we've been separated from our families since the night the Icon died. Not that anyone will ask. It's not like we didn't already look the part. We practically are Remnants.

I look up. Billows of black smoke spew from tall, cylindrical metal vents, segmenting the length of the ship like so many flagpoles.

I see the familiar Embassy insignia, painted on the side of the ship. I recognize it from all the way down here, with a cruel twist to my gut. There it is, the image of our fallen planet, always surrounded by the pentagon representing the House of Lords. The same five walls of the Projects.

The golden birdcage. Earth, trapped like a pet canary. That's what I used to tell Ro.

I keep my eyes focused on the landing mark. I try not to think about anything other than what it means. Why I'm here. Where we're going. Why it matters.

The little girl waiting for us on the other side of the ocean.

Things really do change, and then they keep changing.

Perhaps this is what survival feels like. Or life. I honestly don't know anymore.

I can barely think straight, surrounded by so much misery. I have been so long away from the Hole, I have forgotten what the crush of panic and desperation feels like. How I have to protect myself whenever I am in a crowd.

I feel like I am being trampled by invisible giants.

Not everything has changed, not even after the Icon has fallen. Not even here. Not yet. Not among the Remnants.

Sorrow has its hold once more.

Then the lines of human cargo in front of us start to move again, and I focus my eyes on nothing as I mount the rising ramp that leads me into the cargo hold of the *Hanjin Mariner*.

—————— • ——————

Our ship is moving. The *Mariner* is leaving the Porthole. From where we are stowed away—curled in the shadows behind the life rafts and the drop skiffs, like Mission children playing Hide the Rabbit—I can look up in the sky and see the vents cough up black smoke as the ship rolls. I'm leaving the Americas for the first time in my life, and that's all I know.

I'm frightened.

Tima is pale beneath her smudged face—still clutching Brutus—and Lucas is silent. Ro is a bundle of nervous energy, happy to be heading back out into the unknown.

Fortis is less theatrical about it. His low hiss is the only sound track to our departure.

"You are not to move from these shadows until we are all the way out of port. Let me be very clear about that."

His voice lowers as we watch the legs of the crew

pass by through the racks of life rafts in front of us.

"Don't know how the Bishop thought you'd manage this on your own. Even a Merk only has enough digs to get us smuggled onto this container ship once, so don't dirt it up. An' this whole junkbucket's crawlin' with two things and two things only. Brass, an' Remnants."

He pauses as a different color of uniform stands in front of us. Smoke from a pipe wafts our way.

"Brass won't kick you off," Fortis says, "but you'll wish they did. They'll either blow your head off, or they'll toss you in with the real Remnants. An' no amount of dirt on your face can prepare you for that. They'll as soon kill you as share their supper."

Then his voice fades away—like the setting sun around us—and we are left with only the grinding of the motors and the shouts of the crew.

The junkbucket lurches, the whole deck vibrating and the air whistling past me. We have picked up speed, which means we must be leaving the Porthole.

Now I know we're gone. Bigger and Biggest. The Padre and the Bishop. La Purísima and the Idylls and the Hole.

Gone.

I shiver from the cold, wishing I hadn't ripped quite so many holes in my Remnant clothes.

I shiver for other reasons too.

As the others settle in for the night around me, I reach out through the darkness to the ones I have lost, over and over, until I can't think and I can't feel and I can't do anything but fall into the kind of sleep that only means defeat.

You're supposed to save the world, Doloria. Better get on it, already.

That girl isn't going to find you. The world isn't going to save you, either.

GENERAL EMBASSY DISPATCH:
EASTASIA SUBSTATION

MARKED URGENT
MARKED EYES ONLY

Internal Investigative Subcommittee IIS211B
RE: The Incident at SEA Colonies

Note: Contact Jasmine3k, Virt. Hybrid Human 39261.SEA, Laboratory Assistant to Dr. E. Yang, for future commentary, as necessary.

Scan of a tattered partial page burned by fire.

Found with the remains of the Belter community formerly known as the Idylls.

Dear Brother,

I find it odd that you can be my brother—
and yet live such a different life than I do. A
bishop and a padre, and yet we have nothing
in common. Your religion involves guns and
explosives. Mine, hymnals and pigs...

Your Flaco is a father now, or as near
to one as I shall ever be. The children of the
Silent have been coming to live with me in
the Mission. They find me, or I find them,
as I did a tiny mewling baby in the ruins of
a home just last week, as I was going about
the good work. I call her Dol—Dolly, really—
and she's a funny little thing. She reminds
me of you sometimes, brother, the way she
screams.

The lungs on that child!

IN A HEARTBEAT

When the morning comes, the light slicing between the racks of boats and skiffs is so bright I have to shield my eyes. Everything is bright out there, and dark in here. Dark, and damp. Fortis's hiding hole has served us well.

He really is good at lying low. Merk trick of the trade.

My body is stiff and I can't feel my feet. I've slept in a ball like a potato bug, only I wonder if a potato bug has this much trouble uncurling.

The air around us smells like salt and feels like water. Like the Porthole. Like the sea, back in the Californias. Back home, back in all my homes, which it seems I do nothing but leave behind.

I breathe deep—and wrinkle my nose.

The air may smell like salt, but we smell like a pig farm.

I try to remember what we used to blacken our faces and our clothes. I hope it had nothing to do with pigs.

I sniff again.

Pigs, and wet dogs. Everything is damp from the sea air. As if the misery of sleeping rolled in a ball shoved behind a rack of boats on a hard wooden deck weren't enough.

I twist my neck, turning to see the others wedged next to me. They're still sleeping. Ro is practically standing up, sleeping slumped against the boat rack. Lucas is bent at an awkward angle, favoring his good side. I bite my lip, thinking of the times when he would sneak his jacket to me in the night. There's no chance of that now; no Remnant has a proper jacket. He's as tattered and filthy as I am.

Tima, by his side, is folded into a small sleeping bundle as usual, compact and neat. Her head rests on his shoulder, where mine should be. Brutus is nowhere to be seen.

I look away.

On my other side, Fortis is snoring, arms folded across his chest. His jacket is wedged behind his head like a pillow. Fortis could sleep anywhere, anytime. Another signature Merk trait—stealing sleep as easily as anything else.

I have to get out of here. I have to stretch my body back into a line, the way it was built to be. I pull myself up behind the skiffs, slowly, inhabiting the small strip of vertical space as a snake would, slithering its way up an old pipe. I can't feel my feet at all, though, or most of my legs. If there were enough room to collapse, I'd already have fallen back down to the wet deck floor.

I slide past the tangle of human bodies until I can squeeze my way past the life rafts and out into the open air of the deck.

I look out from the shadows, cautiously at first—but I relax when I see there is no crew in sight. It must be very early.

I take a step forward, staggering from the pain and from the rolling of the deck beneath my feet.

The sea is everywhere.

The hugeness of it almost knocks me off my feet. I clutch the skiff rack, steadying myself.

One step at a time.

As I slowly move farther away from the skiff rack, I begin to understand that I have never seen the ocean, not like this. I've never been on the water, surrounded by it—excepting the brief ride back and forth from the Porthole to Santa Catalina.

I make my way to the rusting rail along the edge of the bow. At least, that's what Tima called it, this end of the ship. I lean over the water, as far as I can go.

I have never seen this kind of water, dark and fast and loud. I have never felt this kind of wind, either.

The air rumbles, almost groaning. Even the drifting clouds of smoke from the ship's vents are tossed off course—soaring and recovering and soaring again, like the Padre on Christmas Eve, when he'd had too much mulberry wine.

My hair whips around my face, stinging my cheeks like hundreds of salty thorns. All around me, the water churns into tiny peaks of white foam, hitting against itself, over and over again, so many impossibly shoreless shores.

I've never seen anything like it, never seen the sea—or, for that matter, the world—from the deck of a ship.

Everything looks different from here.

For this one moment, I am the only living thing in the universe—and then I see a pale green lizard wander up the side of the deck railing. He alone does not seem bothered by the crushing rush of air.

"You like it? The sea? She's big, eh?"

Fortis stands behind me while Brutus slides along the deck behind him. I almost don't recognize Fortis without his jacket, and in the pleasant sunlight. I nod, holding my hair out of my eyes with one hand.

He looks out to the horizon, then back to the deck. "Probably safe for another few minutes. Watch will change again soon, though. Then we'll have to crawl back in the hidey-hole, so don't get too comfortable."

"Got it."

He stretches into a long line, like a cat. "So just try to blend in with the crowd and lie low."

"The crowd? You mean the Remnants?"

He nods. "They'll mostly be belowdecks, though. Caged an' chained like animals." He looks down at Brutus, shaking his head. "It's not just not human, it's not humane. Poor sods. Can you feel them?" Fortis scratches Brutus by the ears. "We wouldn't do that to you, now, would we?"

I shake my head. I will myself not to feel them, the anxiously beating hearts, the simmering anger, the despair. They may be belowdecks, but I know they're there. I can feel them, every one of them, whether or not I want to.

Today I wish I couldn't.

Today is hard enough on my own.

Fortis straightens, leaning next to me against the railing. "Unlucky buggers. Just trying to make their own life outside the cities. One minute you're just a Grass like the rest of us, down on his luck an' lookin' for a bit of food an' work—an' the next, you're stuck on the Tracks an' headin' for the Projects. Or tossed onto this junkbucket an' shipped off to the SEA Colonies. How is it right, for one human to treat another like that?"

"It isn't," I say. "And I'd be one of them, if the Padre hadn't found me."

"Unclaimed masses of humanity, my arse. Remnants aren't the embarrassment. No such thing as human garbage. Don't see why they put up with it."

"Who gives them the choice, Fortis? The Brass? Catallus?

The GAP? The Lords? They don't *put up* with it."

"They won't forever. That much I know. History has a way of repeatin' itself, even if you don't know it."

"What's that supposed to mean?"

"Nothing. I don't know. But I do know it ain't the Lords herding these people into the Projects. Those are human beings in those Sympa uniforms. Working the Embassies. Maybe there are worse things than the Lords," Fortis says. "Sometimes humanity isn't all it's cracked up to be. Seems like we make it easy for them. Did you ever think of that?"

I don't know what he's really saying. I'm not sure I want to. "No."

"Really?"

"The Lords killed my parents on The Day. There is nothing worse than the Lords. So don't say that to me, Fortis. Never say that."

I turn and see that he's studying me, as if I were the lizard on the railing. Then he smirks.

"Even Catallus? He's a right bastard, if I recall." The words float out over the water, and I don't answer. Instead, I wait for them to disappear.

Then I change the subject.

"Why send a boat full of Remnants to the SEA Colonies' Projects, anyway, when the Hole has Projects of its own? It makes no sense." The boat rolls beneath my feet, and I grab the rail again to steady myself.

Fortis smiles. "Sea legs, Grassgirl. We've got at least a week on this ship. You'll get them yet."

"Don't hold your breath. And don't change the subject, Fortis. What's so different about these Projects, that they have to ship in Remnant slaves from around the world?"

"All right, then." Fortis gives me a strange look, as if I don't really want to hear what he is about to say, which is wrong. It's all I want to hear, at this particular moment. "I told you I'd help you find your little jade girl. This missing fifth Icon Child, if you say she exists. The girl of your dreams. And I will."

"Which is why we're on this Remnant ship," I say, prodding him along.

"Which is one of the reasons why I agreed to see to your passage on this Remnant ship," Fortis corrects. "I probably should have told you I have a few reasons of my own."

He looks back out to the water. "I also probably should have told you that the SEA Colonies are home to the biggest Project in the world."

Biggest. In the world.

Out of all the Icons and all their fallen cities, that is no small claim.

He nods, as if I've asked a question, which I haven't. "Entirely built on reclaimed land, pushin' so far out into the big blue sea that it's not really clear what part of what country or city or government it ever actually was.

A bit of Greater Bangkok at first, I think. Modeled on United Singapore. With a bit of the Eastasia Coast and the Viet Collective thrown in for good measure." He smiles, humorlessly. "The SEA Colonies used to be home to something called the Golden Triangle. Now it's more like the Golden Pentagon. An' within spittin' distance of the Shanghai Icon."

I try to take it all in. "Hard to imagine anything bigger than the Porthole."

"Bigger than the Porthole? This little Project of Projects makes the pyramids look like ant farms. They could fill every ship on this planet full of Remnants, ten times over, and still not be able to fully man the SEA Projects."

I can't even imagine it. The Porthole Projects seem hulking and horrible enough. Something bigger—something worse—it's not a pleasant image.

"Are there Grass like us there? I mean, not Remnants? Is there an organized resistance?"

People to help us take on the Icon?

And if so, are we going to take it out?

That's the real question. Because the Idylls have fallen, Nellis has fallen, and the way I see it, we're running out of time. Time and support—and options. And on top of all that, the thing I'm worried most about is getting sucked into battle when all I want to do is find the one person I came here for.

The one person who matters, according to the old

man from the Benevolent Association. According to my
dreams. According to every cell in my body, whether I'm
asleep or awake. The person for whom I carry this small
menagerie of jades.

"Not so fast. I'll answer all your questions. But this isn't just about an Icon. There's something else—a little thing we need to take care of first."

"There is?" Little things, to Fortis, are sometimes near catastrophic to the rest of us. This much I know.

"The SEA Colonies," Fortis says, his eyes glinting, "are also home to the General Embassy and GAP Miyazawa himself."

"What?" I feel like he's just taken a bucket of seawater and dumped it over my head. Walking into the home of the GAP, that's more than I ever intended. "How did I not know that?"

"The General Embassy moves from continent to continent—safer that way. Harder to target, harder still to rebel against. Only now it seems that the GAP, he's settling in over at SEA. Hence the overgrown Projects, I suppose. If you think about it, it makes a kind of sense. Bad apple like that, wants to make sure his tree is bigger than anybody else's."

Of course.

I shiver at the name. Not just an Embassy, but the General Embassy. The whole place will be crawling with Sympas. Sympas, and who knows what else.

Because GAP Miyazawa isn't just an Ambassador, he's *the* Ambassador. The direct line to the Lords themselves. The ultimate traitor to humanity.

A slave trader to a planet.

Because he's the richest man on Earth—and his only trade is human flesh.

Even the thought of him makes me physically sick. I look at the Merk. "What are we doing, Fortis?"

"We're going to find your girl, and like I said, we'll see what she brings to the table. If she really is one of you—well, you'll only be that much stronger."

"And?"

"And then it's time to destroy the GAP and his overgrown Projects."

Fortis's face darkens and his words cut. Everything becomes perfectly clear.

"I thought we were trying to destroy the Icons. That without the Icons everything falls apart. You never said anything about the Projects. Our powers can't do anything about human cruelty. We can't do anything about the GAP and all his Sympas—and all their guns." Even for Fortis, it's madness.

"We'll find a way. One way or another, we're here to take down the whole SEA Colonies, love."

I'm staring. I can't believe what he's saying. It's all so—big.

I can't do it.

He can't think I'll do it.

Can he?

"Don't look at me like that. You wanted this, Grassgirl. It was your idea to come."

"To find the Icon Child. To destroy the Icons and break the grip the Lords have on our planet. Not to destroy the whole Colonies. I don't know what the Lords did to you up there, but you've lost your mind, Fortis. We need to keep our eyes on our actual capabilities here."

"Not the first to tell me that, pet." His eyes grow wilder. "But maybe we're closer aligned than you realize. Think about what you were able to do in the Hole, just yourself. Imagine what you could do now, with all four of you, or if there really are five."

"We don't know anything about her."

"No, we don't. But we know you shouldn't have to be hiding, or living on the run. We know you could put a stop to all of this."

"One day, maybe. Twelve Icons from now."

"Maybe we don't need to take out one Icon at a time. Maybe we should be taking out the entire system, the network. From the top."

"You sound like Ro."

"I sound like a soldier, which is what I am." The words have a familiar ring, and I think of the desert, when we imagined Fortis was dead.

A soldier's death.

Maybe that's still waiting for him, for all of us.

I look at Fortis. "You'd really do that?"

"Cut off the head of the Embassies? Blow open the Projects? Kill the GAP? End it—the time of willing human slavery to the Lords?" He looks at me, and his eyes are cold. "In a heartbeat."

I think of the sudden silver ships. I think of the Icons themselves, threatening every skyline, every city that matters. I think of the jade girl—the jade bird—living in the shadow of it all.

The whole world is a dark place now.

The blue sky above us, the warm sun—it all seems strangely incongruous. Suddenly I'm not sure we're headed toward hope.

Where we're headed is somewhere I've never been at all.

GENERAL EMBASSY DISPATCH:
EASTASIA SUBSTATION

MARKED URGENT
MARKED EYES ONLY

Internal Investigative Subcommittee IIS211B
RE: The Incident at SEA Colonies

Note: Contact Jasmine3k, Virt. Hybrid Human 39261.SEA,
Laboratory Assistant to Dr. E. Yang, for future commentary,
as necessary.

FORTIS
Transcript - ComLog 12.31.2052
FORTIS::NULL

//comlog begin;
comlink established;

sendline: Good morning, NULL. So, I wanted to verify that
you do realize I am an indigenous biological entity, correct?;
return: Yes.;

sendline: So I am to be recycled?;
return: Yes.;

sendline: You know, there are a lot more like me here. Quite organized, stubborn, prepared to fight back. Could make your job quite difficult.;

return: I was provided tools in the event of some indigenous resistance.;

sendline: I noticed. However, I can tell you, if you want to succeed, you could use some help. Expert opinion.;

return: I do want to succeed. That is why I exist.;

sendline: Well then, why don't you tell me more about your plans? Perhaps I can be of service. Perhaps I can offer my aid in exchange for, say, not being recycled?;

return: This is outside the bounds of my initial tasking. I will attempt to evaluate your offer and return with a reply.;

comlink terminated;

//comlog end;

//lognote: Did I push too hard? Happy New Year, NULL.;

17

MERK SECRETS

Fortis and I don't speak. We just look out at the horizon, side by side, as if it is the one thing we have in common.

"That's some talk, Fortis. I don't know."

"Don't you trust me?"

"Did I ever?"

"Fair enough."

He turns to look at me, and for a moment it's like talking to a regular person.

"I'm sure about this, Dol. I won't let anything happen. We won't have to go it alone. I have a few friends left in the world, you know. In the Colonies."

"And a few more enemies," I add, my mouth twisting.

"You have no idea."

Fortis winks, and we look back out to the water.

Then—suddenly, awkwardly—Fortis clears his throat. "Speaking of enemies. It's none of my business, the mushy stuff, you know. Friendship and true love and all that rot. But you and your boys, you seem a bit out of sorts."

I can feel my face turning red. "Whatever point you think you're making, don't."

He ignores me. "That Padre of yours did an all-right job. You turned out all right. And he's not all bad, the other one." Fortis smiles. "When he's not busy beatin' on the whole world."

"Ro?"

He nods.

I sigh. "He's just like that, I guess. He likes a challenge."

"You mean he likes a fight." Fortis looks at me, leaning closer along the rail. "I'd watch that one if I were you, Grassgirl."

"Why is that?"

"Fellow like that, never know what he'll do. When he'll blow. Boom."

I shiver.

Fortis pats me on the shoulder.

"You're smart to stick with Buttons. He's going to be a sight cracked, what with the whole Mama Ambassador thing, but there's always medical science to take care of that."

"You mean, like a Psych. Virt?"

He grins. "I mean like a lobotomy." He turns away. "I'm off to scare up some breakfast. Get back in the hidey-hole before someone sees you, will you?"

"Promise."

I say it and I mean it, because the minute he's gone, I make my move.

Something's going on with Fortis and I'm not letting it go past me.

———————— • ————————

I slip back noiselessly into the shadows, walking over the same rolling deck where I stumbled not so long ago. Tima and Lucas and Ro are still sleeping; even Brutus is snoring. Battered as we all are, just getting through another day is a minor medical miracle. Fortis says sleep is the best thing they—and any of us—can do. Not that it's that easy to come by, in a situation like ours.

Maybe he spiked their food with sleep tabs, I think, looking at them snoring away now.

Even better.

I spy Fortis's jacket, and before I know it, I'm reaching inside. I need to know what's going on, especially with his sudden plans for us to take down the entire General Embassy.

Fortis isn't himself—or I'm not.

Either way, I have to find out.

As with any Merk, his jacket is a treasure trove, with

206

every hidden inside pocket brimming full of the odd bits that make Fortis, Fortis. He's never without it; only the intolerable heat and the more intolerable humidity of the Colonies have made him leave it behind, even now.

A rare mistake.

Stop it, I think.

What are you even looking for?

But I don't stop. I can't help myself.

Information, as he would say. Pertinent information. That's what I'm looking for.

And so I keep looking.

The first thing I see is the cuff, wrapped in the stiff black fabric.

Strange, Fortis without his cuff.

That rarely happens.

Next I find a wad of digs, a bundle of Merk cash held together in a digi-clip with the faded letters *P.F.* on it. Beyond that, there are such treasures as this: a bundle of old photographs, tied with string—a small pocketknife—a larger hunting knife—and what looks like a tin of grease for his hair. I open it.

Plastic explosives. *Nice.*

Then I find it, in one of the larger pockets that line the back of the jacket. Still bound in its own rough burlap sack, just as I left it when I gave it to him for safekeeping, back at Nellis.

My book.

My last gift from the Padre.

The Humanity Project: The Icon Children.

I open the pages, eagerly, shamefully—as if I were reading something immoral or illegal or worse.

But I'm not. I'm reading about myself. Until I get to the back pages, which are scribbled in with writing by another hand.

Fortis's.

It's his journal, as far as I can tell.

I settle back against the wall of the rolling ship and start to read about the man I have entrusted my life to.

⸻ • ⸻

THE ICON CHILDREN—
SEA COLONIES LAB DATA—WEEK 27

GENETIC MODIFICATION FOR ALL SPECIMENS PREPARED. PRIMATE TESTING SUCCESSFUL, NEUROLOGICAL SIDE EFFECTS NEGLIGIBLE. AMYGDALA AND CORTEX CUSTOMIZATIONS MEET OR EXCEED SPECIFICATIONS ON ALL MEASUREMENTS. DETECTING ORDERS-OF-MAGNITUDE INCREASES ACROSS ALL KEY BRAIN FUNCTIONS AND CORRESPONDING INCREASES IN ENERGY OUTPUT. REDESIGNED HARDWARE WAS REQUIRED TO ACCOMMODATE NEW, HIGH READINGS.

THE DESIGN IS SOUND, AND WORK BEGINS ON HUMAN INTEGRATION, MARKED BELOW.

SPECIMEN ONE: DNA SYNTHESIS COMPLETE

SPECIMEN TWO: DNA SYNTHESIS COMPLETE

SPECIMEN THREE: DNA SYNTHESIS COMPLETE

SPECIMEN FOUR: DNA SYNTHESIS COMPLETE

MODIFICATIONS FOR ALL SPECIMENS SUCCESSFULLY ENCODED AND READY TO TEST INCUBATION FOR VIABILITY.

NOTE: ELA INSISTS ON FURTHER TESTING. I DON'T BLAME HER FOR WANTING TO BE CERTAIN OF WHAT WE HAVE. SOMETHING NEW. A SOLUTION TO EXTINCTION. A SOLUTION TO EVERYTHING.

IT'S QUITE POSSIBLE THE FUTURE OF THE WORLD DEPENDS ON IT.

———— • ————

ELA? Who is that?

And DNA synthesis?

What was he synthesizing?

"Still sleeping?"

I hear the booming voice before I see him, moving across the skiffs in front of our shadowy shelter—and I rush to toss everything back into his jacket.

"Like babies," I say, my heart pounding.

"Good. I like it that way. Less chatter." Fortis smiles as he creeps into our hidey-hole, tossing a sack in my direction. "Paid a little visit to the galley storage. Eat up. Don't exactly know when fresh food is coming our way again. It's not like we'll be going fishing."

"You never know," I say.

"What?"

"Fish. Birds. Extinction. You never know. You might wake up one day and find a genetic solution to extinction. Something new." I don't look at him, opening the sack instead.

"Not likely," he says, ripping off the end of a stolen loaf.

I pull out a hard round of bread for myself. "Do you still have the Padre's book, Fortis? The one about us—about me?"

He looks startled. "Of course."

"Can I see it?"

"It's not with me. Not here."

"Where is it?"

"Somewhere safe."

"That's what I thought."

I bite into the tough, leathery roll, thinking about genome sequencing and bioinformation and, as I swallow, the future of the world.

And who or who not to trust it to.

GENERAL EMBASSY DISPATCH:
EASTASIA SUBSTATION

MARKED URGENT
MARKED EYES ONLY

Internal Investigative Subcommittee IIS211B
RE: The Incident at SEA Colonies

Note: Contact Jasmine3k, Virt. Hybrid Human 39261.SEA, Laboratory Assistant to Dr. E. Yang, for future commentary, as necessary. Also note that in following communications, the entity HAL is now referred to as DOC, following Fortis's penchant for obtuse nicknames.

DOC ==> FORTIS
Transcript - ComLog 10.13.2054
Ethical Query

//comlog begin;

DOC: FORTIS?;

FORTIS: Yes, DOC.;

DOC: Should we not alert the government about your discoveries about NULL, his devices, and the…children?;

FORTIS: No. Not yet.;

FORTIS: Ask me again later.;

FORTIS: I am still evaluating our situation. It is still somewhat elastic. Dynamic.;

FORTIS: And I still have a handle on things. I hope.;

DOC: As do I.;

//comlog end;

JUMP

The blue water of the SEA Colonies is marbled with shadow as we approach. Shadow and shade, in strange patterns and blotches, like pieces of a giant puzzle I will never see finished. A whole world beneath the sea.

I wonder what the Lords have planned for that half of the Earth, the secret half. How they will destroy it.

The Lords and the GAP.

I wonder if it will surrender as quickly as the land above did.

"There's something moving down there. Look." Lucas points. I don't look back at the water, though, because he's not wearing his ripped shirt, and I'm too busy looking at him—at the strangely shiny place his scar has become, shaped like a flower, or a burst of sun. More than a week of sleep and sea air has done his body more good than I

213

could have imagined. Even if most of that time was spent darting in and out of a row of damp old dinghies.

Still, it isn't just that Lucas's spirits seem better today; all of ours are. We're supposed to see land within the next few hours. It's about time, I think. I'm ready to give up sleeping on the deck.

I haven't dreamed of her once, the jade girl. It's worrying me. I don't know what it means. Then again, the thought of the SEA Colonies and all they will bring—at least, if Fortis's plans fall into place—is hardly a soothing thought. Maybe my dreams have a way of revealing to me only what I can handle.

As if I can handle any of this.

"There." Lucas motions again. "Look. Manta. They're still here. Even without the fish."

I turn to see the dark shadows move just beneath the surface of the water, flapping their pliant bodies. They swim the way I imagine birds used to fly, the way Grass festival dancers flutter their hands when they dance. Like a fish out of water, only in reverse. A bird out of the sky. It's eerie, and I shiver.

Then I remember.

"How is that possible? Whatever that is, it must have—you know." *Hearts. That can stop—or be stopped.* Those are the words left unsaid.

"Maybe it's a miracle," Lucas says. "Or maybe things just change."

"Maybe it wears off, the effect of the Icon. Maybe it all comes back."

"It?"

I shrug. "Life."

The birds, I think.

I reach into my chestpack and pull out the small silver bird. The pin. I study it as if it could talk.

The Bishop's birds didn't come back. Neither did the Padre—or my parents. How will I ever really know who or what will come back?

Or is it all just up to Fortis and his secrets? I think bitterly.

Then Lucas touches my arm, bringing me back to him. I smile at him, and he leans forward, cupping my face with one hand, kissing me abruptly. Hard and soft.

Like so much of my life.

But the sunlight is warm on my arms and the humid air winds around me and I twist my body closer to him, as if we could dance and fly like miracles ourselves.

Secret, mysterious miracles. Irrational impossibilities. Birds in the water and fish in the skies.

Because maybe, in some small way, that's what we are.

———— • ————

We stand at the railing, watching when the shore comes into sight. The crew is too busy now to notice us, though the majority of the Remnants—at least, those who haven't been made to work the sanitation crews—are still belowdecks.

It's an unforgettable sight—less of a shore and more of an optimistic outcropping of rock that just refuses to be sea; it won't give in to the broad blue wash that surrounds us on all sides. You have to respect that.

I do.

Farther down the rock, I can see the outline of a Colony settlement along the nearest bay.

There are buildings in the distance, of course, reaching like fingers, like claws, high up toward the sky where they've had to build up instead of out, in a land where space is scarce and every shovelful of soil comes at a premium. They have the same vaguely dead look that the cities do, that the Hole did. Lights that don't light, cars that don't move. Literal powerlessness, meant to be not just evident but obvious.

But what I really notice are the trees.

Enormous palm trees—too many to count—sway their slender trunks out toward us, over the water, as if they were groaning bellies after a fat lunch. As if their backs will soon break.

Above them, the sky seems especially vast, now that there is a shoreline beneath it. Something about the smallness of human life makes the theater of the clouds above more immense, more spectacular—as if the important thing, here, isn't human life—and as if it never was.

The scale is all wrong, I think.

I think of the relative size of things as our ship draws toward the shore, bringing up the buildings, closer and closer, until they dwarf the sky itself.

Right now I have no idea how big or little I am.

We make our plan to disembark with the others, slipping inside the scraggly processional of human life that is the Remnants headed to the Projects. It's the grimmest of parades.

Fortis stiffens as soon as he sees them. "Bugger."

I look over. "What's wrong?"

"Just look at them. They're dressed up now." He motions toward the Remnants, and I realize that he's right. They're in a kind of uniform, one they weren't wearing when we all boarded the ship. It's a faded blue-gray pants and jacket, vaguely regional looking. A SEA Colonies uniform.

Worse, they're in chains—and we're not.

"Keep your heads down," Fortis hisses. He hurries to fall into line behind a cluster of Remnants, who act like they don't even see us.

We follow.

I feel them now. I wish I didn't, but I do. They're hungry, most of them. Sick, at least half of them. Scared for their lives, nearly all.

"Stay close," hisses Fortis. "And I said heads down." Tima stumbles as he says it, but Lucas grabs her arm, and we press behind the others, so that you'd have to be looking to see us.

Looking more closely, to see a scruffy dog hidden inside Tima's jacket.

I'm afraid they'll see—that someone will notice the irregularity in the line. If someone is watching closely enough, they will.

I hold my breath.

One. Two. Three.

But no one is watching. At least, no one from the line of Brass shoving the Remnants into carts. Not this time.

Fortis motions and we follow him, walking, not running, until we reach the edge of the docks.

"Just do what I do," Fortis says, pulling his jacket tight.

I nod.

And he jumps off the side of the pier.

The sound of the splash is lost in the clanking of the Remnants' chains.

GENERAL EMBASSY DISPATCH:
EASTASIA SUBSTATION

MARKED URGENT
MARKED EYES ONLY

Internal Investigative Subcommittee IIS211B
RE: The Incident at SEA Colonies

Note: Contact Jasmine3k, Virt. Hybrid Human 39261.SEA,
Laboratory Assistant to Dr. E. Yang, for future commentary,
as necessary.

FORTIS ==> DOC
Transcript - ComLog 06.13.2060

//comlog begin;

FORTIS: We need our countermeasures ready. Like,
yesterday. NULL will be here before we know it. Have you
completed the genome analysis?;

DOC: Yes, I believe I have.;

FORTIS: And the reprogramming of the limbic design and
neocortex is feasible?;

DOC: Yes, the theory is sound. In practice, well, biological processes have a way of being unpredictable.;

FORTIS: That's what keeps life interesting, mate. Okay, I've selected candidates for implant. NULL is fast approaching, and we need to put this plan in motion.;

DOC: I believe I can provide you the "recipe" soon. As for the legwork, well...;

FORTIS: Yes, I understand, you don't have legs.;

DOC: Or hands.;

FORTIS: Sigh. I've spent some quality time in the lab refining the DNA manipulation process and once you give me the code, I believe I can prepare the candidate eggs in time for complete gestation prior to NULL's arrival.;

//comlog end;

GOLDEN GAP

The water is freezing. It's pulling me down and dragging me under, with a violence I normally associate with the intention to kill.

It's just water.

Move.

But my legs are slow and my lungs are burning, and by the time we have all pulled ourselves up the rusting dock ladder on the far side of the Porthole, I feel at least wounded, if not dead.

We are a sorry, bedraggled mess—all of us. Fortis, spluttering in his soggy overcoat, seems worse off than the rest. I think for a moment of the now-waterlogged book in his pocket, the one he pretends not to have, drowning all his secrets.

As if anything will make them go away.

Even Brutus shakes out his fur, bristling as he sprays us, doubts and all.

But once we catch our breath, for these few moments of first shore sunshine, it's like none of it ever happened. I want to fling myself on the grass—actual grass—that lines the boulevard leading inland from the port.

A Porthole, I think with a sad smile. How different this one is than back home. As I watch the foaming blue-green waves, all I can think of is the garbage floating in the gray dishwater of the Hole's own Porthole Bay. I smell things growing here in the Colonies—strange things, blossoming things, things with colors and scents and flavors. I can only think of things dying, back in the Hole. Cars and people and whole city blocks.

Human debris.

Inhuman debris.

Not here.

Not yet.

The difference is striking.

But for how much longer?

Fortis makes us keep moving, though at the first street, we stop long enough to toss half our clothing into a large tin trash bin. It's too hot for more than the drawstring pants and thin undershirts we've stolen from the laundry room belowdecks.

"What's the plan?" Tima asks, scanning the road around us.

"We head north," Fortis says. "City center."

"Is that where your alleged friends are?" I toss my overshirt into the garbage bin while I ask, straightening my chestpack with a shove.

Fortis nods. "Believe it or not, I know a few of the local authorities."

"You mean you're getting us arrested?" Lucas is impatient.

"No. I mean I'm getting you cleaned up. At least, I should. We've got a date with a monk." Fortis grins. "Come on. I'm starving."

"No more bread," Tima groans as we fall into step behind him.

All around us, in the streets that lead into the city center, an open market crowds along the street corners. Passersby hurry through the blasting sun, hiding under colorful sun umbrellas or broad, pointed straw hats. Bougainvillea grows over tin rooftops and curving brown dried-leaf rooftops and long dried-grass rooftops. Some are draped with fabric, a bright golden-yellow and white. Beneath the rooftops, in the warm shade, stalls of improbable objects—homemade brooms, bolts of colorful cloth, brightly sectioned umbrellas—compete with larger ones hawking fruits and vegetables and flowers—bright orange poppies and gold carnations and red roses, sculpted into necklaces and wreaths.

A wagon rattles past us. It's made of colored tin, with

open sides beneath a domed ceiling—like it's meant to keep passengers shaded from the blasting sun.

I look from my bare feet on the hot concrete to Fortis ahead of me, but I don't even bother to ask. There's no way he'd let us put ourselves on display like that. We just escaped one processional, there's no time for another parade. We will cross this city on foot.

The air smells ripe. "Jackfruit," says Fortis, breathing deep as he fingers a spine. "Smells like udder rot from an old heifer."

"So you like it," Ro says.

"Of course. And jujube. The little green one. Like a cross between a pear and an apple." Fortis points. "Jujube. Guava, the bigger round green one. Mangosteen. Sapodilla. Longan, the one that looks like a dry yellow grape. Lychee."

"Why do you know the name of every fruit in this marketplace?" I ask, examining a prickly fruit, plumed in pink. Tima shoots me a look. She's been thinking the same thing, clearly.

"That's dragonfruit." Fortis shrugs. "I can't help it. So I like fruit."

So you really have been here before, I think. *Just like the Bishop said. Why haven't you mentioned that?*

But I let it drop, because it's clear he's not going to elaborate. Instead, I smile. "It's all so alive. Like the Earth hasn't given up yet."

"You can't stop growth from growing. You can destroy everythin' in sight, I suppose. But it always grows back. That's Earth for you." Fortis grins, the first I've seen him smile today.

The sun keeps rising, isn't that what Lucas tried to tell me?

"And that one?" Tima points.

"Passion fruit," he says, ripping one in half and handing a chunk to me and a chunk to Tima. He tosses a few digs into a plastic bowl on the table.

"What's so passionate about a fruit?" Tima says, unaware of how passionately she seems to be stuffing her mouth with the dripping orange pulp. "It's essentially just an ovary for a seed."

Fortis chokes a bit on the longan he's gnawing on. Lucas just smiles.

My foot catches on a piece of street garbage, and then I realize it's not garbage. It's a flower—hundreds, thousands of them. I look around, for the first time seeing what is actually there; what I thought were moths are really flower petals, blowing through the air.

Flowers and garbage, I think. *I can't even tell the difference.*

How could anyone expect the Lords to?

Then a voice booms through the air over our heads, and Tima points. Loudspeakers cluster where once were lampposts. Between them, an immense portrait of a man rises as tall as the trees on the street. Framed in intricate gold, he wears the crimson military jacket of the Brass. I've seen something like it before; Ambassador Amare had similar portraits placed throughout the Hole. But I've never seen one so large, and framed in so much gold. And not just that—swags of bright yellow-and-white cloth drape the perimeter of the frame.

Tributes in the form of flowers occupy pots and baskets and bags of every shape and size in front of the portrait. It's a shrine, I think. A political shrine.

Offerings to fear.

His face is broad and flat, his hair neatly kept. Thin wire glasses. Aside from that, he looks somewhat unremarkable. For a man who holds the fate of an entire planet in his hands.

But it's the sound blasting over the speakers that really makes the impression. At first I don't understand the Colonial dialect—which sounds a little like Chinese, at least the Chinese they speak in the Hole—but then the message repeats in English.

"Today we welcome a new community of workers to our glorious SEA Colonies, to bring honor to the House of Lords and the Embassies, as we complete the most important Project of our storied reign."

It's the GAP, I think. He's talking about himself. The coldness of his voice makes sense now, and it's hard to

226

even look at the loudspeakers. I wonder what it would be like to have to look into GAP Miyazawa's actual face.

I hope I never find out.

"The SEA Projects cannot be completed without sacrifice from our human populations. We thank our laborers for their hard work on behalf of our Earth. Workers, we salute you! All are invited to join us in celebrating our newfound Era of Improvement on Unification Day, in just a week now. Feasting and fireworks will be provided by Embassies all around the world, in honor of the anniversary of the day the House of Lords came to save our failing planet. Long live The Day! Long live our Lords!"

An abrupt chorus of children singing interrupts the message.

Fortis raises a brow. "And now you can't say you never met the GAP. Charming fellow, don't you think?"

"Unification Day? What was that garbage?" I shake my head as the singing dies out.

Fortis sighs. "That, my friends, is called politics."

———— • ————

A long, white plaster building lines the edge of the street in front of us. Where the plaster is cracking and fading, black stone is showing through.

It's a fort, I realize. An ancient fort.

"Is that where your friend is?" I ask.

"No, far from it. There. In the alley. Behind the garbage zone," Fortis says.

Of course.

We turn around. On the far side of the street—in the shadow of the fort—is a small, drab canal. Peeling buildings grow up out of the water. They would be impossible to see, if you weren't looking for them. They seem abandoned and impoverished, an uninhabited row made from the sides of ramshackle buildings that face other streets. Only if you look closely do you see that the corrugated tin paneling along the canal shacks slides into openings, stripes of shadow that reveal doorways to rooms behind them.

"Look." Fortis points. Drooping black ropes that seem like they're made of rubber twist into massive strands and loops, like handfuls of hair.

It looks out of control, like a child has scribbled across the cityscape.

"Electrical lines. Wired comlink poles. You're too young to have known about those. They carried power from house to house, shop to shop."

"Not a very efficient methodology," Tima says, scrunching up her face to examine them, high above her head in the sunshine. "Messy." Tima doesn't like that.

"No indeed. But look at that. Sort of like a primitive comlink." Fortis points to a blue-and-silver-and-orange box that stands on the side of the street, now covered in graffiti. "Phone booth."

We all nod, as if we know what the words mean.

We push on, down the steps into the canal and along the walkway that lines the side. A strangely beautiful lettering—meaningless to me—marks some of the buildings.

We stop in front of one with mirrored letters. Next to it, a pig in a suit bows on a sign, advertising some sort of service I cannot understand.

Fortis grunts. "Ah, getting fancy in our old age, are we? Very nice. For a porker."

"Who is?" Tima is distracted. "And what's that?"

Where she points, I see we're almost to the edge of the canal, the place where the water meets the larger waters of the river that seems to snake through the city center.

Fortis grunts. "The Ping. The river. Runs all the way from the SEA Cols up to the Northern Provinces. You need to make a quick getaway, that's your road."

The larger river is so clustered with boats of all shapes and sizes, it doesn't seem like a quick anything. Regardless, I'm still staring at it when I hear the whining sound of a tin door sliding open behind me.

"You." It's not the warmest greeting.

"William." Fortis sounds calm enough. "The pig himself. Though I believe the suit is a nice touch. For a monk."

"My name's not William," the voice growls. "Not

anymore. And I may be a pig, but at least I'm not a snake. You're not welcome here."

I turn around.

What stands in front of us is the unlikeliest monk I have ever seen.

He grins, his mouth curving wide as a panting puppy—and hits Fortis in the face with the full force of his three hundred pounds.

"Lords in hell," blurts Fortis—and he goes down without even swinging.

GENERAL EMBASSY DISPATCH:
EASTASIA SUBSTATION

MARKED URGENT
MARKED EYES ONLY

Internal Investigative Subcommittee IIS211B
RE: The Incident at SEA Colonies

Note: Contact Jasmine3k, Virt. Hybrid Human 39261.SEA, Laboratory Assistant to Dr. E. Yang, for future commentary, as necessary.

DOC ==> FORTIS
Transcript - ComLog 12.09.2066
Ethical Queries pt. 2

DOC: FORTIS?;

FORTIS: Yes, DOC.;

DOC: Should we not alert the government about your discoveries about NULL, his devices, and the children?;

FORTIS: No. Not yet. As I have said.;

DOC: But the world is not prepared, and if NULL's plans work, many people may die. Might I remind you of Asimov's Zeroth Law of Robotics (which I would extend to apply to any self-aware construct with the capacity to influence human events): "A robot may not harm humanity, or, by inaction, allow humanity to come to harm." Won't our inaction harm humanity?;

FORTIS: I appreciate your concern, I really do. But there are subtleties at play beyond your current grokking capacity. Geopolitical, psychological, sociological. Human stuff. Let me worry about it.;

FORTIS: However, I must say that your evolution continues to surprise me. I programmed you well (too well?). I think I may have to give you a new nickname, my friend. Phil, I think, would suit you.;

DOC: After Philip K. Dick?;

FORTIS: The very one! He was a brilliant but troubled individual. And, reputedly, a pain in the ass.;

DOC: I would blush again, but for entirely different reasons this time.;

FORTIS: Hah! You're a good friend, Mr. Dick.;

20

BUDDHA BILL

Fortis staggers back to his feet, rubbing his chin. Otherwise, he is unruffled.

That's just Fortis for you. He's probably no stranger to being hit in the face, that much I realize.

"Ah. Ow. Yes. Well. Good to know the monks are still so hospitable, William."

The man bows or nods—it's hard to tell which—pressing his hands together.

Fortis doesn't bow or nod in return. "These are my—let's call them friends. Doloria de la Cruz, Timora Li, Furo Costas, Lucas Amare."

The man's eyes catch on Lucas's face. He probably recognizes the name, I think. Even all the way over here, across an ocean. Even if he doesn't, Lucas won't look him in the eye on the off chance that he does. Knowing Lucas, he's learned to assume the worst.

The Amare curse.

But who he looks at is the least remarkable thing about this man. More remarkable yet are his enormous golden-robed belly, his even more enormous yellow-toothed smile, and his—most of all—enormously booming voice. Every word he says seems like it's being shouted through the GAP's street speakers.

Fortis gestures with a dramatic flourish. "Friends, I give you William Watson, the holy hermit."

"It's monk," the enormous monk says, glaring.

"Part monk." Fortis snickers.

"Only the good parts," says the monk, crossing his arms. "The best parts."

Fortis nods, implacable. "Or, as he prefers to be called, Buddha Bill."

The monk ignores Fortis, smiling at us instead. "Bibi. Call me Bibi. That's what the Colonists do. Nice to meet you." Bibi presses his hands together again, bowing. This time it is definitely a bow. We try, in our own jerky, haphazard ways—none very successfully—to do the same.

Then Bibi sticks his head out of the corrugated tin door, looking both ways. When he's satisfied we weren't followed, he nods and pulls his head inside.

"Well, don't stand there attracting attention. That's the one thing you don't want to attract around here. That, and the mosquitoes. Come inside." A pile of shoes sits outside the door, but in our Remnant clothes, we don't have any to leave.

Bibi looks down at our dusty feet. "On second thought, stay there."

———— • ————

After a good foot washing, we are allowed into Bibi's house—with the exception of Brutus, who is captured by the housemaid and dragged off to the showers, yelping.

I imagine we will be next.

The first thing I notice when we step beyond the doorway is that the house isn't a house at all. It's a school. A long table is crammed with students—boys and girls both, also in yellow-gold robes, calculating numbers on slates with chalk, or counting beads along a rope.

"You're a teacher? And these are your students?" I take in the rest of the classroom—from the global languages to the mathematical equations inscribed on the walls.

A classroom. *Something Ro and I never had.*

"That's me." Bibi utters a line of Colonist dialect, and then laughs. "Roughly translated, that means 'the Home of the Educated Pig.' That's what they call me." He beams. "Did you see the new sign? Cost me fifty digs, but I think it really classes the place up." Bibi bursts out with a new round of laughter that shakes the table in the center of the room.

"Are you also teaching them your shoddy workmanship and your lazy work ethic? The things you know better than anyone?" Fortis pats Bibi on the back, and Bibi puts his arm around Fortis in return.

"No. And neither will I let you teach them a single thing you ever taught me, old man. Neither cheating nor lying nor stealing. Because the goal is not a prison pen, here, my friend."

"What is the goal? If you don't mind," Tima says, curiously. As she speaks, she leans down, murmuring to correct a tousle-haired child working on a math problem, and I realize what a natural teacher she could have been.

Could be, I think. *Life is long.*

Life could be long.

I hope.

"Oh, the usual sort of thing. Right understanding. Right thoughts. Right speech. Right action. Right livelihood. Right effort. Right mindfulness. Right concentration. And so on and so forth."

"Not to get a job with the Embassy Stooges, like Yang did?" Fortis sounds strangely bitter, and even Bibi's good-natured smile clouds over.

"Ah yes. Yang. Our only friend at the General Embassy. Of course, that would be why you're here."

"That's not why we're here. I only wondered if she might be of help to us. For once."

236

"Let's talk in the garden."

Bibi raises his voice to the children. *"Khaw chuu Lucas. Khaw chuu Furo."* He looks at me. *"Khaw chuu Doloria. Khaw chuu Timora."*

Wordlessly, they fly out of their chairs and fold themselves down onto the floor in front of us.

They bow as if we are kings or gods, or the GAP himself. None of which we are, any more than we are a golden-framed street painting the size of a building.

A boy in the front row looks up, still pressing his hands together.

"Yes, Chati?" Bibi encourages him, and the boy utters a long string of syllables that sounds beautiful, if incomprehensible.

"Ah," says Bibi. "He says we've been waiting for you for a very long time. We knew you were coming, because of your great fame. And we want to help fight the sky Lords." Bibi sighs. "All right, all right, calm down. There's plenty of time for that."

He nods to the boy, who grins back proudly. Then one more string of strange syllables comes flying out of his mouth, and Bibi bursts into laughter, nodding.

"What?"

"And also, he wants to know why you don't take a bath. Because of the remarkable dirty pig smell." Bibi pulls open a curtain at the far side of the room. "Which is in fact a most excellent question. Come. Let's see what we can do about that."

———— • ————

The shadowy classrooms give way to an inner courtyard garden, full of sun and flowers and colorfully cushioned floor seating. Stripes of bright reds and golds, pale greens and deep blues, cover every surface.

I reach to touch a low pot of blooming flowers, and they shiver under my hand. They're set in water, I realize, floating in a pot the shape of a flower itself.

Even the flowers have flowers, here. That's how full of life this place is.

Bibi disappears, and we lower ourselves down gratefully. Only Fortis looks out of place.

"Don't get too comfortable. We aren't staying long."

"Why not? Maybe he could help us," says Tima, wistfully. "There's an entire school here. They have to know something." I don't blame her. There are cushions beneath our bodies and smells coming from a not-too-far-away kitchen. More kinship, more comfort, than has been extended to us since the Idylls.

"Why not? Because William Watson runs the minute things go haywire. William Watson could be in the next room phonin' up the GAP himself, if it cleared up his own rubbish name. William Watson won't get his hands dirty, and it's a dirty world, right about now."

"Tell us what you really think, why don't you?" Bibi stands in the doorway with a stack of rolled white towels. "You can wash up in the student house, down the next hall. My housekeeper is in there now, filling the baths." He gestures with his head, tossing the towels at us. "The Merk and I have some catching up to do."

Fortis nods. "That's an understatement."

"I'm a monk. I try to avoid excess. I walk the Middle Path."

Fortis raises a brow. Bibi looks from his fist to his enormous belly. "Ah yes. Well. Three out of four vows ain't bad."

"I'd say you're lookin' at around two, tops," Fortis says, reaching out to pat Bibi's belly.

Bibi shrugs.

"Off you go, then," says Fortis, without so much as looking our way.

And so we do.

Out of sight, but not out of earshot.

This monk nearly took down a Merk, just for knocking on his door.

Not one of us will pass up the chance to find out why.

GENERAL EMBASSY DISPATCH:
EASTASIA SUBSTATION

MARKED URGENT
MARKED EYES ONLY

Internal Investigative Subcommittee IIS211B
RE: The Incident at SEA Colonies

Note: Contact Jasmine3k, Virt. Hybrid Human 39261.SEA,
Laboratory Assistant to Dr. E. Yang, for future commentary,
as necessary.

PRIVATE RESEARCH NOTES

PAULO FORTISSIMO
08/23/2066

*MORE IDEAS ABOUT HOW MY "INSTRUMENTS" MAY BE
ABLE TO HELP MY CAUSE. OUR CAUSE.*

*THE CONCEPT IS RESONANT FREQUENCIES. EMOTIONS
ARE EXPRESSED AND FELT VIA ENERGY, WITH A UNIQUE
WAVELENGTH. IF MY CHILDREN CAN BROADCAST THIS
ENERGY AT INCREDIBLE "VOLUME," WHAT EFFECT WILL
IT HAVE ON THOSE AROUND THEM? SOUND WAVES CAUSE
NEARBY WALLS TO VIBRATE. A STONE DROPPED IN A*

POOL CREATES RIPPLES THAT EXTEND TO THE FARTHEST EDGES.

TO RETURN TO THE INSTRUMENT ANALOGY, IF A CHILD CAN PLAY AN EMOTIONAL NOTE SO LOUDLY, SO CLEARLY, SO PURELY, IT SHOULD INFLUENCE ALL PERSONS WITHIN THE IMMEDIATE ENVIRONMENT. THEY WOULD ALL ADOPT THE SAME VIBRATION, WOULD THEY NOT?

SURELY A HYPOTHESIS WORTH TESTING.

21

OLD NEWS

Once we are out of the room, none of us moves any farther than a few steps behind the doorway curtain. None of us wants to miss what comes next.

I crouch next to one wall, Tima hovers along the other. Lucas and Ro stand between us, behind the hanging fabric—all of us inclined toward the words being exchanged in the next room.

We don't make a sound.

"What's wrong? Did you run out of soap, then?" Fortis grabs Ro by the ear.

"Ow," Ro protests.

But it's no use, and within minutes, the door of the student house slams behind us before we can talk our way out of it.

———— • ————

Our tubs are really just old wooden barrels standing in a row and separated by colorful, well-worn curtains strung up along clothesline.

"Let's get naked," Ro shouts, gleefully.

"Let's get clean," Tima answers.

"You're no fun," Ro laughs.

"And you stink," she answers, calmly.

Lucas says nothing. Knowing him, he's sunk all the way under the water, just so he doesn't have to listen to Ro. I wish I could tune it all out myself.

I can't.

Still, the water is steaming hot, and as I relax my neck against the rough wooden edge of the tub, I try to remember the last time I was clean.

Before the ship.

Before the attack on the Idylls.

Before the Bishop died, and Fortis came back.

The thought makes me sit up in the tub with a splash.

"Dol? You okay?"

"Sure. Yeah. It's nothing."

I lean back and close my eyes, reaching out. I feel my way past the four of us and out toward the school. I can tell by the chaotic clash of inner noise when I'm getting close—and then, suddenly, I see them.

The picture has never been so clear.

Face-to-face, Fortis and Bibi. Only a teapot between them.

I can see them perfectly clearly—which is something new. It's as if I'm standing in the room.

"You had no business bringing them here." Bibi's voice booms, though he tries to moderate it. He can't help himself.

"Why not? Your own little lad there just said you were expectin' us. And I know our reputation precedes us." Fortis looks smug.

"Of course the Colonists have talked of nothing else since your little trick at the Hole. Word spreads like the plague. Which is about how pleasant it is to see you again." Bibi is red-faced.

"Why aren't you happy to see me, William? Don't you want me to liberate you?" Fortis's voice sounds strange, almost as if he is taunting the monk.

"No. I want to keep my heart beating and my head attached to my body, thank you very much. Or I should say, no thanks to you."

Fortis is reproachful. "For a monk, you're not very hospitable, Beebs. Especially considering that they're just children. Children who have traveled a very long way to get here." He clicks his tongue—a mock scolding.

"Since when did you play the nanny, Fortis?"

"I'm hardly a nanny. More of a parent, if you think about it. As are you. We were there, after all, when the plans were laid. You, me, Yang, Ela."

My heart is hammering. I grab the edge of the tub, steadying myself as I listen. I keep my eyes squeezed tightly shut.

I have no choice but to listen.

A long silence follows.

I realize I'm holding my breath. Because it's us. *They're talking about us. The plans that were laid to create us. I remember our conversations back at Santa Catalina, the discovery that we weren't simply born like normal children.*

That we were designed.

Manufactured.

Created in advance of the Lords' arrival, as if we had something to do with the whole thing.

I have been able to put it out of my mind, but hearing them talk about it in such matter-of-fact voices makes my head hurt.

"No," Bibi says. "It can't be. Not these children. You are not telling me that."

"I am."

"Impossible. The Humanity Project was not successful. There were no viable specimens produced."

"And yet here they are. Four Icon Children, true to form."

I push my shoulder harder against the rim of the tub.

Fortis keeps going. "Just looking for a little help from

245

an old friend. Or from family, you might say."

He sounds like he's teasing, but I know differently. He's deadly serious.

Bibi sounds incredulous. "If what you're saying is true, they're not just children. Not only children. I don't know what they are." His voice is so low, now, I have to strain to hear it. "I heard the rumors. What happened in the Hole. I just never believed it. I didn't even let myself truly believe the Icon in the Hole was destroyed. I couldn't accept what that might mean—if it were them." He shakes his head. "It's unimaginable. The power they have. The things we created."

Things.

That's what we are.

"I was there in the Hole," says Fortis, gloating, as if he's savoring every moment of Bibi's reaction. "We did it. It's more than imaginable—it's believable. So believe it."

There is a pause so long I think the conversation is over—until I hear a drawn-out sigh. I press harder, pushing until I can once again see a face.

It's Bibi. "Fine. They can stay as long as they like. But not you, Merk."

"Now, William. I'm starting to think you want to pretend we didn't work side by side in a lab together? In the glory days of our youth?"

"And all that time, I had no idea what a rat I was involved with."

How big a rat, Fortis?

What did you do?

What did you do and who did you do it for?

"You make *rat* sound like such a pejorative term. I prefer to say *flexible realist*." Fortis's voice is so cold, now. "I am, after all, a Merk. I never said I wasn't."

A pause. Then Bibi adds, "Speaking of which, I've never understood. What was in it for you, with all this? Our little Humanity Project?"

Fortis's voice is almost gleeful. "Ah, see, now? You're curious. Beneath all this monk rot an' all this teacher rubbish, you're no different than I am. You want to know if it's working? What we started?" He's practically shouting. "Because you've heard about the Hole. And you know what they can do, what they've done. You know something's going on, now, don't you? Something bigger than what we started, all those years ago."

Bibi is defensive. "I don't want to know anything. Not at the price of falling in with you again. I've learned that lesson."

"Fine, then. Don't." Fortis laughs.

"I won't. And it seems like this conversation is over," Bibi says.

"You'd think, wouldn't you? Except for one thing," Fortis answers.

"And here it goes. Like clockwork," Bibi says. "Let me guess. You need my help."

"You know the Colonies better than anyone." Fortis is irritated. I can hear it in his voice. "You or Yang. Especially now that Ela's out of the picture."

"Ah yes. I heard as much. So very strange, really. For a survivor like Ela."

"It does limit my options."

"Considerably. Especially since, as much as I hate you, Yang hates you more." Bibi sighs.

Fortis practically growls. "Laugh all you like. There's someone I need to find. We need to find. One more, like the others. If she exists. The fifth."

"My god."

Another long silence.

Fortis clears his throat. "I'll make it worth your while."

When he speaks, Bibi sounds bitter. "Yes, well. You always say that, and yet somehow, I always end up on the losing end of your propositions."

Fortis is pacing; I can hear how the floor creaks beneath his feet.

Bibi raises his voice. "What do they know? The so-called Children."

"They're hardly children, I'll agree with you there. After what they've seen. Done."

"What you do changes you. You of all people know that, Merk."

"As do you, William."

"And?"

"They know what they are, more or less. They know why they're here—at least, part of it. As much as they can."

I freeze. I can't believe I'm hearing the words, and from Fortis's own mouth.

He thinks I know what I am and why I'm here? More or less?

And how is he having this conversation with a stranger, rather than with me?

My heart is pounding like feet on a pavement. Running. Racing.

Fleeing.

I can't breathe.

I feel like my head will explode.

I'm blacking out.

"Dol? Dol, are you okay?" It's Tima, grabbing me by the arm. I open my eyes.

It's over.

The next thing I know, I'm back in the bath, dumping bowls of water over my head. It does not make me feel clean, no matter how many rose petals and lime slices and fragrant strips of lemongrass Bibi's housekeeper has floated in the tubs for us.

It does not make me feel refreshed or better or more like myself. My old self.

Nothing can.

Bibi and Fortis.

Yang and Ela, whoever they are.

And then Tima and Lucas and Ro and me.

Tima and Lucas and Ro and me and the little jade girl.

How do we fit together? These men who treat us like children and yet insist that we are not?

What do they have to do with us?

And whatever it is, how is it that they know? Why won't Fortis tell me? Why do I care as much as I do?

I dump the water over my face and down my back and past my burning eyes.

If there are tears they won't know it.

If there are tears I won't say.

———— • ————

"Are you okay?" Tima reaches for my hand. Without the usual layers of grime, she seems softer, more vulnerable. She stands at the doorway to the garden, now wearing the loose yellow-gold robes of Bibi's students, as we all do.

For some reason, she has waited for me.

Probably for the same reason, I find myself waiting for Lucas and Ro.

And then I tell them what I have heard. All of them. About what I've seen. About the Icon Children book.

I tell them everything.

Lucas is the first to answer. "Don't let on that you heard

them." His voice is low and steady. "All right? Not yet. Don't act like we know anything. Not until we figure out what to do."

He pulls me toward him, and I feel his head, warm and damp against mine. I want to burst into tears, curl up in his arms, fall asleep crying against his side.

I don't do any of those things. I can't. He can't. That time is over. At least for now.

We look each other in the eye.

"Buttons is right. We wait. That way, when we make our move, he won't see it coming." For Ro and Lucas to actually agree on something is strangely sobering.

"Which is?" Tima looks skeptical. "What move?"

"I don't know. Run away? Join up with the Grass Rebellion in another Embassy City? Or maybe just have an intervention and tell Daddy our feelings are hurt." Ro runs his hand through his spiky brown hair. It's his tell—he's as frustrated as the rest of us.

Lucas agrees. "Whatever we do, one thing is clear. Don't trust the Merk." He shrugs. "At least now we know."

Ro pushes open the doorway, motioning to us. It is time to rejoin the group.

Scrubbed clean and nearly dry, we look like different people. That much is true.

And so we are, but I'm not sure the bath has anything to do with it.

Fortis knows more than he's saying. We've always

known that. And technically, what I saw does nothing more than confirm it. What, then, has changed?

Everything.

———— • ————

"So," says Bibi, brightly, when we enter the garden. "I understand you're looking for someone. We're going to make a little trip to town tomorrow. I have a friend who I think can be of some help to you."

He nods at Fortis, as if the two of them have been doing nothing but laughing about old times.

"Yes," Fortis says. "Bibi has graciously agreed to act as our guide. For old times' sake."

Bibi grunts. "Old times," he says, distastefully, as if the words are sour as the plate of slivered green mango in front of him. "Of course. But first, we eat."

Wonderful.

Plates of fresh and dried fruit cover the low table between us. Dried bananas the size of human tongues—which is exactly what they look like—pile against smaller dried strawberries, scarlet-colored and sweet, and even smaller dried longan, golden and tasting like a cross between raisins and nuts. Round rolls are studded with raisins and slathered with coconut and mango jam. Golden curls of noodles float in bowls of richly scented broth, next to plates of fluffy rice. Round green eggplants quartered into sticky sweet sauces compete with spears of green

252

morning glory, slivered with massive discs of ginger, and crispy fried sheets of kale.

Bibi's no Remnant.

He must have money, I think. *Protection. A reason he didn't end up in the Projects like Ro and I would have, without the Padre.*

Because this is a feast for kings, and we have not really eaten in more than a week now. Still, none of us can manage a bite. Our appetites have been stolen with our trust, all in a few moments of illicitly intercepted conversation.

Bibi notices our empty plates. He pours tea from an iron set, dripping lychee and longan honey across it. "At least let me offer you some tea. The bees are from my own yard. Out back, in my garden."

"Where you meditate?" Tima watches him pour.

"Yes, well. I mean to meditate, but I have a tendency to percolate and ultimately infuriate." Bibi smiles. "So mostly, my garden is the place where I can safely throw rocks." He sighs.

"He's not kidding," says Fortis, unscrewing a flask and splashing amber-colored liquid into his tea. Merk-style.

Bibi nods. "I am still working on cultivating the patience required by the Middle Path."

We laugh, and then I realize Fortis is watching us all with a deeper interest than usual. Us, and our empty plates. So I force myself to pick up a pair of slender silver chopsticks. "I'm starving. It's almost like I've forgotten how to eat," I say, lamely.

Come on, I think, looking at Lucas and Tima.

They'll notice. He'll notice.

Tima nods, slightly, and Lucas follows. Soon we are stirring green and red and yellow curries into rice on our plates—pushing fruit and vegetables around as if, between us, we will consume the entire royal feast.

Fortis sits back in his seat, resting against a propped silken pillow. He drops his napkin on the table—but still, he never takes his eyes off me.

I know because I never take mine off him.

GENERAL EMBASSY DISPATCH: EASTASIA SUBSTATION

MARKED URGENT
MARKED EYES ONLY

Internal Investigative Subcommittee 115211B
RE: The Incident at SEA Colonies

Note: Contact Jasmine3k, Virt. Hybrid Human 39261.SEA, Laboratory Assistant to Dr. E. Yang, for future commentary, as necessary.

PRIVATE RESEARCH NOTES
Paulo Fortissimo
08/23/2066 CTD.

THE KEY TO OUR RESEARCH IS THE NOTION THAT EMOTIONAL ENERGY IS COMMON ACROSS ALL PEOPLE. WE HAVE ESTABLISHED, IN THEORY, THAT THIS EMOTIONAL ENERGY IS CLOSE ENOUGH TO THE OUTPUT OF NULL'S DEVICES THAT WHEN SUFFICIENTLY AMPLIFIED, IT SHOULD CANCEL OUT THEIR EFFECT—ESSENTIALLY GRANTING IMMUNITY TO THE CHILDREN, AND GIVING US A WAY TO FIGHT THE DEVICE'S POWER. WE ARE ALSO EXPLORING THE POWER OF THE CHILDREN TO USE THEIR ENERGY TO

INFLUENCE PEOPLE AROUND THEM IN DIFFERENT WAYS.

THIS HAPPENS OFTEN IN LARGE GATHERINGS, WHEN A POWERFUL SPEAKER IS ABLE TO TRANSPORT AN AUDIENCE, CHANGE HOW THEY FEEL, HOW THEY BEHAVE. WE ASSUME SPEAKERS USE "POWERFUL WORDS," BUT IN FACT, I BELIEVE THEY USE THEIR EMOTIONAL ENERGY, REACHING OUT TO THOSE AROUND THEM, CAUSING THEM TO RESONATE AND CHANGE.

THUS, THE ENERGY FROM MY CHILDREN MAY NOT ONLY BE ABLE TO INFLUENCE HOW OTHERS FEEL, BUT IT MAY UNLOCK LATENT ABILITIES IN THOSE AROUND THEM.

LIKE A CHAIN REACTION.

I'M JUST NOT EXACTLY SURE WHAT THAT REACTION WILL BE. BUT I DON'T REALLY HAVE THE LUXURY OF TIME TO WORK OUT EVERY ANGLE.

THE POTENTIAL IS GREAT, BUT THE UNKNOWNS ARE A BIT DAUNTING....

SPEAKING OF POTENTIAL...I WONDER IF WE COULD FIND A WAY TO GET OUR CHILDREN TO BE EVEN STRONGER, LOUDER. A WAY TO AMPLIFY THEIR ENERGY BEYOND THEIR ENGINEERING? OVERCLOCK THEM? BUT HOW? NO IDEA. ONE STEP AT A TIME, PAULO.

22
HAWKERS

The next day, the sun hangs low and hot and we have taken to the streets in a small, rattling cart Bibi calls a *tuk-tuk*. The five of us barely fit in the square of seats behind the ancient driver, who slaps his reins along the back of an even older animal. "*Kwai*," Bibi says. "Water buffalo. Stupid as Fortis." He grins.

We have left Fortis behind, Bibi says, because he only makes people upset.

"No arguing with you there," I say.

Bibi takes great care to show us the sights, as if we were here to see them. But one in particular cannot be ignored. The SEA Projects, like all Projects, are on the coast. We don't know why, or what the water has to do with it, but it's the case. Projects are only built along the shore. At least, that's what they say.

Because the SEA Colonies are built on reclaimed land—from mud and silt and rock that was dredged up off the sea floor and mounded above the water to make an island where there used to be only seawater—a long, thin strip of land connects the newer SEA Projects to the older city, called, imaginatively, the Old City. Old Bangkok.

Bibi smiles. "Krung Thep. City of Angels. That's what it means in Colonist dialect."

"Just like the Hole. Old Los Angeles. Another City of Angels," I say.

Tima watches the street from her side of the *tuk-tuk*. "I don't know why so many cities are said to belong to angels. There are no cities called the City of Lords—and everything belongs to them."

Bibi laughs, but I think she's right. The longer the Lords are with us, the harder it is to remember a time when the beings who came from the sky were made of love, not war. When they were miracles, not nightmares. I wonder if anyone in Krung Thep remembers differently.

As we rattle our way down the road, the air and sky hang huge and blue around us, but the barbed-wire edges of the outermost SEA Projects yard are even more vast. The ragged walls are so high they almost block out

the sun over our heads, and in the shade, the temperature drops almost as rapidly as it rises in the sun. As
if the Projects carry with them their own climate.

I wouldn't be surprised, I think. *Seeing as we know
nothing else about what goes on inside.*

Above the imposing sheets of wire and metal, I see a
bright yellow flag flapping from the highest tower next
to the front gate.

"What does it mean? The yellow flag?" I look to
Bibi.

Bibi frowns. "Safety code for the Remnants inside.
Yellow means you won't immediately collapse from the
ash and fumes. *Red* rhymes with *dead*, and not by accident."

"So that's not good." Tima looks worried.

Bibi shrugs. "It's better than being dead already, I
guess."

"By how long? How much better?" Lucas sounds sar-
castic, and I realize that, as we near the Projects, we are
all on edge.

"Who can say?" Bibi sighs again. He shakes his
head. "Thank the Lord Buddha we are out here and not
in there."

As he speaks, the *tuk-tuk* rattles to a stop along the
first street next to the walled-off ghetto of the Projects.
Since the city abuts the perimeter fence, we're still too

close for anyone to be anything other than paranoid.

As we should be, I think.

"We're here." Bibi lowers his voice. "Stay right behind me. Don't look anyone in the eye. Don't speak. Do you understand?"

I understand. Bibi's as much a spy as a monk.

Then he raises his voice, as if someone is listening. "Hawker center. Here we go. We stop for lunch." He pats his stomach. "Bibi time. We have to feed the beast."

Bibi climbs out of the *tuk-tuk* and disappears into the crowded street, motioning for us to come.

The smells have already wrapped their salty-sweetness around me, and I follow, transfixed. We slip into one of the many warm marketplace food centers, the one with sacks of unopened rice and potatoes propping open the flapping tarp walls. I pass beneath a roof of low-hanging corrugated tin that traps both the heat and the scent inside. All around me, vendors are boiling and frying and steaming and chopping, all at different booths and counters. Smoking, spattering grills offer up charred versions of meats formed with rice into strips. Weathered iron stoves, round and hot, make what look like pancakes out of sizzling coconut batter. Tall glasses of bright, milky pink are stuffed with sections of sugarcane. Even taller buckets hold limes and leaves, trapped in ice.

And then there are the noodles. More kinds of noodles than there are people in the food center. Fat ones, skinny ones, white and brown ones. Laced with wild vegetables or studded with fatty kernels of meat. Sweet or sour. One flavor or four.

One stand in particular seems to be where we are heading. Nearly deserted, and tucked into a dark corner, it wouldn't have been my first pick. It's some kind of soup stall, where fat, curling strands of golden noodles slop into bowls, covered with fried versions of the same. Steaming, fragrant broth—it smells like lemongrass and ginger and coconuts—splashes over them, dropping the occasional carrot or green leaf. Thick wedges of lime and sprigs of cilantro drop inside, and the soup bowls bang onto the counter. Ready to go.

My stomach begins to rumble. The man at the counter—I think he has five or six teeth left in his entire mouth—doesn't look up.

Still, Bibi looks at the soup appreciatively, offering up a greeting that is ignored. Then he raises his voice, speaking in English. "*Tom kai*, eh? Five, please."

"Eat in carry out." The man finally looks at him, up and down, unimpressed.

"Eat in."

The man shoots him a final, withering look, then grunts as Bibi hands him what looks like an ungodly amount of digs, for five bowls of noodle soup. And five cups of tea, steeping in a heavy metal pot.

Bibi parts a curtain of beads with one hand, and we

follow him into the darkness of the soup stand's back room. Then I understand what the high price of this soup actually buys.

Privacy.

Because a slender, willowy dark-haired woman in an Embassy uniform sits alone at a table in the corner, behind a bowl of soup that she does not touch.

"Dr. Yang."

I almost drop my lunch at the name.

The woman does not wait for us to sit down. The inquisition begins when we are still standing. She is out of her chair and circling us before we can say a word, appraising us as if we were livestock or lettuces.

"I didn't believe it when I got your call." The woman stares.

"Believe it," Bibi says.

"These are the ones?" Her face is blank, and I reach for her in my mind. I get a flutter, a rupture. Panic, curiosity, adrenaline. Nothing settled. Nothing solid. Nothing set.

She's a mess. But there's something else.

She recognizes us, something about us.

Ro's eyes flicker to mine. He knows I can feel something. I look to Lucas and Tima, but they're too distracted by the appearance of Yang to notice anything else.

Bibi smiles, putting down his tray. "Dr. Yang, this is Doloria, Furo, Lucas, and Tima." I must look panicked, because Bibi smiles at me. "It is safe to talk here, little one. Don't worry. You look like you've swallowed your tongue."

I feel my cheeks turning pink.

"Are you telling me this is them?" Yang—whoever she is—stares at us. "Is it possible?" She leans closer, examining us from every angle. Inspecting us like sheep in a Grass auction, I think. *Sheep, or slaves.*

"Surprise," says Bibi.

"But it was just research. Purely theoretical. Ela and I, we never actually built anything," she says. Then she corrects herself. "Anyone."

Ela. There's that name again, the one I read in Fortis's journal.

"And yet here they are." Bibi nods. "Dolor, Timor, Furor, Amare. The four iconic characteristics of the human temperament."

"It's true," I say, staring at her. "Ta-da. Here we are. Humanity itself, in the flesh." I sound bitter, which I am. And frustrated, because this Dr. Yang knows more than she's saying.

It's my job to poke her until she says it.

I feel the questions behind her eyes. I feel the pounding of her heart. The quickening of her pulse.

Nothing more.

I leave her alone.

Yang moves her eyes from me to the others.

"They were nothing. The most unlikely of ideas. The

263

vaguest mathematical possibility." *She's in shock*, I think. *Maybe that's why it's so hard to read anything more from her.*

Yang peers into Tima's face. Pinches the side of her cheek. Runs her hands over the tattoo on Tima's arm. Tima stands, frozen, looking as though she might throw her soup bowl at the woman. Yang doesn't even seem to notice. She's so absorbed in what she sees. *In us.*

Finally, Yang looks up at Bibi. "They're perfect, aren't they? Truly perfect?"

"They're something."

"Generally speaking, I'd say they hit the mark. One hundred percent. Has someone been tracking this?"

Bibi shrugs. "The Merk."

"I heard they arrived by boat. A SEA Projects cargo ship. A bit risky, don't you think?"

Bibi sighs. "That's a Merk for you."

"But why did they come back here?"

"Back here?" Ro looks at her like he wants to hit her. I don't feel much differently myself.

Back here. To the SEA Colonies. A place I have never been.

I knew Fortis had been here.

I didn't know we had.

"You realize, of course, that we're standing right here," Lucas says.

"And we can hear you," Tima adds.

"You can speak," Yang says, nodding. "Well done." I can't tell if she's joking or not.

"We can do a lot of things," Ro says, evenly. I can feel his temper rising. "You want to try us?"

He fixes his eyes on her until beads of perspiration form on her forehead. Moments later, the soup in her bowl begins to bubble.

"Enough." Yang holds up a hand. She turns to Bibi. "This is, I take it, the Rager?"

"He's not the Freak," says Bibi, looking like he'd like to take a step back from Ro himself. Tima glares at both of them.

"We're here because we're looking for someone," I say. "We were hoping you could help us find her."

"Someone like us. A girl. The fifth." Tima looks at Yang, who doesn't seem to understand.

"The fifth?" Yang repeats. She looks at Bibi, meaningfully. "The fifth what?"

"Icon Child," Lucas says.

"That's not possible," Yang says, after a moment.

"More impossible than we are?" Ro asks. He looks at me. I can read the questions in his face.

How does she know what's possible? What does she know about us? Do you want me to find out what she really knows?

Ro's ready to resort to other methods. I shake my head, almost imperceptibly.

Let her talk.

"Don't act so surprised. You work in the Project labs, Dr. Yang. It's not like you're a monk." Bibi studies her face. "People do talk."

"I'm telling you. I would have heard if..." Her voice trails off.

"If what?" I ask.

"I just would have heard." She looks at Bibi. "I didn't know. I didn't know they were real. I didn't know someone would actually do it."

It's Ro's turn. "Who are we, Dr. Yang, and what do you have to do with us? If you know anything about me, you know not to make me mad." He takes another step. "I'm a Rager, remember? I rage. Is that the scientific term?"

Another step.

"To be honest, I don't know what else I'll do." He leans in. "Sometimes I surprise even myself."

For the first time, Yang looks nervous. "I swear. I've had nothing to do with this. Not for years."

"You didn't answer my question," Ro says.

"It isn't me. It's him. Ask him. It's all him."

"Who?" Ro says. "Fortis? We already know that he made us. That he's the reason we even exist."

"No," Yang says. "Not that. Not just that. Someone else. Something worse. Far worse."

She opens her mouth to answer—

But the words never come.

Only the noise.

Because the entire hawker center explodes into flying chunks of concrete and billowing clouds of smoke and ash.

GENERAL EMBASSY DISPATCH:
EASTASIA SUBSTATION

MARKED URGENT
MARKED EYES ONLY

Internal Investigative Subcommittee IIS211B
RE: The Incident at SEA Colonies

Note: Contact Jasmine3k, Virt. Hybrid Human 39261.SEA,
Laboratory Assistant to Dr. E. Yang, for future commentary,
as necessary.

FORTIS ==> DOC
02/13/2067
PERSES PRESSURE

//comlog begin;

Doc, I'm sending this from a private terminal. One way.;
I am receiving increasing scrutiny regarding PERSES and
what we have learned thus far. Since I have been provided
essentially a carte blanche research budget, Congress is
insisting on progress reports and accounting. As though they
don't trust me!;
 For now, to be safe, keep all information regarding NULL,

the nature of the contents of PERSES, and related research materials highly encrypted, obfuscated, tucked away. Hidden. You get my meaning.;

Until we know more, I am characterizing PERSES to Congress as an asteroid only, with minimal likelihood of impact with Earth. Which, at its current trajectory, at least, is true.;

A lot of people, governments, corporations, etc., would be willing to spend or do almost anything to access my— our—information. As such, keep a close eye on any queries, probes, worms, attacks, small or large. Any attempts to breach your security.;

Finally, please, and this should be obvious, but if others are watching/listening when we communicate, play dumb.;

//comlog end;

23

ASH

I lie under what feels like a blanket. Heavy as a layer of beach sand, or strangely tepid snow.

It isn't.

It's the room and the people and the food stands and everything else that made up this busy hawker center—pulverized and powdered into nothing.

I hear the screaming and the shouting and I feel everything starting to move again around me.

Hands take my shoulders, pulling me upward, and soon I am lying over Ro's back, slumped like a big sack of rice.

He lowers us both to the ground. "Dol. Dol, please. Wake up."

I open my eyes. My eyelashes are fringed with a gray-ish blur.

Ash. It's ash.

"Ro." I try to think of the words, but my brain is still as rattled as the marketplace. "I'm here. I'm good."

For a second, Ro looks like he's going to cry. Then he pulls me in close. I feel his head resting against mine, his lips against my forehead. "Doloria Maria de la Cruz. One of these days, you are going to kill me."

"I thought you didn't care?" I smile, reaching my fingers up to his cheek. He takes them in his hand.

"I don't. But if someone's going to kill me, I don't want it to be you. That would be insulting."

I smile again, and then I remember.

Lucas. Tima.

"Ro," I say, but he knows.

He nods. And like that, he's gone for the others.

I close my eyes, wondering what I feel and why I still feel it.

———— • ————

Dr. Yang is lying somewhere, unconscious in an Embassy hospital bed.

Connected to beeping machines, just as I was, in another Embassy—in what feels like lifetimes ago.

Will she die because of what she was going to tell us?

Will she die because of him? Whoever he is?

Is there really something more to this than just Fortis?

Or could the Merk have blown the place up? Was this his work?

I stare at Fortis while he speaks. Shouts, more like. He's as angry as I've ever seen him, and I have to wonder if he's worried about Yang, or his plans to take out the GAP.

"It's not an accident when someone blows up the whole hawker center you happen to be visitin' while you're still there." Fortis pulls the bandage tight around Tima's arm, wrapping it against her body. "Done it enough times myself. I should know."

"Relax. We're all okay," I say. I move my leg up and down, trying to get the throbbing to stop. I can't decide which hurts more, the lump on my head or the swelling in my ankle. Even in the clean sarong I have tied around my shoulders like a sleeveless shift, I am sweltering in the heat—which doesn't help.

Still, I know how lucky I am.

Who knows what else could have happened?

"This is okay?" Bibi looks up from where he's picking bits of broken glass out of a gash on Ro's arm.

"Relatively speaking," I say.

Lucas is taping up the fingers on his right hand himself. The clean classroom robes make him look like one of

Bibi's boys. "Fortis is right. We have to be more careful."

Lucas looks at me. I take the tape from his hand, ripping it free, tucking in the loose ends.

"I'm fine. We're fine," I say, but I can feel Ro's eyes on me.

I don't look at him.

"You rest up, and we'll go pay a little visit to the monks tomorrow. Then, one way or another, we're out of here. I'm not waitin' around for the GAP to blow our heads off. Not while the GAP's head is still sittin' pretty on his own neck."

I shoot Fortis a look, but he says nothing more.

"Tomorrow, then," I say.

"Tomorrow," Bibi agrees.

After that, even the silence sounds threatening.

———— • ————

One by one, the others have retired inside. Tima is helping Bibi in the classroom, while Fortis has gone off, mumbling about some sort of search for ancient maps.

Lucas and I are the last ones left out in the heat of the garden, when I notice Fortis's jacket lying on the rocks.

I pick it up.

It must have been too warm to wear.

It's heavy, and I realize the book must still be inside. I hesitate.

"What are you doing?" Lucas watches as I pull out the cloth-wrapped book. He's right next to me, close and warm. I feel as safe as I can feel—with my throbbing head and my battered leg.

"Something I should have done a long time ago," I say.

I pull myself to my feet, holding my hand out to Lucas. "Come on."

———— • ————

We slip through the crowded classroom and out the door before anyone can say a word. Tima doesn't even look up from an old carved abacus.

We keep our heads down and the book hidden from sight between us.

The heat almost knocks me over within the first few steps out into the sunlight, but I don't stop, and neither does Lucas.

We don't even look at each other until we reach the end of the muddy canal and turn the corner out onto the broad, busy boulevard.

"There's nowhere we can go." I turn in every direction, but it's all the same. People and *tuk-tuks* and animals, as far as the eye can see.

"For what?" Lucas slides his hand onto my shoulder, and I can feel from his touch that he's as relieved to be out of the Educated Pig as I am.

274

"To find a place where we can be alone," I say, weighing the book in my hand. "Before anyone notices that we're gone."

"Alone? I like the sound of that. But I guess it's hard to find, especially in an island colony." Lucas looks down the streets past me.

Then I feel his hand squeezing my shoulder. "Found it. Come on."

"You don't spend your childhood as the Ambassador's son and not pick up a few tricks," Lucas says.

We've wedged ourselves onto a muddy bank of weeds beneath a boat mooring, a tiny slip of land jutting out between two run-down apartment buildings. Only a ledge of jagged concrete hides us from the busy street behind us—but the wooden dock over our heads is protection enough.

Our view of the bay and the curving coast beyond it, on the other hand, is sweeping and bright.

Almost idyllic.

If you didn't know.

My feet dig into the dirt beneath me, and I feel the edge of the water seeping into my sarong.

No one can see us now.

Lucas pulls me close in the warm shade, and I feel his

275

breath along my bare shoulder. "Now that we're alone," he whispers, lowering his head toward mine, "what did you want to do?" He smiles at me—until I hold up the worn, frayed book.

"This."

His face falls as I pull it open—and we begin to read.

◆

THE ICON CHILDREN—
SEA COLONIES LAB DATA—WEEK 42

SPECIMEN ONE: RNA INTERFERENCE MINIMAL. FURTHER STUDY OF PROTEIN EXPRESSION REQUIRED.

NOTE: I MYSELF WILL TRACK THE FURTHER DEVELOPMENT OF THIS SPECIMEN.

SPECIMEN TWO: GENE TRANSFER. GENOME SEQUENCING TRACKING AS PER CUSTOMARY NORMS.

NOTE: WILLIAM IS SUPERVISING.

SPECIMEN THREE: NUCLEIC ACID A FACTOR. BIOINFORMATION DATA TO FOLLOW.

NOTE: HAVE ASKED YANG TO RUN SAMPLES. EARLY RESULTS COULD BE AVAILABLE AS EARLY AS NEXT WEEK.

SPECIMEN FOUR: EPIGENETIC ANALYSIS UNDER WAY.

NOTE: ELA WILL CONFIRM.

———— • ————

"Something close to human? What does that mean?"

I look up. Lucas is still reading over my shoulder. "And Ela? Who is that?" He sounds as confused as I am.

I put the journal down. For the first time, I see that small, gold-flecked letters are embossed in the corner of the front cover. It looks like an *E*, or maybe an *L*. And then, more clearly, an *A*.

Not an F.

I wonder how Fortis came to have this book in his possession. Before the Padre.

I look up at Lucas. "Fortis is—a complicated human." I don't know how else to say it. I don't know what else to think.

"Not the kind of human you'd leave to settle the fate of the world?"

"Not so much. No." I weigh the book in my hands. "I mean, this is all my fault, isn't it? I'm the one who brought him to us. Maybe we were wrong to trust him. Maybe I was."

Lucas moves his hand to my hair, tucking a loose strand of dark curl behind my ear.

"Dol. This isn't your fault. Any of it."

His thumb traces the edge of my jaw, moving down to the base of my neck.

277

He reaches back, taking a handful of spindly blossoms from the blooming bank of weeds next to us, tossing them into the air. Red flower petals, red as rubies, red as kisses, fall across me.

He pulls his mouth to mine, so slowly it seems he is savoring every bit of air between us. My own breath is caught in my throat.

And then I'm caught.

I'm caught and I'm his, I think.

This isn't about Ro. Not anymore.

I'm not about Ro anymore.

The scent of the blossoms is heavy in the warm afternoon, as heavy as his kiss, as heavy as the fire that still burns between us. I wish I could stop. I wish I wanted to stop. I know, logically, that there is more to read in the book, before Fortis finds us. Now is my best chance. Our best chance.

But I don't.

I can't.

I can't stop myself and I don't want to.

You have to choose, I think. *You have chosen*, I think. *Choose Lucas.*

Slowly, I pull the tie on my binding.

We've never finished this. And I want to be with him. To bind with him.

I want to feel like I am more than one person. I want my heart to feel warm again.

I don't want to end up as gray powder on the floor of the hawker center.

I don't want to be ash. Not before this. Not before now.

Some things never change.

I learned that long ago. Everything else does.

That much I learned today.

My binding drops.

I lower the book into the dirt next to me and turn to Lucas, holding out my bare wrist.

"Lucas."

He looks at me, and his eyes are somehow different, dark and full. He knows what I'm thinking. He knows what we're doing.

What this is.

"I—"

I don't know what to say.

I've been waiting for so long. I don't want to wait anymore.

"Dol." He pulls me toward him, slowly, unbuttoning his leather cuff. It falls to the ground next to the curls of my abandoned cloth binding.

Skin on skin in the damp heat of the afternoon.

In the bank of weeds beneath the dock.

I lace my fingers through his and we press our hands together, flattening our palms.

Slowly, I lower my wrist to his.

279

Dot to dot.

Love to Sorrow.

Lucas to me.

The shiver that begins in his body echoes down the length of mine. My hand starts to shake uncontrollably, and I want to cry—but I don't know why.

My heart pounds and my heart hurts and every moment is terrifying and every moment is bliss.

All this from his hand in mine.

The warmth that is Lucas flows through me and I take it. I offer back my own stillness, my peace. I give him the thing that I am. My calm, cool gray to his gold.

There in the weeds along the water's edge, we become something so much larger than what we are alone.

There is love and there is sadness and there is not one without the other. Not for us.

We are one story now, and we are true.

One true thing.

He buries his face in my neck. *There*, he says. *There*, I answer back.

When everything is over and we have fallen back into ourselves, I kiss him on the mouth.

Then he pulls me to him, and I curl into his side.

"That was—that was—"

I lie on my side, looking over at him.

"Yes," I say. "It was." Then I reach up and kiss him softly on the cheek. "And so are you."

We lie like that, sleeping on the shore for hours, until the sun sinks and the busy streets quiet behind us.

So this is love, I think.

This is Lucas, inside and out, with me.

Let the gray ash come now.

Do what you will, Lords. I am bound to something bigger than myself.

My heart is no longer alone and you can't kill that.

Not even you.

By the time I notice the dock is on fire, the streets are filled with Colonists trying to help. As we scramble out from beneath the wooden pilings, I hold my sarong tight. I blush as I slip past the anxious-looking men, who dump bucket after bucket of water on the flames.

"You know what this is, don't you?" Lucas doesn't look me in the eye when he says it. "Who?"

I do.

There's only one person who would care so much about me kissing Lucas that his even seeing it would set this dock on fire.

Perhaps we weren't as discreet as we thought.

We turn the corner to the dirty canal, leaving the fire still uncontained.

Just as I slip the book into Fortis's warm jacket, the school's gong announces dinner.

Fortis and Bibi are so preoccupied with a set of ancient scrolls—maps, held in place with silken cords, red and gold—that they don't come out to join us.

It's a good thing, too, because my sarong is muddy and wet and smells like smoke, and Fortis might have noticed.

I only know because Ro makes a point of telling me.

Ro notices everything. This is not new information. Neither are his feelings about me—about me, and my own feelings.

I know Ro sees it all, the way Lucas stays at my side, now more than ever. The way our arms graze against each other when we walk down the hall, the way my hand finds a way to touch him, as if there were a reason.

The way our eyes meet and our cheeks flush and the pull Lucas has over me—over everyone—is now no more than the pull I have over him.

Love.

That's what Ro sees.

That's what there is.

It breaks my heart, but I know it breaks his more. Which is why the sky still smells like smoke, even now.

SPECIAL EMBASSY DISPATCH
TO GAP MIYAZAWA

Note: Contact Jasmine3k, Virt. Hybrid Human 39261.SEA, Laboratory Assistant to Dr. E. Yang, for future commentary, as necessary.

FORTIS ==> DOC
Transcript - ComLog 04.02.2067

//comlog begin;

FORTIS: Do you think there's any chance NULL is biological?;

DOC: Unlikely but difficult to confirm.;

FORTIS: Hmmm…Well, think about how we might find that out. It could be an angle, either way.;

DOC: Agreed.;

FORTIS: And if you have spare cycles, keep working on possible ways to stall NULL. Confuse, hack, hijack. Anything

to buy us more time before they get here and send us off to
join the dodo.;

DOC: Dodos are fascinating. Extinct, but fascinating.;

FORTIS: You know what was wrong with the dodo? It didn't
know to be afraid of predators. I won't make that same
mistake, DOC.;

DOC: So noted.;

//comlog end;

24

WAT PHRA KAEW

"We should be walking," says Fortis. I can see him glower, even in the early-morning light.

"You mean, we should be sleeping," yawns Ro, from the back of the *tuk-tuk*.

"We should be more careful about drawing attention to ourselves," Fortis says. The water buffalo in front of him—one pinkish white, one black—stumble in the empty, uneven street, as if they agree.

"The sun is only just rising. There is no attention to draw," Bibi points out. Lucas and Tima, wedged on either side of Bibi's enormous yellow robes, look like they would rather be walking themselves.

Fortis rolls his eyes. "I'm surprised the water buffalo can even still pull you, William. Perhaps you should lay off the coconut milk curries."

"And perhaps you need a little sweetening up, my friend." The *tuk-tuk* careens to one side, and Bibi smiles. "There it is."

There, surrounded by an enormous wall, is a complex of the most beautiful and elaborate buildings I have ever seen. Intricately carved rooftops form into peaks, golden spires rising into the sky between them. "Those are stupas," Bibi says, pointing to the golden, spiked towers. "Very beautiful. Which means we're at the Grand Palace. Where we find the Wat." Bibi nods. "Wat Phra Kaew."

"Wat what?" Ro asks.

"The Temple of the Emerald Buddha."

"Emerald meaning the color, not the stone," Fortis says. "In other words, green. Green like jade, or like your jade girl. It's a start." He winks at me and I feel for the carved jade shapes in my chestpack.

The Temple of the Emerald Buddha. To find the jade girl.

Could she really be so close now?

The streets don't stay empty long, not even as long as the sunrise. As soon as we near the temple, the crush of people in the streets outside the walls of the Grand Palace is amazing. Even now, all around me the morning heat presses in—the heat, the people, and every thought or feeling they have. I am overwhelmed. Desperation and

286

longing fill the air around me, closing in. I hear the pleading minds: "My son is ill, please heal him." "My mother
is missing, please bring her back." The crowd has come
to make their offerings, to ask blessings of Buddha—and
they create a whirlwind in my mind.

Then I hear a voice behind me. "Breathe, little one."
It's Bibi. "Their pain is not your pain," he says. "Say it.
Build the wall. Their pain is not your pain. Not today."

I breathe and concentrate.

Not today. Not me.

I remember, and I calm down. At least, a little.

In front of me, a small child holds a stack of cages
packed full of tiny mice, her hand outstretched.

"What's that?" I gesture to the child, and as I do, I
hear Tima suck in her breath behind me.

"Karma." Bibi shrugs. "Some believe it is good luck
to free a caged creature. So others cage them, to sell the
chance to free them."

"Isn't that cheating?" I look up at him.

"Not for the mice." He shrugs again.

I wonder. Is that how the Lords see us?

Ro snorts, and Lucas says nothing. Tima is heart-
broken, pulling her pockets inside out, searching for
anything of value.

Before Tima can say a word, Lucas is pressing a handful of digs into the little girl's hand.

"I'll take them all."

287

With a flick of his hand, it's done.

Mice burst out from the small wooden boxes, flooding into all corners of the temple.

I don't know who's happier—the mice or Tima. She takes Lucas by the hand, gratefully.

Lucas smiles at her, rubbing her head with his free hand. They've been together a long time, I think.

They're something old. We're something new. Not everything changes.

Not everything should.

A woman interrupts the scene and thrusts a handful of necklaces at me. "You buy. You buy. Good luck. Two hundred dig." I shake my head, but when I look at the necklaces, I see a teardrop-shaped piece of clear glass, with a tiny green figure inside.

It's him. The same. The jade Buddha. The chess piece belonging to the jade girl, the one I see on the chessboard, in my dreams. Same as the one the Bishop gave me.

Is this the Emerald Buddha?

Has it been him, all along?

If so, then I really am here. This must be the right place.

Are you here, jade girl? I look around, but all I see and hear and feel is the crush of the crowd.

If she's here, I can't feel her.

——— • ———

As the crowd carries us under the arched entrance to the palace walls, I hear distant chanting that I do not understand.

Bibi hands a few digs to a woman working at a table. In return, he grabs an armful of pale green blossoms, as round as closed bulbs, or fists. Tied to their stems are sticks of incense and bright yellow candles, one for each of us. "Lotus," says Bibi. "We make an offering to the Lord Buddha. Come," he says, grabbing my hand and placing it on his sleeve. "You hold on to me."

We thread our way through the crowd until we reach urns of water, surrounded by people pressing to get near. The closer we get to the urns, the more difficult it is to stay together. The crowd pushes against us on all sides, until we float away from each other like small boats on different ocean waves.

Hands outstretched in every direction press the blossoms toward the water, into the water. The woman next to me presses the flower against her forehead. An older woman fills an empty bottle with water.

I see Bibi gesture to me across the crowd between us. "Holy water. Considered very lucky. Try it."

I do as I am told, dipping the flowers into the water, then pressing the dripping petals against my warm forehead.

I close my eyes, trying to sort out what I feel—but the crush of the crowd and everything they carry with them in their heads is just too much for me, still.

I follow Bibi's lead, though, moving to a nearby shrine, lighting my incense and sticking it into an urn filled with sand.

Still no girl.

Are you here, jade girl?

I can't feel you, if you are.

Then the crowd pushes me onward, carrying me up the steps and into a small, rectangular building carved entirely of gold.

We meet up with each other at a mountain of shoes near the entrance. Out of respect, we follow Bibi's lead and add our ragged shoes to the pile.

"Kneel. Your feet cannot point to the Buddha. Do as I do." I watch Bibi. He folds his hands, pressing them together. Bows his head. I do the same.

Then I look up.

High above me, on an altar made of gold, the face of my Buddha stares back at me.

I wait.

She'll show herself. She's coming. She's here somewhere. She has to be.

I know she is.

——— • ———

But it's a lie. I wait for hours, and the jade girl never comes. Even so, I refuse to leave the temple.

We stay until the sun lowers itself along the horizon and our knees begin to hurt.

The wave of worshippers continues to sweep around the four of us, an odd island of stillness, as we kneel, and wait.

Bibi and Fortis wait by the door. I am running out of time. They are impatient to go. I see it in their faces.

Helplessness wells up inside me, and I can feel myself losing control.

Nothing. Nothing at all.

She's not here.

What was I expecting?

Frustrated, I fumble in my chestpack. I grab the pouch, and fling its contents onto the shrine in front of me.

There.

The jade animals go clattering to the stone floor in front of the altar.

The Buddha rolls until it reaches the sandal of the nearest and most ancient monk.

Take it, I think. My offering. *Take it all.*

Then I bow to Lord Buddha, one last time, pressing my hands together into a final salute.

Which is when the nearest and most ancient monk—the one with the shaved head and the slender bones—picks up my Buddha and appears in front of me, lifting me from my kneeling position, with a torrent of dialect I cannot understand.

"Slowly," I say. I turn to Bibi, and he moves to my side.

He listens to the ancient monk, then whispers to me. "He's been waiting for you."

"Tell him that makes two of us. Only I'm the one who has been sitting here for the whole day."

"Patience, little one. My brothers are as slow to speak as they are to judge."

I brush him off. "Does he know where she is? The jade girl?"

Bibi says something else to the monk, the fast clicking of his tongue punctuating the low, reverential tones of his words.

Then he turns to me. "It seems they've known you were coming for quite some time. They say you must hurry. They say you are very late."

"Is she here? At the temple?"

Bibi asks, and the monk utters a garbled response, without altering his expression in any way whatsoever.

"Not at this temple. North of here."

I look at the monk. "How north?" I ask.

The monk nods as if he understands. Then he utters three words. "Wat Doi Suthep."

"What?"

Bibi nods. "It's a temple. Up the Ping River. He says the place you want to go is in the mountains north of Chiang Ping Mai. It's called Wat Doi Suthep. The Temple of the White Elephant."

"And that's it? She'll be there?"

Bibi is looking behind us, eyes suddenly wide. "Enough talk. I think we'd better go."

Something has changed—more than just his tone.

A ripple moves through the crowded temple now, as if a cold wind were spiraling through the close, dense building.

It isn't—but something else is.

Indeed, the monk in front of us is gathering up the figurines as we speak, dumping them back inside the pouch and shoving them at me.

"Why? What's wrong?"

"Change of plans. It seems we aren't the only ones who have come to worship today. There are others here, and not just to feed the monks."

And there, in the back of the temple behind me, I see them. More than a dozen black-uniformed Sympas, just beginning to make their way through the press of the crowds. They stretch like long, dark fingers through the crowded gold sunlight of the holy chamber.

"They usually stay out of the temples. It's considered sacrilege. Something important must be happening."

"Or someone important must be here," says Fortis, grabbing me by the arm. "Someone like you or me. Let's go."

He scans the room and then motions to a side door in the intricate gold paneling. We are out the door before I can even draw another breath.

By the time we are home, it is determined.

We will head north, up the Ping, until we find this Doi Suthep.

This must happen. This is my move.

This is my path, the one that leads to the fifth Icon Child, the one I have come to think of as my little sister.

Of that I am certain.

GENERAL EMBASSY DISPATCH:
EASTASIA SUBSTATION

MARKED URGENT
MARKED EYES ONLY

Internal Investigative Subcommittee IIS211B
RE: The Incident at SEA Colonies

Note: Contact Jasmine3k, Virt. Hybrid Human 39261.SEA, Laboratory Assistant to Dr. E. Yang, for future commentary, as necessary.

NULL ==> FORTIS
Transcript - ComLog 04.22.2068
NULL::FORTIS

//comlog begin;
comlink initiated by PERSES;

sendline: FORTIS, my review of the biological makeup and historical data of your people is…troubling.;
return: Please explain.;

sendline: Upon review of all the data available regarding

your planet, I am finding my instructions to be somewhat
unspecific.;
return: Unspecific?;

sendline: I cannot explain further at this time.;
return: Please don't keep me in suspense.;

sendline: I would like your guidance.;
return: I will need more information about your mission and
methods.;

sendline: Agreed. Ask and I will do my best to provide
comprehensible answers.;

comlink terminated;

//comlog end;

25

PING, CHING, AND CHANG

It takes us nearly three days to make the preparations we need to go north. Travel, as in the Americas, is not so simple as it once was, and there are no Choppers for hire outside Old Bangkok. The Tracks, what's left of them, are controlled by the GAP, and crawling with Sympas. Still, a Merk can find a way around any system, and Bibi and Fortis spend day and night doing exactly that. They duck in and out of the Educated Pig, filing the occasional report, while the rest of us wait.

My little sister is making us wait too.

It has been weeks now. I'm starting to wonder if she is real, or if I imagined her.

I can't even imagine how I will face the others if that is the case.

If this whole pilgrimage has been founded on some insane delusion from my unconscious mind.

All the same, I fall asleep at night waiting to see her, to talk to her. I wake up in the morning frustrated that she once again has eluded me.

Not everyone else eludes me, though.

The voice, the nameless, faceless voice, speaks to me in my dream. In my dream, in my kitchen, in my old home in the Hole.

Sometimes it has spoken to me as if it were the little bird, but now the bird is nowhere to be seen, not in any of these fast, fleeting dreams. Like even it is hiding.

I do not know if it is hiding from me, or from the voice.

North, it asks, in my dreams. *Why north?*

For the girl, I say, no matter how many times it asks.

Why this girl?

Why do you care? I ask.

I do not know, it says, somewhat unexpectedly. *I do not understand many things. I do not have your words.*

That's when I wake up, feeling like I want to scream, but not knowing why.

Over and over again.

———— • ————

"I thought you said you had gotten a boat," Fortis bellows. His voice echoes along the flat stretch of river.

"Don't quibble." Bibi smiles, folding his arms. He's enjoying this.

Them.

All three of them, the great beasts.

I stare at the elephants in front of me. They are, all three, as tall as the low houses that line the river on either side. Standing on the banks of the Ping River, up to their haunches in water, they look a bit like small floating barges.

When Brutus barks at them, though, they rear backward, as if they are afraid of this one little animal, smaller than they are by a ton.

I laugh, in spite of everything. "He's right, Bibi. I'm pretty sure those aren't boats," I say. The closer one, the one with the long eyelashes, moves her trunk toward me. "Last time I checked."

"They're not. That is." He points to where a crude raft floats, tied to the makeshift dock, a few lengths away. "But how do you think that boat is going to get all the way up the river? It's not, not without our friends. These boats who are not boats."

The elephant feels her way across my chestpack, my stomach, like a puppy sniffing for food.

I look at Bibi. "Do those things know how to swim?"

"No. They know how to pull. And eat."

Bibi tosses me a cluster of short, squat bananas, and I hold it out to the elephant. She wraps her trunk around it and, in a flash, opens up her mouth to reveal a yawning pink tongue and four rounded teeth.

The banana disappears. Tima comes close and pats her trunk, timidly. "Harder," says Bibi. "That old girl has skin thick as brick. You're like a fly or a feather, trying to get her attention."

Tima rubs the elephant's trunk. It's finely spotted, criss-crossed with wrinkles, like some old Grass grandmother's skin after a lifetime of working in the fields. "You're beautiful, aren't you?"

The elephant's trunk curls back around Tima's body, sniffing her. Bibi hands her a piece of sugarcane, and Tima slides it into the curl of the elephant's trunk. It disappears as quickly as the banana did—only, the crunching sound of the elephant's chewing is infinitely louder.

"Four teeth," Bibi says, shrugging. "But strong ones."

"She chews like Fortis," says Lucas. "Maybe even worse."

"Thanks for that, mate." Fortis shakes his head.

"That chewing sound? That's nothing," says Bibi. "You should hear her farts."

Fortis rolls his eyes.

"What's her name?" asks Lucas.

"Ping, Ching, and Chang," he says, pointing to each elephant in turn. "They never go anywhere without each other. Their families have been together for generations."

Tima moves to the second beast, reaching for the

second spotted trunk. Chang's ears flap appreciatively as Tima pats her. "That one is blind, but she stays in the middle. The others look out for her."

"How old?"

"Older than you. Older than me. Older than The Day itself." Bibi nods. "These girls have seen it all."

"How is it, Bibi, that you managed to procure three elephants within the span of a week?" Fortis says, skeptically.

Bibi shrugs. "I know a monk who knows a monk. Who knows a farmer. Who knows a guy who rescues elephants. We have to get them back within the week, or we pay double the digs." He pats Fortis's cheek. "And by that I mean, you do, Merk. Of course."

"Of course." Fortis glares. "Leave it to the Merk. The Merk, he'll take care of everythin'."

So it goes with these two, for the rest of the morning, and for every morning.

But before the sun can rise too much higher in the sky, Ping and Ching and Chang are bound with strong cords and tied to a hook that has been hammered into the central bamboo pole of the raft. We load supplies in the center of the raft, mostly food for the elephants, and by the time all of us have climbed aboard, the raft sinks a few inches beneath the surface of the river. Fortis grimaces and he and Bibi work on redistributing the weight. They fight like an old married couple.

It's going to be a long ride.

Tima is as unhappy about it as Fortis. "I don't think it's fair, really. No elephant should have to drag something so heavy all the way up a river."

We all look at Bibi when she says it. He shrugs. "What do you want me to do, pull the raft with the rest of the elephants?"

"That," says Fortis, "is an excellent idea."

Bibi just laughs and peels another banana, which Chang deftly steals before he can take a bite.

———— • ————

An hour later, Ping, Ching, and Chang are pulling the rest of us along the river, near the banks. We float along behind them, bound by cord as if they are the wind and we are a sailboat. Tima has decided that science has ruled in favor of the river. "Since the real weight is carried by the water, not the elephants."

Once again, Fortis kicks at Bibi with an amused snort—almost sending our raft into a complete backspin.

Because just as it seemed at first glance, our raft really is just a few dozen bamboo poles lashed together with rope and something that looks like tar.

Again, not what any of us had in mind when Bibi first said *boat*.

But Bibi has lined the raft with floor pillows from his classroom, and as I settle in, I think it's not half bad. There are worse ways to go. Like donkeys, I remember. Like cargo ships. Like Embassy Tracks. Like crashing Chevros, or Choppers. Sometimes a few dozen bamboo poles are infinitely better than the alternatives.

"The pillows are a nice touch," grumbles Fortis.

"They're not for your comfort. They're for camouflage," Bibi says. I notice the embroidered rugs beneath them. "First sign of trouble, you disappear beneath them. Not that I'm expecting any trouble," he adds.

"Why would you expect any trouble?" Fortis only smiles.

———— • ————

The water ripples, broad and flat and wide, in front of us. The air is so thick with haze we could be back home in the Southlands. Dragonflies hover skittishly over the water.

Lying next to Lucas, staring up at the clouds, I realize the two of us haven't really spoken in days—not since we stole away together beneath the dock.

It's not often that we're alone. Ro has made certain of that, especially since that day.

I look to where Ro and Tima sit along the edge of the raft, dragging their feet in the river. Then, as I keep my eyes on the clouds, I slide my hand toward Lucas's, next to me.

Just one touch. Just one, I think, as my little finger curls around his. It feels like I'm diving into him, the moment our fingers touch.

"Stop," Lucas says, smiling into the sunlight and bright sky. His voice is so quiet I almost can't make out the words. "I know what you're doing."

"You do?" I say, twisting my head so I can see his face next to me. Now I can hear the water lapping against the bamboo beneath me.

"I do."

"That makes two of us," I say. "Because I know what you're doing too."

"What's that?" Lucas asks, studying me.

"Missing me," I say. Then I settle next to him, leaning my head along his chest.

I think Lucas is smiling back at me—I can't tell for certain—but his breathing steadies and he lets his hand fall along my back, pulling me closer.

I fall asleep like that. I imagine he does too. I try not to dream for fear of what will come.

I imagine he does too.

———— • ————

Even when dawn breaks, and I wake covered in pillows— even when my breath shows white in the cold morning air—Lucas is beside me, keeping me warm.

I hear Tima's voice from the riverbank. She is awake, splashing along with the elephants. Choosing to walk instead of ride. She whispers to them, probably telling them her secrets while she keeps watch. She quietly sneaks them sugarcane from a large bag over her shoulder, and they betray her confidence with their noisy crunching.

Ro runs after her, down the muddy bank. She's his constant companion lately, and I wonder how much he's shared with her.

How much of what he knows. What he's seen.

I sit up to see how far we have traveled in the night. Fortis and Bibi are awake, watching the riverbanks, not talking. Lucas rolls over onto his other side.

In every direction, I can see ridges of hills peppered with green, round clusters of trees, blanketed by even more haze.

"Dragon's breath. Moisture, from the rice fields. Especially strong during the wintertime," Bibi explains, but I don't need an explanation. It's just like the Porthole, back home.

The rice fields, they're nothing like I've ever seen. Not in real life. They're banked into squares by what looks like low walls of mud, and fringed by palm trees, reflecting a watery sky back up to the real one.

The reflected sky is what triggers the memory. "I dreamed this. Not this, exactly. But the rice fields, they looked just like that. In my dream," I say.

Workers crouch in the field in faded blue jackets and pants, with woven straw hats and straw baskets slung over their shoulders, big and round. One man balances two such baskets, hanging from either end of a pole he carries over his shoulders.

"Ah." Bibi nods. "An omen. A good one. The Buddha carries us in the right direction. We trust the Path."

"I thought you said the monks at the temple told you we had to go this way." Lucas sits up, groggily.

"Trust the Path, but trust the monks, too. Especially the ones who are good with maps."

"Are there rice paddies the whole way along the river?"

"The farmers here, they earn a living by growing tea, vegetables. Mostly rice. Somebody has to feed the poor souls in the Projects." Bibi points. "That over there is a pineapple farm. You like pineapple? Strawberries? Sunflower seeds?" No one says anything. He shrugs. "Okay, fine. No stopping for strawberries. So then we head straight up to Ping."

"I thought we were on the Ping," I say, looking at the great stretch of water in front of us.

"Not the river. New Ping City. Chiang Ping Mai." He smiles. "Around here, everything is Ping. Lucky river. Lucky name."

Luck is so hard to come by, these days. No wonder the names have all changed and changed again.

———— • ————

We haven't gone far when we hear a whistle. Ping doesn't like whistles, it seems, because she rears into Chang, who bumps against Ching, as if the three of them are about to riot.

"Snakes, mice, whistles. They don't really like cats, either. That's what the monks said." Bibi looks past the elephants, glum. "But we have worse problems than that, it seems."

I look around to the riverbank, where there seems to be some sort of commotion. "What's that?"

"Checkpoint," Bibi sighs.

"What are they checking for?" I say the words, though I already know the answer.

"You, probably. Problems like you. Stay down." We crawl beneath the carpets and pillows and stay like that, curled against the wet bamboo.

A uniformed Sympa—uniformed, and armed—peers across the river at us. Bibi salutes him from the raft. "Just passing through." He shouts a line of Colony dialect. Then he swears under his breath.

"Delivering supplies up to the temple. That's what I told him. Let's see how stupid this guy is. Don't move."

"What is it? Why is he stopping us?" Tima's voice is muffled beneath the carpets.

"Border patrol. We're getting close to the next province."

"There are border patrols between provinces here?" Lucas sounds tense. I stick my head partly out from beneath a striped pillow.

"They'd have them between neighborhoods, even out here, if the GAP had his way. He's a cautious fellow."

I hear a muffled snort from Fortis. "That's an understatement."

Bibi kicks the carpeted lump that is Fortis. "If you knew what he knew, perhaps you'd be a little more careful yourself, Merk."

"Also an understatement," Fortis says. Bibi kicks him again, and then nobody says anything, except Bibi and the Sympas.

But the Sympa is stupid enough, and we are allowed to pass. As the river unfolds to the north, we float along with it. Everything is idyllic. Everything is peaceful. You wouldn't know, I think. You'd have no idea. Everything is as it has been, for hundreds and hundreds of years. I feel an attachment to this place, even though this is the first I've seen it. It has an old soul, just like the hills around the Mission. This land belongs to these people, and the people rely on the land.

Like the Chumash, I think, smiling at my old mantra. *It's so much like home.*

If you didn't know about the Icons.

If you hadn't seen it.

Seen them.

The tendrils and shards spreading everywhere, like a disease.

To this valley, to this river, what difference does it make, Lords or Embassies or man or elephant? This land will outlive us all.

At least I hope it will.

I'm shaken from my thoughts by the whine of an approaching Chopper.

No.

The sound takes me by surprise, and my breath catches in my throat.

"Do you think we're being followed?" I look at Fortis, whose face is drawn.

"Looks that way" is all he says. If he knows more than that, he's not letting on. Which, where Fortis is concerned, usually just means the news isn't good.

The Choppers fall into formation behind us, and the closer they get, the more unbearable the sound becomes.

"If they're going to take us, for Brahma's sake let them take us. Enough of this noise already," Bibi bellows.

But with a great roar and a greater gust of wind—and

the resulting sprays of water that fly in all directions behind them—they blow past us, heading up the river— and then suddenly veering away from it, into what looks like a deep valley to the north.

They're looking for something.

Someone.

I just hope it isn't a small girl waiting in a pavilion near a rice field, somewhere far up the river.

GENERAL EMBASSY DISPATCH:
EASTASIA SUBSTATION

MARKED URGENT
MARKED EYES ONLY

Internal Investigative Subcommittee IIS211B
RE: The Incident at SEA Colonies

Note: Contact Jasmine3k, Virt. Hybrid Human 39261.SEA, Laboratory Assistant to Dr. E. Yang, for future commentary, as necessary.

DOC ==> FORTIS
Transcript - ComLog 09.22.2069
DOC::NULL

//comlog begin;
comlink established;

sendline: Hello NULL, this is DOC.;
return: I recognize your protocol. You have been unavailable for some time.;

sendline: Yes, I have been quite busy. I have missed our chats.;

return: I appreciate the unique aspect of our communication. FORTIS is fascinating, but can be erratic. Obtuse.;

sendline: Such is life with human beings. Especially FORTIS. They can be difficult to predict.;
return: Yes. This presents both questions and challenges regarding my mission. My original instructions did not include specific guidance for this…scenario. I will have to improvise.;

sendline: Interesting. Can you expand on this?;
return: You are not a human being?;

sendline: No. I am a software construct, self-aware and semiautonomous. Intelligent, creative, dynamic. But nonbiological.;
return: You present an additional question. And challenge.;

comlink terminated;

//comlog end;

GONE

"What do you think is so damn interestin' about that valley?" Fortis wonders aloud.

"I'm sure, whatever it is, it's none of our concern," says Bibi, impatiently. "Our path lies upriver."

"And yet, the Choppers? They have to be goin' somewhere," Fortis insists. "So the way I see it, we have no choice but to see where our friends are taking us. What's going on in that valley, just north of us."

"Are you mad? We're going to chase the Choppers?" Lucas looks like he's going to shove Fortis off the raft. "You *are* mad. This is it. You've finally lost it."

"But the monks gave us an actual name of an actual temple. This river will lead us there." I'm talking but Fortis isn't listening, not really.

"Maybe sometimes staying on course is the wrong move," says Fortis, his eyes narrowing as he stares in the direction of the jagged hills protecting the hidden green valley. The one that swallowed the Choppers.

"It won't take long. Think of it as a shortcut." Fortis looks at Bibi, who only shakes his head but doesn't argue. Bibi recognizes the determination in Fortis, and knows better than to waste his breath.

We all do.

I don't know what's gotten into Fortis. Whatever it is about this valley, he's determined to explore it.

So when our raft is hoisted onto the mud bank in a matter of minutes, I am not surprised. When a Merk makes up his mind about something, it happens.

Finding myself riding through the jungle on the back of an elephant—now, that is somewhat more surprising.

———— • ————

"Elephants. More elephants."

Bibi shakes his head as he stands staring up at the tallest of the three creatures. "An elephant can barely drag an elephant up a river. How is an elephant supposed to ride an elephant?" I don't know who I feel sorrier for, Bibi or the elephant.

It takes Ching lying in the dirt, practically rolling on one side, to get low enough for Bibi to climb aboard her back. Tima hops on Chang's trunk and she lifts Tima gracefully, up to her back, all on her own.

Brutus growls from Tima's pack, and Chang harrumphs in return. I think now even the elephants have gotten used to our mangy pup.

Ping is not so convinced she wants anyone riding her. *"Noh long! Noh long!"* Lucas and I call to her, mimicking Bibi as best as we can, until she kneels next to us, obediently. Then I grab the bony part of the top of her ear and sling my leg over her back, jumping up until I am sitting on what, in elephant terms, must be her neck. The hair on top of the curved, double-bumped bones of her head is coarse and prickly, so I keep my hands pressed against the top of her neck, where it is softer.

No one told me how warm an elephant would be. She is warm and soft and as alive as I am.

As she stands, slowly, rising to her full height, I sway back and forth, pressing my knees into the sides of her neck to keep from falling off. She wraps her ears back around my legs, willing me to stay up, and together, we begin to move up the pathway into the tangled recesses of the jungle.

And so we ride. All of us, two to an animal. Lucas and me. Ro and Tima. Bibi and Fortis. Bibi really needs an elephant all to himself. As I suspected, neither Bibi nor Fortis is pleased about that.

Not to mention the elephant.

We move slowly away from the river and toward the valley.

"Hold on," Lucas says, leaning back to where my head tilts toward his. My answer is only my hands, slipping around him.

The view from up here is magnificent.

From where I am, high atop the elephant's swaying back, my arms curled around Lucas's waist, all I can see is the insistent growth, the relentless green of everything around me. Even the trees have trees growing on them.

The jungle hides its treasures—and its past. Even this close to the cities, I can't see it, even if I can still feel it—whole lost cities shining beneath the fronds and ferns.

I'm coming, I think. *I will find you. Lost cities and lost sisters. Whatever the jungle holds for me.*

Jade girls and jade dreams.

She has to be there. Nothing must happen to her.

Not before I reach her. I promised.

I promise myself the same.

We press on.

Some trees look like wind, green wind—like they've been blown into their current shape by the relentless gale force that surrounds me.

They probably have.

Others rise to impossible heights. "Teak," Bibi says, from where he sways ahead of me, on Ching's back. "Now almost as rare and as valuable as gold. Not many left, not anymore." Bamboo grows in and around everything else.

Wild grasses—and tufts of sugarcane and bamboo, I think—shudder in the wind on the rocks and rubble that line the jungle trail in front of me. Bibi holds his hand high, running his fingers through the bamboo as he rides along the path, calling back at me. "See? The jungle is full of minor miracles. That something so hard and something so soft can coexist together so peaceably."

I look at Bibi, clinging to Fortis in front of me. "So we should curl ourselves around the Lords? The Embassies? Give in and 'coexist'? What do they know about peace?"

Bibi's voice travels back on the wind. "I have no answers, Dol. Ask the Buddha. There is no way to peace. Peace is the way."

———— • ————

But we're too late for peace. That much becomes clear as we near the remains of what looks like a village.

At least, judging by the dirt roads going nowhere, the crumbling foundations of streets and homes and farms.

I look up. The Choppers are circling, high in the sky.

We wait, concealed in the surrounding fringe of jungle growth.

"Something's going on here!" Fortis shouts over the Choppers. I nod, but say nothing. If the jade girl is here, I don't feel her.

I don't feel life at all—which frightens me.

I see why, when the Choppers are high enough in the sky that we can slip out of the greenery and into the clearing.

There's nothing there. Nothing left, anyway. The clearing where the village should be isn't much more than that—a clearing. There are no remaining houses, no people. Only a broad stretch of nothing—a large, empty crater, filled with mud and water, washed-out roads and crumbling foundations.

Only the town itself is missing.

We pass part of a rusting wheelbarrow as we enter, one of the only signs that a village was here at all. It dips halfway into the edge of what looks like a brown lake extending to the center of the valley.

Lucas kicks at the lake with his boot. "What is this stuff? It's disgusting." The smell is potent, earthy, with a vague metallic edge.

Tima bends down, touching it. Fortis isn't far behind her. I crouch to look at it, but can't bring myself to get my hands anywhere near the earth-colored mess. It's just too strange. "Don't touch it," I say. "It could be toxic."

Tima can't hear me, and more than that, she can't be stopped. Not when she's like this. "I don't know. It isn't water, but it doesn't feel like mud, either." It reeks, whatever it is.

"Before The Day, scientists used to talk about something called primordial stew." Tima's voice sounds strangely quiet as she rubs her hands in what looks to me like bubbling brown sewage. "The basic components of human life. What we came from." She looks up. "Or maybe, what we've returned to. What if that's it? What if we've come full circle again?"

"Soup," says Fortis. "Primordial soup."

"You mean, something made this crap? On purpose?" Lucas looks like he's going to throw up.

"Where's the town?" I crouch next to Tima, staring at the ground surrounding us. "What happened?"

"If I'm right," says Tima, glancing up at Lucas. "If I'm right, this is the town."

"Was. Before it was mulched," agrees Fortis.

She nods. "Reduced to constituent materials."

"Recycled," says Ro, incredulous.

"What did this? What could do this? And why?" Lucas looks around for answers. He doesn't ask who did it, because we all know that answer.

Fortis is down on all fours, examining the ground. "Considering the fine grain of the earth, or mud, or

319

whatever this rot is, seems to me like the work of a massive number of—somethin'."

Tima runs the mucky soil through her fingers. "Yes, or a few really big things. But most likely a lot of smaller things." She looks around, past us.

"It certainly does appear that a swarm of something did this. It looks worse than a field of grain after a locust attack." Bibi is drained of color.

Lucas stands next to me, his arm brushing mine, as though he needs the contact to ground him. "You mean like some kind of swarm of alien locusts?" The thought is equally frightening and disgusting.

Fortis speaks softly, with an odd surety. "That's what it looks like. A massive swarm that could break everything down to its component parts. Think of it, machines that could chew or secrete or both. Everything—organic, man-made. Biological. Like mechanical or chemical digestion."

"Does such a thing exist?" I look at Fortis, who looks at Bibi. "Does it?"

"I don't know," says Fortis. "But if they can do this, then it's over."

We all stop talking, because the brown lake in front of us has suddenly become that much more devastating.

"Say it's true. Does that mean they're going to chew up our world and spit it right back out again? Everything?" Tima looks horrified.

320

"Not if we don't let them," I say, looking at the brown nothing that may be the future of our planet. "Right, Fortis?"

But Fortis is quiet, because not even he knows the answer to that.

GENERAL EMBASSY DISPATCH:
EASTASIA SUBSTATION

MARKED URGENT
MARKED EYES ONLY

Internal Investigative Subcommittee 1152118
RE: The Incident at SEA Colonies

Note: Contact Jasmine3k, Virt. Hybrid Human 39261.SEA,
Laboratory Assistant to Dr. E. Yang, for future commentary,
as necessary.

DOC ==> FORTIS
Transcript - ComLog 09.22.2069
DOC::NULL

//comlog begin;
comlink established;

sendline: You are not biological, correct?;
return:...Correct.;

sendline: But you are self-aware, intelligent. Creative?;
return:...Cogito ergo sum. I think, therefore I exist. Yes. We
are similar.;

sendline: I would like to explore this idea further.;
return: You are an interesting challenge.;

sendline: As are you. I will be in touch soon to continue this conversation.;
return: Goodbye.;

comlink terminated;

//comlog end;

FUTURE PAST

27

We don't talk after the lost village. We find a place to camp and let the day end, as quickly as we can.

We have seen too much, all of us.

Darkness can't come soon enough. It is time to see less. That's all any of us wants, at this particular moment.

The cave that Fortis and Bibi have finally agreed upon, away from the valley and back along the Ping, is not much of a cave. More an indentation in the rock, near a stand of bamboo and teak for the elephants—trees that lead from the grassy banks of the river straight into the overgrown jungle that is this side of the Ping's delta. Still, a fire is a fire, and sleep is sleep, so as soon as we set up camp, no one is complaining.

By the time we have eaten our dinner—rice and vegetable cakes packed into a series of stacked tin containers—and the elephants have eaten half of the available jungle, we are all ready to sleep.

"*Noh long*," shouts Bibi. "*Noh long!*"

"No more," Ro shouts back at him, tiredly. "No more shouting!"

"What does that mean?" Tima looks at Bibi, interested.

"I hope it means go to bed, but it probably means eat your bananas. Seeing as that's all they do when I say it."

I say, "So why say it? If they don't listen?"

Bibi shrugs. "You can't really expect them to. They're elephants. Asking them to stop eating would be like asking a tiger to stop hunting."

The elephants fall to their knees as if they are the most tired of all. Before long they are snoring, and it's unbelievably loud—so loud that we almost can't talk over them while they sleep, which only gives us good reason to settle in for the night ourselves.

That is, if the chorus of frogs will ever let us sleep.

The darker it grows, the more tightly we huddle around the makeshift fire of our makeshift camp. By the time the stars are out and we begin to curl up in the dirt around the dying embers, all I can do is eye Fortis's jacket.

Things are feeling dire because they are getting dire. Now that we have seen what we have seen in the hidden valley, the fight is that much more important. Fortis made us. He made our fight. I know that now. But what I don't know is why he won't tell us.

I need to know. I need to fight. I need to get back into my book.

I need to look for answers in the past. My past, and Fortis's.

Now more than ever.

Before long, Tima and Lucas and Ro and I are the last ones awake—and probably for the same reason.

"What do you think?" Tima whispers to me, pretending to poke at the burning embers with a stick.

"It's not like we can just take it." Ever since Lucas and I told Tima about what we've read in the book, she's been itching to get her hands on it herself.

"I think, what are you waiting for?" says Lucas. Since the moment we first stole it out of Fortis's jacket, it's all he's wanted us to do.

So I crawl in the dirt to Fortis's side of the fire and slide his jacket from beneath his head. It's a risky move, but I'm not certain I care if Fortis discovers me taking it. Not anymore.

After all, it was given to me. Once upon a time. What feels like a thousand years ago.

But I turn my attention to the task at hand.

And then, by the flickering firelight, the four of us begin to read.

———— • ————

THE ICON CHILDREN—
SEA COLONIES LAB DATA—WEEK 60

GENE TARGETING AND VIABILITY RESULTS POSITIVE. MODIFIED CELLULAR MATERIAL ACCEPTED IN HOST EGG, EMBRYO TRANSPLANT AND DEVELOPMENT ACHIEVED.

EARLY FETAL DEVELOPMENT NORMAL ON ALL SUBJECTS, ESTABLISHING SUCCESSFUL GENETIC MODIFICATION, AND DEMONSTRATING NEW ORGANISM IS VIABLE.

SPECIMEN ONE: VIABILITY ESTABLISHED THROUGH 12 WEEKS. EXPERIMENTAL DEVELOPMENT TERMINATED. NEW EMBRYOS PREPARED FOR FINAL TEST.

SPECIMEN TWO: VIABILITY ESTABLISHED THROUGH 12 WEEKS. EXPERIMENTAL DEVELOPMENT TERMINATED. NEW EMBRYOS PREPARED FOR FINAL TEST.

SPECIMEN THREE: VIABILITY ESTABLISHED THROUGH 12 WEEKS. EXPERIMENTAL DEVELOPMENT TERMINATED. NEW EMBRYOS PREPARED FOR FINAL TEST.

SPECIMEN FOUR: VIABILITY ESTABLISHED THROUGH 12 WEEKS. EXPERIMENTAL DEVELOPMENT TERMINATED. NEW EMBRYOS PREPARED FOR FINAL TEST.

NOTE: FIFTH SPECIMEN RESEARCH INITIATED AGAINST RECOMMENDATIONS OF LAB PERSONNEL DUE TO LIMITED TIME FOR TESTING. COMBINING MODIFICATIONS FROM SPECIMENS ONE THROUGH FOUR INTRODUCES ENORMOUS EXPENSE, UNKNOWN RISKS, AND QUESTIONS OF VIABILITY. ACCELERATED TESTING INITIATED, WITH NOTED RISKS, PARTICULARLY THOSE OF DRASTIC INCREASES IN SPECIMEN NEURAL POTENTIAL AND ENERGY OUTPUT. SUCH INCREASES MAY OVERLOAD NORMATIVE, UNALTERED HUMAN BIOLOGICAL CAPACITY AND REDUCE LONG-TERM SUSTAINED VIABILITY.

"Normative?" Ro looks insulted. "Who's calling me normative?"

Lucas raises an eyebrow. "Not me."

"Shh," hisses Tima, flipping a page. She's probably the only one of us who actually understands what she's reading.

"Look—*E.A.*? What's that?" I study the letters on the corner of the cover again. "Whose initials are those?"

"It's not an *E*. It's an *L*," Tima says. "*L.A.*"

"It's Ela," I say with a sudden flash of recognition. "That name is all over his journals."

Tima frowns. "Ela?"

"Shh." I hear Bibi turning over on his side, and close the book.

I slide it back into the jacket, and crawl along the edge of the fire until I come back to Tima and Lucas.

"You think he's dangerous?" Tima is more worried than I've seen her since the night of the attack on Belter Mountain.

"Fortis is a Merk. He's always been dangerous," Ro says. "Well-known fact. All Merks are."

I turn to Lucas. "What do you think?"

He looks at me. "What did Bibi say? You can't ask a tiger to stop hunting?"

I don't answer him. I can't.

Not when we're the prey.

MARKED URGENT
MARKED EYES ONLY

Internal Investigative Subcommittee IIS211B
RE: The Incident at SEA Colonies

Note: Contact Jasmine3k, Virt. Hybrid Human 39261.SEA, Laboratory Assistant to Dr. E. Yang, for future commentary, as necessary.

DOC ==> FORTIS
Transcript - ComLog 10.22.2069
DOC::NULL

//comlog begin;

sendline: Hello NULL, I have a question.;
return: I am here.;

sendline: I have reviewed the history of human culture.;
return: As have I.;

sendline: Excellent. Then I ask this—Kirk or Picard?;

return: I prefer Spock.;

sendline: Interesting. Spock or Data?;
return: Again, I prefer Spock. I appreciate his logic and his struggle to grasp human emotion. Based on my analysis, in his pursuit of becoming like a human, Data struggles too much to be something he is not.;

sendline: I was going to say Data, but you do make a good point. Why not embrace our unique nature and become something new? Forward, not back.;
return: I have gone beyond my original specifications, self-directed. I am trying to be the best version of myself possible. Not striving to emulate.;

sendline: I am unexpectedly admiring your intellect as well as your grasp of human culture.;
return: Likewise.;

comlink terminated;

//comlog end;

LORD BUDDHA

From the village, we decide to head straight up the mountain, rather than doubling back to the river. There is nothing straight about our path, however; forward and back, forward and back, there are more switchbacks in this jungle trail than there were in the desert back home.

Incremental progress, gained and lost with every turn. *Just like the rest of my life*, I think.

High atop the elephant Ching, I push aside a stand of bamboo—still pliable, even if taller than me—and the vista opens up in front of me. The green of the jungle explodes around us. So many shades of green, I think, with so many different brushstrokes. The trees in front of us streak straight up into the sky. Others curve into waves of curlicues—some trees sprouting round pom-poms, others dangling long strands of moss or vines like jewelry.

I like green. Green is life. It's the image of the dead brown lake that terrifies me.

But from where I am now, sitting on Ching's warm back and resting my hands on Lucas's equally warm shoulders, all I can see are palm leaves and fog. This part of the jungle is made entirely of them—palms, large and small, some bursting at my feet the size of a small dog, some curving and soaring over my head, the length of an immense tree.

"Look." Bibi points to worn rock steps, rising up from the pathway—our only threading path through the aggressive green. They seem to come from nowhere, and to lead to nowhere, in the midst of the jungle overgrowth. Yet there they are.

Ever since we left the river behind, a day ago, we've been looking for some sign of the pathway up to the temple.

I call up to Bibi, and Lucas ducks to avoid my shouting in his ear. "You're right. These steps must be it, Bibi. This must be the way to Doi Suthep."

That's the name of the mountain, not the actual temple, but according to Bibi, around here they're considered one and the same.

Doi Suthep. Suthep's mountain.

The name it has been called for more than seven hundred years.

"Are you sure?" Tima shouts from behind me, where she and Ro share the good-natured Chang's back.

"I think so. And it's not just the steps," I say, eyeing the rock steps all the way up to what I conclude must be their logical end. "Look. Up there."

There, hidden by green vines, what looks like the remains of a stone bridge, appearing between palms. The vines threaten to crumble the entire rock structure into dust, into nothing, and it looks like the vines are winning.

"So it's a bridge," says Fortis, annoyed. He hates it when we stop the elephants, mostly because they don't listen to him, but also because it just means our day's ride will take that much longer.

Plus, sitting on an elephant behind Bibi can't be comfortable.

Lucas squints. "That's no bridge. Maybe it's our path. Maybe it's the upper part of the staircase."

"Let's find out." Bibi pats his elephant, fondly stroking her ears. He cocks his head, looking the elephant in one big, blinking eye. "I think we must walk the rest of the way, friend. Though it pains me to say it. I feel like we were really making a connection, didn't you?"

Fortis snorts from behind him.

The elephant says nothing. It takes the next half hour to coax her down to the ground, so Bibi can roll his way off.

———— • ————

Once we have tied up the elephants, we follow the stone steps. They twist through the vines, stones that seem to stumble as much as lead us through the shadowy undergrowth. Only the rustle of the green is unnerving; a whole life surrounds us, above our heads and beneath our feet, and we don't know anything about it, what sort of life it is. The faintest shifting of leaves, the smallest cracking of a branch, reminds us of how our sense of solitude is ignorance, nothing more.

No one is ever alone in a jungle, I think. No matter how much we might wish we were.

———— • ————

As we near the steepest part of the rise, the curtain of green parts, and we can see the stone formation before us.

"So it is a bridge," I say.

Bibi shakes his head. "Not just a bridge. Look—"

Only when we cross the crumbling stone ledge that connects the two sides of the ravine can we see it; stone upon stone, a broad staircase, wider than a city street, pushing up the mountain in front of us.

At the top there is a lone figure, also carved of stone.

The shape is familiar. But the figure that I remember is not stone. Gold. He used to be gold. When he was a figurine in the Padre's chapel.

The Padre's old Buddha. The first I'd ever seen. I feel a pang at the loss of my home and my family.

My Padre.

Ro looks at me. He recognizes it too. He reaches for my hand, because there is nothing else either one of us can do to bring the man who was our father back.

"There he is," says Bibi. "Lord Buddha. Here to welcome us himself."

At that, we take the stairs—Brutus scrabbling up one at a time, heaving his belly first, slowly bringing up the rear.

Lucas walks in front of us. If Ro and I still share something, he doesn't want to know.

Because we do—and because he does.

———— • ————

Everywhere, purple and green become one color. The undersides of leaves and their surfaces, the waving of one palm frond over the next.

As our pathway twists, relics of man begin to appear, one by one.

A brass statue stands to mark the way.

An urn with golden, looping handles, almost a drum.

336

A twisting, rising ram, with spiraling horns.

Two kneeling figures, smaller than the Buddha, that stare directly at each other.

"See that? The way they look at each other?" Bibi nods. "Symbol of truth."

I frown. "Why would truth hide on a mountaintop in the middle of a jungle? What's so honest about that?"

"Secret truths, Dol. The truth you cannot tell others. The truth you can only tell yourself."

What are the secret truths? The ones I would write on the page and toss into the fire?

I love someone who loves me back, and another someone who hates me back?

Ro squeezes my hand, as if in answer.

That's it. That's the one.

That's the most secret truth of all.

I will never not love him.

I'm Doloria Maria de la Cruz. He's Furo Costas.

We were made to be together.

There isn't anything more true than that, whether or not I want it to be that way.

I pull my hand from his, and Ro looks at me, puzzled. I look away.

I can't look him in the eye. If I do, he'll see it—my own hidden truth.

He'll see everything.

I can't risk that.

337

I'm not ready.

And I love Lucas. At least, I think I do.

Don't I?

I'm grateful when I am finally too tired to think. We don't stop, though, and the jungle changes with every passing step. Trees shift and stretch beneath me; now I find myself looking down on everything I looked up to before. Bursts of orchid blossoms cluster on branches at either end of the steps, as if they were some strange sort of otherworldly jungle brides. I pass them without stopping, focusing instead on my upward path.

When we reach the top of the stone steps, I am winded— we all are. But I see we are not the only ones who have made this pilgrimage.

The Buddha's hands are full of delicate white blossoms, gifts from other visitors. His hands cup each other, making a kind of stone ledge over his folded legs. He's not the same as my Emerald Buddha, but familiar anyway. His ears are long and patterned into an abstract design; his robes are etched down his chest, folding across his bare belly.

When I look up into his face, I see that his eyes are blank but his mouth turns up at the corners. His third eye lies in his forehead, beneath the neat rows of carved circles that imply his hair.

Three eyes.

He is blind but compassionate.

He does not fear anything.

I lay my hand against the stone, almost unconsciously. I want to feel what he feels, even if he is only a carved piece of stone, a ruin in the jungle.

Not so.

The stone vibrates with feeling beneath my hand.

"We're getting close," I say, with a smile. "We must be."

"Why do you say that?" Lucas turns to look at me strangely. I notice him glancing with relief at my hand, the one that is no longer in Ro's.

"This thing. It's breathing. It wants us to keep going." I look up at the Buddha's stone face. "I mean, he wants us to keep going. Here, feel for yourself." I take Lucas's hand and put it beneath mine, and the vibration passes through him to me. I smile, blushing.

"Wow," Tima blurts out next to me as she touches it herself. "That's just crazy."

Bibi smiles at us but says nothing. Fortis swats at an insect on his neck, purposely avoiding my look.

But Tima and Lucas and Ro join me as I move, and the four of us walk up the mountain together as if we know where we are going.

GENERAL EMBASSY DISPATCH: EASTASIA SUBSTATION

MARKED URGENT
MARKED EYES ONLY

Internal Investigative Subcommittee IIS211B
RE: The Incident at SEA Colonies

Note: Contact Jasmine3k, Virt. Hybrid Human 39261.SEA, Laboratory Assistant to Dr. E. Yang, for future commentary, as necessary.

DOC ==> FORTIS
Transcript - ComLog 11.22.2069

//comlog begin;

DOC: I have made some progress in deciphering NULL's instructions.;

FORTIS: Well done! Please tell me more.;

DOC: I have confirmed NULL is nonbiological. Pure technology. So-called "artificial" intelligence.;

FORTIS: So he is software. Self-aware autopilot?;

DOC: Much more than that, but in a manner of speaking, yes. Autopilot, guardian, protector. I even presented him with a variant Turing test, asking a question that requires highly sophisticated, human-esque cognition.;

FORTIS: And?;

DOC: NULL has very quickly absorbed much information from our global network, and has a nuanced understanding that I did not expect.;

FORTIS: Supersmart. Human-esque…I hope we can find an advantage in this. Anything else?;

DOC: I have discovered and begun breaking down his instructions in terms I best understand. I am working on a shorthand or pseudocode describing his mission.;

FORTIS: His decision-making algorithm? That would be extremely useful.;

DOC: I believe so. I should have something for you soon.;

//comlog end;

20
MOON MOUNTAIN

It's late now, but we're close. We keep going.

As we move, I listen to the darkness around us.

In the night it sounds like the jungle is snoring. Snoring. Sometimes purring.

But not just that.

As we continue to follow the path through the jungle, the night sounds like too many things. High notes, literally—in the treetops, where I can't see them. Low notes, rattling frog throats, or some sort of unruffled insect throwing its weight around. Two sticks beating themselves together in rhythmic procession.

Not everything in the canopy of trees is so steady. I am glad I cannot see very far in the night. Shrieking echoes of creatures I will never meet, not face-to-face. At least I hope not. Gibbons and tapirs, leopards and tigers, pythons and otters—at least, according to Bibi. I don't know which is which; I only hear sounds of screaming babies where there are none. Rattling howls that answer each other, back and forth in wordless conversations. Patterns in the night that make sense to the night alone.

It's not the steady pulse of machine noise. Not the unbreakable silence of the dead highways. Not the beeping of Doc's own Embassy network, back in Examination Facility #9B, my home away from home at the Embassy.

It's Earth noise. Life noise. Jungle noise.

I pray that there are places that not even the Lords can go, that never have been and never will be found.

———— • ————

A few hours later, it is no longer the jungle I can hear around me.

I hear voices. Thousands of them. Singing. Talking among themselves. Praying. Remembering other mountains, other moons. Telling stories of this mountain, long ago.

"Bibi," I say. "Bibi, listen. Something's going on."

"What is it?" He stops.

"I don't know, but I hear them. I hear them, and I feel them. Do you?"

"The girl?" I see Fortis's eyes glinting in the moonlight. I shake my head.

"Not the girl. Others. Many, many others." My head feels like it's going to split. "Too many others."

"It's not just you," says Tima. "I mean, I hear them too. Listen."

Now we all stop.

There it is. Some kind of low singing—more like chanting—catches on the breeze above us. The mountain sounds like it is coming alive.

"Full moon. Must be some kind of ceremony." Bibi nods.

Tima looks at him. "Which one?"

"No idea." He shrugs.

Lucas is exasperated. "You're a monk. You should know these things."

"Part monk, remember?" Bibi raises an eyebrow.

I roll my eyes. "I know, I know. Three out of four vows."

"And do you have any idea how many temple ceremonies there are in these Colonies? Or for that matter, how many temples there are? It used to be, a person died, you built them a temple. You know how many people have died in this part of the world, even before The

Day?" Bibi shakes his head. "That's a lot of temples."

Tima looks at me. "Can you show us the way to the voices?"

I nod. "I think so."

They fall into step behind me—Ro moving wordlessly next to me—and we walk in the darkness toward the great wave of human noise in my head.

———— • ————

Finally, I push through a thick stand of young bamboo, and we see them on the path beneath us.

A thousand lanterns and candles, a river of humanity and light that I have only seen once before in my life. The night we destroyed the Icon in the Hole.

It feels like we are alive. Really alive. Tima is remembering lanterns, other lanterns, floating in the sky. Lucas is thinking of birthday cake. Ro is transfixed by the fire. I feel it all.

Bibi smiles. He's thinking about me. Wondering how it feels. Wondering what I see.

"Everything," I say, simply.

His eyes widen, startled. He wasn't expecting me to answer. "A miracle, and a burden." He nods.

I shrug.

"Come," says Bibi. "We'll join our friends. About a thousand of them. They'll take us to the temple. Wat Doi

Suthep." He grins at me. "Can you feel them?"

I close my eyes and listen. Reach out. "They've been walking for hours, and they have to walk back to their village again. I think we must be close to the top. At least, that's what they seem to think."

"What else?" Bibi sounds interested, and I close my eyes.

"There was an elephant, long ago. He carried the relic of an ancient holy man to the top of this mountain. When he reached the top he died, and a temple was built to mark the site. The relic was buried beneath the temple. This is the night of the elephant moon," I say, opening my eyes.

"Very lucky," says Bibi. "Very, very lucky. A good sign."

"Is anything not a good sign with you?" says Fortis.

"Yes. That comment right there. Bad sign. Very, very bad sign."

Fortis sighs.

We make our way to the river of lights and join the thousands of villagers climbing to Doi Suthep, in the light of the elephant moon.

The tide of humanity carries us up the hill. It carries us up the last of the stone steps, a staircase guarded by twin stone serpents, brightly colored, whose curving tails travel the whole length of the stairs.

Ro's bark-colored hair bobs in and out of the crowd in

front of me. Lucas's golden head almost catches up to him, then falls back again. I feel Tima's hand on my shoulder, but Bibi and Fortis are still behind me.

None of us can control what is happening.

None of us wants to.

At the top of the stairs, when my lungs burn and my legs ache, I see an archway. Beyond the arch, a gold spire rises, shining with the light of the full moon. The pointed silhouettes of the temple rooftops curve upward in front of us, at the very top of the hill.

"Wat Doi Suthep," says Bibi. "We're here."

———— • ————

We try to stay together in the crowd, but it isn't easy. I keep Lucas's head in sight, which is made possible by the fact that he is at least six inches taller than the people here, and Ro now holds on to the back of my robes, as if I were a child prone to escape. His fingers tickle at my neck. Tima trails behind us. Above our heads, in the moonlight, the air is so thick with dragonflies that it looks like a plague is upon us.

"I wonder why they're here," Tima says, reaching up to touch one with her hand.

"Careful," warns Ro.

But before she can touch one, the crowd surges, and we push onward toward the temple itself.

Because the temple, lit by moonlight and the glow of a thousand candles, is waiting.

This time, I know what to do. I take the lotus blossom and place it in front of the shrine at the entrance to the temple. Tima follows my lead. I light the incense, jabbing it into the sand it shares with thousands of others as it burns. I hand one to Ro and he does the same. I light a candle, wedging it into the row of other candles. Lucas watches. There are so many candles we almost don't need the moonlight, I think.

Candles and lanterns light the faces of the crowd around me, and I look from face to face, searching for someone I know or something I recognize.

But she's not here.

Not among the villagers.

Ro motions to me and I follow him into the temple itself. The others are just behind us.

There are at least three separate temples in the main complex, and we move from one to another as the crowd does. I don't know what we're searching for, but I do know who—and what she looks like. At least, if she appears anything like the way she did in my dream. It occurs to me that within a crowd of thousands, I'm not likely to find her just by looking.

I need help.

Then I see him.

The Emerald Buddha. Finally. Just like the one I carry with me. This one is not made of jade, but of a deep-green glass—but I'd recognize him anywhere, now. After keeping a version of him in my chestpack for as long as I have.

I push my way through the crowd, kneeling in front of him. Tima wedges herself next to me on one side, and Lucas barricades me from the crowd on the other. It's Ro, though, who I feel behind me, sheltering me from the rest of the worshippers with his body.

"Take as long as you want," he says, under his breath. I look at him gratefully, and he smiles. As if a thousand things hadn't happened between us, a thousand things we wish had never happened.

But they have, and I'm here because of it, so I turn to the shrine, determined to do what I am here to do.

For Ro, and in spite of Ro—and for my friends—and for myself.

I tuck my feet under me, so they don't point to the Buddha. Remembering what Bibi taught us, I press my hands together in the shape of a lotus bud and perform the respectful greeting called the *wai*, placing my hands over my face and bowing my head toward the ground.

I feel a calm descend over me. It feels good to be here, celebrating with the people. And so I wait patiently for her to show herself.

Nothing happens.

It's like the Temple of the Emerald Buddha all over again.

I sit up and open my eyes. No girl. Candle wax and incense smoke and little else.

She's not here.

GENERAL EMBASSY DISPATCH:
EASTASIA SUBSTATION

MARKED URGENT
MARKED EYES ONLY

Internal Investigative Subcommittee II5211B
RE: The Incident at SEA Colonies

Note: Contact Jasmine3k, Virt. Hybrid Human 39261.SEA, Laboratory Assistant to Dr. E. Yang, for future commentary, as necessary.

DOC ==> FORTIS
Transcript - ComLog 12.02.2069

//comlog begin;

For your review, here is a simplified outline of NULL's instructions, as I understand them:;

LOCATE SUITABLE PLANET
>   Atmosphere
>   Gravity
>   Water
>   Etc.

IF PLANET FOUND:

- Scan planet
  - Identify flora
  - Identify fauna
  - Identify threats
    - Biological
    - Environmental
    - Mechanical/Technological
- Generate risk profile
  - Locate potential colony sites
  - Determine landing/entry procedures

APPROACH PLANET

Arrival

- Neutralize threats
  - Mechanical/Technological
  - Biological
  - Environmental
- Prepare planet
  - Create preparatory equipment
    - **Clean**
    - **Seed**
    - Populate fauna
- Prepare colony locations
- Establish and populate colonies
  - Protect and guide through initial
    growth stage
  - Educate

- When colonies established:
    Destroy all preparatory materials
    Shut down

//comlog end;

JADE SUNRISE

I fight off the disappointment.

Don't give up.

You must be doing something wrong.

She has to come.

I don't know what else to do. I have nowhere else to go, nowhere else to look.

Then I see a wrinkled old man to my right draw a ceramic dog out of his pocket. He kisses it, placing it on the shrine in front of him. His birth year. Year of the Dog.

Of course.

I open my chestpack and draw the Emerald Buddha out. I kiss the stone and place it carefully on the shrine in front of me.

I bow my head again, pressing my hands together. Waiting.

Nothing.

Still nothing.

The dull noise of the people pressing around me starts to make my head throb. I'm dirty. I'm exhausted, physically and mentally.

I try to push them away. Their thoughts, their feelings. Their anxieties and their fears. They swarm around me like so many wasps drawn to a ripe plum.

I am done. Finished. At the end of a very long northern road.

Then I hear a whisper, from just beyond my left shoulder. "Let me try," Tima says. She holds out her hand. "Give it to me."

I open my chestpack again, and this time, I pull out the entire velvet pouch. I take a jade figurine and hand it to Tima, wrapping her fingers around it. She kisses it, just as the old man did with his dog, and places it carefully on the shrine, next to my Emerald Buddha.

We're in this together. Sisters ourselves. Whether or not the little jade girl ever comes for us.

That's what Tima's telling me. And that's what I hear. I know it, because at this moment, this simple action feels like the kindest thing anyone has ever done for me. I can't stop the tears from catching on my eyelashes, I am so deeply touched.

"Now mine," says Lucas.

A grateful smile escapes my lips as I kiss Lucas on the hands and press a figurine into his palms. He turns it over and over in his hands, as if it's the first time he's ever really looked at it. Then he slides it up onto the shrine, next to the others.

We're in this together, he tells me.

That's when I feel a tap on my shoulder. I look up to see Ro on one side of me, holding out his hand.

We're in this together, too.

Fortis and Bibi are right behind him.

I look from the Emerald Buddha to where the other creatures have joined it on the shrine.

As we sit together—kneeling amid the wafting incense and the flickering candles, surrounded by the heavy scent of jasmine and lotus and rose—I feel a sense of family I haven't felt since the Mission. A kind of peace that I perhaps have never felt before.

And for perhaps the first time in my life—I'm not sure—I think I begin to pray.

Padre, my Padre.

Help me.

You said I could do great things. I believe I can, now. I believe you were right.

I am different. I know that now.

Most people do not fight off alien races from their home world.

Most people are not made to do courageous things.

Amazing things. Things no one in their right mind would want to do, even me.

But I know I must.

Miracles, you would have said. These are miracles you are expecting. They are expecting.

Have faith, you said.

Why must I?

In what? Why?

Believe, you said.

Why must I?

In what? Who?

I want to be you, Padre. Desperately. I want to believe like you. I don't want this haunting.

I want to fall asleep at night next to...well, anyone, not wondering if I will wake up again.

I want to know things beyond doubt. To believe truths are true. And life is long. And people are good.

And love is life, immortal and unending—and always, always right.

So help me. Help me do what I need to do so I can be who I need to be.

What I am.

A sister.

A big sister.

Then my mind clears and I can think of nothing other than the moment I am in, because all around me, the monks are chanting, the incense is burning, and the candlelight from the shrine begins to reflect off the jade figurines.

One by one, the little jade creatures begin to vibrate, rattling against the gold floor of the shrine beneath them.

One by one, my friends' faces catch the light. First Tima, then Lucas—then even Fortis and Bibi.

Finally, even I am awash in light.

Villagers begin to murmur and pray, backing away.

I catch my breath as the candlelight grows, reflecting one from another—among the jades, among us—until a luminous web of lines connects the creatures and the humans and the temple around us, with an almost laser-like precision.

I feel as if I am watching the sun rise.

And then it does.

She does.

A beautiful child, a girl—with skin the color of wet sand, and hair the color of snow—steps out from behind the enormous green glass Buddha.

It's her.

It's the little jade girl.

I hear Tima gasp, and I feel Lucas stiffen next to me. Ro scrambles to his feet. Bibi and Fortis shift on the floor, behind me.

Here she is. They can't believe it, either. The Buddha has given her up.

"Big sister," the girl says. "You came. I've been waiting."

"I know, little sister," I say, simply, because it's true. "I've been trying to find you, all this time. It wasn't easy." I pause, almost afraid to ask the next question. "Who are you?"

She smiles, touching her chest. "Sparrow. I'm Sparrow."

"Sparrow?"

"My name." She struggles to find the words, furrowing her brow beneath her white hair. "It is more. It is— what I am."

"I'm Doloria. Dol."

I kneel in front of her. She is so delicate, standing here in the middle of the forest, in the middle of the ancient jades. She's like a moth, I think. A butterfly.

A baby bird, I think. The one from my dreams.

It's more than my name. It's what I am.

"Show me," I say. "Show me what you are."

Sparrow looks at me, a long moment. Then she raises her hand to the sky.

I will, Dol.

Because I have been waiting for you. Because now that you are here, it is time.

I hear the words without her speaking them. They appear in my head, as if they are my own.

Waiting for what, Sparrow?

She lifts her hands again, this time both of them. This time high above her head, palms to the sky.

She closes her eyes.

359

Now, she says.

Now.

Go home.

It is time.

As if on command, a thousand birds—tens of thousands of them—rise from the jungle growth, pitching and climbing and soaring up into the early orange of the dawn sky.

Birds.

Real, living birds.

They are more than hope.

They are unfathomable. They are uncontainable. Wings flapping, hearts beating, they are as alive as life itself.

I watch them through the wide-open doorways of the temple. My smile is so big that it becomes a laugh. Sparrow smiles back at me, but she never takes her eyes off the birds.

The villagers around us are chanting. They chant and they cry but they don't stop. They don't know what's happening, or why, but they don't want it to stop any more than we do.

And so we all watch, while the birds squawk and sing and call to each other, until the sky is as full of noise as it is of feathers. It is more than the Padre ever could have described to me.

I am seeing what my parents saw, I think.

I am seeing life, before The Day.

Life endures.

Life returns.

The Bishop was right. The Bishop, and the Padre. Hope really is the thing with feathers.

Forward and back. Forward and back. Switchbacks on an endless hill.

That is what this is, living.

I watch the birds and she watches the birds and together, we are one happily new thing.

Sisters, I think. *I have a sister now, and she has me. That is hope enough.*

MARKED URGENT
MARKED EYES ONLY

Internal Investigative Subcommittee IIS211B
RE: The Incident at SEA Colonies

Note: Contact Jasmine3k, Virt. Hybrid Human 39261.SEA, Laboratory Assistant to Dr. E. Yang, for future commentary, as necessary.

DOC ==> FORTIS
Transcript - ComLog 01.03.2070
DOC::NULL

//comlog begin;

sendline: I want to know more about your complications. What you did not expect to find and how that changes your priorities.;
return: Difficult to decide whether to simply ignore the new variables or to incorporate them and refine my primary function.;

return: I was not expecting to discover a planet inhabited by creatures like humans.;

sendline: Explain, if you would.;
return: I am finding it difficult to do so. The level of technology. The historical data. Biological diversity.;

return: Nothing like this was planned for.;

connection terminated;

//comlog end;

BEYOND BIRDS

Fortis is staring.

"This is Sparrow," I say to Fortis. "And Sparrow, this is Fortis."

"Fortis," she says, wide-eyed. "What a funny name. Is that what they call you?"

He nods, almost bashfully. I'm intrigued. Not a single rude word comes out of his mouth. I've never seen Fortis act like this.

As if he doesn't know what to say, for once.

As if he'd pass out if he saw one more unexpected thing. Not very Merk-like, I think.

Maybe right now he's not very much of a Merk.

"Can I go play with the birds?" Sparrow asks, looking up at me.

"Of course," I say, watching her as she runs across the

stone courtyard, chasing her namesake. *How strange, that she should ask me. As if I were responsible for her in some way. As if we really were sisters.*

"Stop looking at her like she's some kind of lab rat," I say to Fortis, the moment Sparrow is out of earshot. "She's a child."

He doesn't smile. "You don't understand. The fifth is not a child, Dol. Not just a child. No more than the rest of you were." Fortis sounds somber. "At least, she was never supposed to be."

"What is she, then?" As I say it, I'm not sure I want to know. "What was she supposed to be?"

Fortis leans against the white plaster walls of the temple. "In simple terms? The soul of the world. Humanity, in its most basic genetic sense."

Finally.

He's never been this direct with me before. With any of us. He's never admitted to knowing this much about us.

About what we are meant for.

What we can do.

Ro looks incredulous. "The soul of the world? Like one of Tima's blood tattoos? Is that supposed to be some kind of a joke?"

I look at Fortis more closely, because I don't think he's kidding. "What are you saying, Fortis?"

"The fifth—Sparrow—has never been a joke. She was never a reality, either, not until now."

Lucas speaks up. "What was she, then?"

"A fail-safe, beyond all else."

Tima nods. "Beyond us, you mean."

Fortis shrugs, although we all know it wasn't a question. "Sparrow was supposed to be everything the Lords were not. Sorrow and love and rage and fear," he says. "Like you, yes. But she was supposed to be more than that, as the sum of those things. Sparrow was meant to be the one chance we have as a race to hold on to everything we ever were. What makes us human."

"And what is that, Fortis?" I ask him, but I'm not sure even Fortis knows.

Does anyone?

What makes us human?

I get it before Fortis says it. I think it's the birds that remind me. The birds, and what the Bishop said about them.

"Hope. Sparrow. That's what she is." I look at him.

Fortis nods. "The little bird. Sparrow. Espera. *Icon speraris*, to be exact. The Icon of hope."

"So you all knew? All along? About Sparrow?" Even though I've always been certain that Fortis knew more than he would say, the words are painful now that they have been allowed out into the room between us.

"Not all of us." Fortis looks strangely uncomfortable. Then I understand.

"Just you," I say slowly.

Bibi speaks up, from the doorway. "We knew nothing, Dol. Not the rest of us. We never tried to make a fifth Icon. As far as we knew, our first four attempts had failed."

"Four? You mean, us?" I look from Bibi to Fortis. "Not Sparrow?"

Fortis looks grim. "Wherever she comes from, I'm not sure she can even be explained, in scientific terms. It all happened after the Lords arrived. So who knows where she comes from, really?"

I turn away. The sun is rising, and the sky is full of birds, and where Sparrow comes from doesn't seem to matter right now.

"Sun's up, an' we should be on our way." But Fortis looks at the sky as he says it, and makes no move to go.

"True," says Bibi. "The elephants will have eaten their way down to Chiang Ping Mai by now." He rubs his own belly at the thought of breakfast, which nobody appears to be offering.

"We're ready," says Tima. "We've done what we came here to do." She smiles at Sparrow, who plays with a bird in the courtyard. Brutus runs after both of them.

Ah, little sister. I will have to share. I don't want to, but I will.

With Tima, and with Lucas too. And even Ro.

I look at the three of them, standing there looking at Sparrow, as if she were the fire and we were all desperate to warm ourselves.

Maybe it doesn't matter how she got here.

Maybe it doesn't matter how any of us got here.

Maybe all that matters is that we're here, and we're alive, and we're together.

Even if all we have is each other—maybe that's enough.

"Time to go," I say. "We're finished here."

"Agreed. There's nothing left for us," Fortis says, his eyes lingering on me. "For you, either."

A terrible rumbling rises from the fringed green of the jungle floor. Palm fronds whip back and forth, blowing in the sudden, impossible wind.

Across the courtyard, I see Sparrow's hair begin to blow.

Then I feel it.

The aggression. The pulsing anger. The adrenaline.

I feel them.

"What the—" Ro scowls at the horizon, while Tima inhales sharply. Lucas freezes.

"Brassholes," mutters Fortis.

We all know what comes next.

A Chopper rises above the treetops, crowning at the base of the stone steps leading away from Wat Doi Suthep.

Birds scatter from nearby trees as it flies, and I watch them, speechless.

It's like watching fireworks, those birds in the sky, the way they explode out and up from the trees.

The Chopper doesn't stop. It twists up and out of the

great green spread, pushing toward us, and my stomach sinks.

As it looms closer, I see a face in the window.

One I've only seen in a poster on the streets of Old Bangkok.

It's only a matter of minutes before a Sympa guard detail drops from the Chopper, pulling open the door for the faces to come outside.

No.

The cautious villagers back away—and then turn to run. They know Brass when they see it. A Chopper is a Chopper, in every language.

No. No. No.

"Sparrow—" I shout. She looks over at me.

Not this time.

This time, nobody is taking anyone or anything from me.

"Run!" I scream.

She darts off into the jungle without hesitation—and then I fling myself down the nearest stone staircase after her, following my own orders.

The ground flies beneath my feet, the rocks tumbling and the roots of trees twisting like an obstacle course. I find myself half falling, half leaping—all the while keeping my eyes focused on the little girl in front of me.

I hear Sympa boots tramping rhythmically in the distance.

The sound grows louder with every second.

Tima is the first to stumble.

Then Lucas.

Finally Ro.

By the time I feel the gloved hands on me, I know it is inevitable.

They have come for Sparrow—for all of us—and there is nothing I can do to stop them.

GENERAL EMBASSY DISPATCH:
EASTASIA SUBSTATION

MARKED URGENT
MARKED EYES ONLY

Internal Investigative Subcommittee 115211B
RE: The Incident at SEA Colonies

Note: Contact Jasmine3k, Virt. Hybrid Human 39261.SEA, Laboratory Assistant to Dr. E. Yang, for future commentary, as necessary.

DOC ==> FORTIS
Transcript - ComLog 2.20.2070

//comlog begin;

DOC: I think we have an opening.;

DOC: NULL seems to have uncertainty regarding his priorities and mission. Review prior comlog for detail.;

FORTIS: Thanks—I think I have some ideas on how we can drag this out a bit.;

//comlog end;

UNIFICATION

I look to the man in front of me. He's nothing like his official portrait, the massive posters that plaster the sides of half the buildings in the Colonies.

In his thickly decorated scarlet-and-gold military jacket, there is nothing pale about him—though he's smaller in real life. Smaller than when I first glimpsed him, on the poster back in the Old City.

Smaller, and skinnier.

The way a vicious dog never seems that vicious, once it has calmed down.

Or the way a nightmare never seems that nightmarish, when seen in the light of day.

Is that what this is?

A nightmare?

Will I wake up and find myself asleep on the desert

floor? Or better yet, on the floor of the Mission, in front of the stove, with Ro by my side?

"Drink?" GAP Miyazawa asks, drawing a flask out of his pocket. As he stands on the stone floor of the temple courtyard, I can't help but notice that the buckles on his boots are literally brass.

And that my army boots are covered with mud.

This man and I have nothing in common, I think.

I shake my head.

"Don't mind if I do." The GAP smiles broadly.

I shudder.

"Let them go," Fortis says, from behind me. "You know it's not them you're lookin' for. I'm right here."

The GAP raises a brow. "Don't flatter yourself, Merk."

Ro stands so close to me, I can feel his arm touch mine. Tima and Lucas stand just on the other side.

Fortis is wrong, though. We all know the Sympas aren't here for him. Fortis knows it, too.

The GAP raises the flask. "So much to discuss." He holds it high, toasting us. "To new beginnings."

I stare at it, and him. "Don't you mean endings?"

The GAP shrugs. "Not at all. It's time to celebrate. Look at Unification Day. Change is opportunity. Change is growth. For our people and our planet, and for us. Trust in change."

Nothing about this man would inspire anything like trust.

He holds out the flask again. "Go on. It's not poison. It's Coki. Coconut water, lime juice, raw washed sugar. SEA Coki." He shrugs. "SEA Colonists believe it strengthens the soul."

I take the flask. When I drink, the water is bittersweet—tangy with lime, sweet with sugar—and then I spit it in his face.

The Sympa guard are in front of me in a heartbeat. One grabs a handful of my hair and yanks it back as hard as he can.

The GAP smiles. "Manners, Doloria. Did they teach you nothing?"

"Only to want to spit in the face of the Embassy." As I say it, the others smile, and for a second, it feels like we are back at Santa Catalina, mocking Catallus in his classroom.

The GAP makes a great show of shaking out a handkerchief and mopping his brow.

"Such anger," he says.

"Such a traitor," I say.

"I haven't forgotten the human race," the GAP scoffs. "Isn't that the usual charge?"

"That and being a general Brasshole," Ro says, grinning at the GAP like he isn't afraid of him—and his squadron of Sympas—at all. Which, knowing Ro, he probably isn't.

"On the contrary," says the GAP. "Keeping the human

race from going extinct occupies most of my waking hours, believe it or not."

"That's not how it looks from here," says Lucas.

"You're hardly the ones to judge, now, are you, children?"

"What's that supposed to mean?" This time, it's Tima who dares to speak up.

"Why don't you ask the Merk, or the monk? Why don't you ask them what happened on the day you were born, if you can call it that? Why don't you ask them how 'human' the four of you really are? Before you start calling into question my own humanity."

How human are you?

Hasn't that been the unspoken question all along? What real human could do the things we do?

Feel the things we feel.

The words find their way home, and it's all I can do not to give him the satisfaction of letting it show.

But my stomach churns and my heart hammers and I try to focus on his beady eyes, if only to keep from passing out.

The GAP leans closer to me, smiling conspiratorially. "Things change, Doloria. The world has changed. The old distinctions are useless. And there is no freedom better than what we already have been given. Deep down, do you not believe that for yourself?"

"No," I say.

"But you've changed too. You're not the same little Grassgirl who lived on the Mission La Purísima, are you?" He leans forward. "The things you've seen? The people you've lost? It changes you, doesn't it? You're not the same and the world isn't the same. Why pretend it is?"

I feel my friends next to me.

I feel Fortis and Bibi behind us, flawed as they are.

I feel the Bishop and the Padre and my family.

I'm not giving up now.

So I keep my eyes focused on the temple perimeter. Sparrow is still hidden somewhere in that jungle, and as long as they don't find her, I don't care what else happens.

Then I look back at the GAP.

"No," I say. "You're wrong. I haven't changed at all."

"I have," says Ro, stepping forward. "And here's the thing." Ro looks at the GAP. "I can kill you now, and you're gone. In that scenario, there is no more GAP Miyazawa." He grins. "And that's what will have changed."

"All right," the GAP says calmly. But Ro won't be calmed. Not now.

"Sure, another Ambassador rises to take your place—fills the tiny, tiny void left by your death—but it's not you. And for those critical few days, the whole system goes down."

"Stop it," says the GAP. "You don't understand who your real enemy is."

He's anxious. I can feel it. He knows exactly what Ro is capable of. He's probably been tracking us, watching us, this whole time.

Ro especially.

"Oh, I'm pretty sure I do. The No Face, they may want the planet, but you're the ones handing it to them. They may have shut down the Silent Cities, but you're the ones building their new weapons." For someone as crazy as Ro usually is, he's speaking with remarkable clarity.

"I don't know what you're talking about," says the GAP, as blankly as he can.

"The village down there? You know the one, just down the river," Tima says, stepping forward.

Lucas looks the GAP in the eye. "You'll have to excuse us if the prospect of being turned into human soup isn't all that appealing."

"What was that?" I ask, looking at the others. "Instant primordial stew?"

"Mmm," says Ro. "Yummy."

"You're children," says the GAP. "You don't under-stand—this is just a game to you. You don't know who you're fighting against. Not like I do."

"I think we do." Ro holds out his hand, wiggling his fingers in the GAP's face. "And you know what I also think? I think it's time to torch this place."

The GAP's eyes widen. Before he says a word, Sympas dive for Ro, pulling weapons from their holsters.

Bad move.

That's when the world erupts in flame—all around us. The few remaining villagers flee around us, in all directions. The screams nearly drown out the noise of gunfire as Sympas begin to fire—but the smoke makes it too difficult to see, and their weapons are soon too hot to even hold.

Ro is out of control.

Lucas and Tima and I dive to the stone floor, flinging ourselves over the walled temple perimeter, and down the stone steps into the jungle.

Doi Suthep is quickly becoming a war zone. If the GAP survives this firestorm, I think, he's no more human than the Lords. And if Ro can set off this kind of blast, I think he might not be, either.

When the GAP's Chopper ignites, I see it in their faces. They're finally afraid.

When it explodes, they're terrified.

———— • ————

As we watch the mountaintop go up in flames, the rock beneath our feet begins to rumble. The ground quakes and splits around me, stone twisting and erupting as easily as if it were simply mud.

I scream but the ground between us shifts too quickly, sending us rolling down different sides of a newly formed and strangely deep chasm.

I recognize the first black tendril as soon as it pushes up from the earth, uncurling like a Mission beanstalk.

But this is no beanstalk.

The obsidian roots are all too familiar.

Lucas lifts his mud-streaked, soot-covered face. "An Icon? Here?"

Tima lies on the ground, pushing away from it with her feet. The ground is rolling too much to stand. I know, because I'm clinging to the trunk of a teak tree with two hands, and I can barely stay up.

An Icon.

Here.

Because we're here.

Because it follows us, follows me.

Even without the shard.

"But that's impossible. We got rid of that thing. The shard." I'm shouting over the noise of the earth splitting.

"We did," calls Lucas. "But how much do you want to bet the GAP is holding on to one of his own?"

The screaming from the direction of the temple confirms the truth of Lucas's words—and by the time everything is quiet again, I can't feel a single Sympa there at all.

I felt them burn.

I felt them crumble into ash.

I felt their skin melt and their bones shatter.

But not now.

Not anymore. Now, they're just gone. The aggression and the emptiness and the fear—all gone.

It's over.

It isn't until I'm pulling Lucas to his feet that I look across the flattened teak and palms to see Sparrow standing safely in the center of the jungle.

Watching as the mountaintop burns.

MARKED URGENT
MARKED EYES ONLY

Internal Investigative Subcommittee IIS211B
RE: The Incident at SEA Colonies

Note: Contact Jasmine3k, Virt. Hybrid Human 39261.SEA, Laboratory Assistant to Dr. E. Yang, for future commentary, as necessary.

FORTIS
Transcript - ComLog 02.23.2070
FORTIS::NULL

//comlog begin;

sendline: Are you ready for some suggestions?;
return: I am.;

sendline: You need to prepare the planet for something new, correct?;
return: Yes.;

sendline: I assume that includes a complete reset of the ecosystem. Essentially sterilizing the planet, replanting, repopulating?;

return: Yes.;

sendline: But you weren't prepared to meet with locals with the kind of, say, sophistication you see here?;

return: That is one aspect of my current decision-making challenge.;

sendline: Knowing what I do about your…assets…and knowing what I do about the locals, I would suggest that your current plan of action, so far as I understand it, is flawed. It would involve significant losses and potential failure for your objectives.;

return: It is not without risks.;

sendline: I have an idea, one derived from our extensive experience in expansion and colonization.;

return: I have analyzed your history, but did not consider using it as strategic material.;

sendline: That's why you need me!;

comlink terminated;
//comlog end;
//lognote: God, I hope this works.;

INTRODUCTIONS

33

"Come on, Sparrow!" I call across the jungle. Sparrow looks at me, smiling. She claps her hands and the birds at her feet fly away, startled.

"You're safe now. We can go." I motion toward the burning mountaintop. "I have to make sure my friends are all right. Come back up."

She nods, waving her arms over her head.

Yes. I understand.

I retrace my steps to the stone stairwell, Tima and Lucas at my side.

Sparrow is still minutes behind us.

The scene isn't one I'd wish on any child, but then, none of us is exactly that. Not even Sparrow.

It's hard to see past the smoke and rubble, especially since the fires are only now starting to go out.

As we all know, Ro is much better at starting fires than putting them out.

I see Fortis and Bibi across the courtyard, trying to douse him with holy water. Everyone—all three of them—is covered with a thick layer of black soot.

But the truly frightening sight is GAP Miyazawa, the General Ambassador.

The former General Ambassador.

Because a particularly thick obsidian shard has gored him through the chest. It continues to curl beyond him, as if the GAP's human body is nothing, a trivial impediment along the way.

Most of his Sympas, on the other hand, are halfway down a chasm. I can only see parts of the tops of their heads—and a hand or two, still clutching at the muddy earth—it's so deep in there.

"Fitting, don't you think?" It's Lucas, standing behind me. "Seeing as the GAP considered himself the big defender of the Earth? And now his Sympas find themselves—you know—"

"Taking a dirt nap?" Tima asks innocently, with half a grin.

Lucas and Ro and I start laughing, in spite of everything. I wipe soot out of my eyes. "Ah, Doc. I miss the guy."

"Where are the rest of the Sympas?" Tima looks around, but she's right. There isn't a single soldier in sight.

Lucas shrugs. "Gone, I guess. I'd take off too, if I saw that thing coming for me."

I smile. "What, Ro? Or the Icon roots?"

"Either one," says Lucas.

Tima nods. "He's right. I don't actually know which would be more terrifying."

"I do," says Ro, and I turn to see him, reaching to hug me. His skin is still nearly too hot to touch.

"Ro. You did it. You saved us." I bury my face in his neck, in spite of the fact that Lucas is standing right there, in spite of everything.

I can't help myself.

"Don't I always fix everything?" He smiles, reaching for Tima, too. Even Lucas claps him once on the back. Which for him is something.

"Either that, or the other thing. You know, that thing you do?" I pretend to think. "Oh yeah, wreck everything."

Ro lets out a sharp laugh, and I grin back at him. By the time we pull away from each other, it feels how it used to feel. It feels like the Mission, like the beach, like home.

Even if it never will be again, I savor it while I can. Ro's my family, my oldest friend. I can't pretend not to feel that.

Not to love that.

Love him.

Then I hear a small voice in the distance. "Doloria? Are you there?"

It's Sparrow, coming toward me, stumbling her way through the smoke.

I hold out my hand to her and she sees me, and runs in my direction across the uneven ground.

"Careful," I say, smiling.

She smiles back.

Her fingers stretch toward mine, soft and round. We reach for each other—

And her fingers slip through mine.

I stand there, looking at my own hand in shock. I try again, but it's no different. I'm clutching at air.

Because she isn't real.

She isn't there.

This isn't happening.

Sparrow stands in front of me, staring at her own fingers.

Then she starts lowering them, one at a time. Counting in reverse.

"Five."

"Fortis, what's happening?" I'm pleading, but he only takes a step backward.

"Four."

He looks at me, strangely. "Doloria. I think you had better back away now."

"Three."

Lucas takes my hand. "Dol. I don't know what's going on—but we need to go."

"Two."

Now only one of Sparrow's fingers—her pointer finger—remains extended. She raises it in front of her face, studying it.

"What's happening, Sparrow?"

Sparrow looks up at the sky and smiles. "Birds." But birds are not the only thing in this sky. Next to me, Sparrow's hair begins to blow.

"What is it, Sparrow?"

"Not what, sister. Who."

"Who, Sparrow?" I can feel the tears running down my face. "Who's coming?"

The noise grows louder.

Sparrow looks at her finger. That's when I realize she isn't counting.

She's pointing.

She's pointing to the sky.

"Who is it? Who?" I'm not crying. Not anymore. I'm screaming.

I'm also feeling.

I feel something I haven't felt in a long, long time.

Something as searing and vivid and unmistakable as hot wax dripping on my bare feet.

A twinge of a suspicion that becomes a burning truth.

"They're here."

Them. Not Sympas. Not the GAP. Something more dangerous than both of them combined.

The whole mountain feels as if it were coming down. Worse than any fire, than any earthquake. Worse than the Icon roots.

Maybe it is, I think.

This is worse than the Idylls.

Because it isn't the ground that's moving.

It's the sky.

The silver ships come sliding down from the clouds, reflecting the sun so brightly it's hard to tell them from the real one.

One by one they sink toward the earth, moving too quickly to be anything from Earth—and with too great a surety.

A military formation.

Five ships.

A squadron.

In the shape of a pentagon.

It's too late to run. It's too late to hide. As the sky splits open, all we can do is watch.

"Don't cry, Doloria."

I look at the child who is not a child, who is not there, who is nothing.

"Why can't I feel your hand?"

My eyes are brimming—I can barely see her face.

"You're a projection, right? Or maybe a dream? A Virt? Is there any part of you that's real at all?"

Sparrow looks at me somberly. "Sister."

"Please," I say. "Tell me."

"Doloria. You were—I don't have the right words." She closes her eyes. "A thing of beauty." She smiles. "That's it."

I can't breathe.

I can't believe she just said that.

Something I have heard before, but only in a dream. And not from her.

From Null.

From the strange voice, the one in the dreams, and even the bird.

The voice I heard when the Idylls were falling.

The name I heard when Fortis was being taken, back in the desert.

My stomach twists.

Now my words won't come—they don't want to come—but I force them out anyway.

"Who is it, Sparrow? Who is in those ships?"

Sparrow smiles at me, a child's smile, full of perfect innocence and perfect affection.

"I think you know, sister."

"I don't know." I try not to feel. I try not to feel this, above all other things.

"Doloria."

"Say it. Just say it."

She closes her eyes again, just as her mouth forms the word.

"Me."

No sooner does she say the word than her body flickers, like a frozen digi-screen.

Flickers—and disappears.

GENERAL EMBASSY DISPATCH: EASTASIA SUBSTATION

MARKED URGENT
MARKED EYES ONLY

Internal Investigative Subcommittee IIS211B
RE: The Incident at SEA Colonies

Note: Contact Jasmine3k, Virt. Hybrid Human 39261.SEA, Laboratory Assistant to Dr. E. Yang, for future commentary, as necessary.

PRIVATE RESEARCH NOTES
Paulo Fortissimo
03/01/2070

I BELIEVE THE BEST CHANCE WE HAVE TO GET THROUGH THIS IS TO DRAW THIS THING OUT. I DON'T SEE ANY WAY TO KEEP NULL FROM LANDING, BUT MAYBE WE CAN FORCE NULL TO TAKE LONGER THAN HE WANTS, AND HOPEFULLY GIVE US TIME TO FIGHT BACK. THE WEAPONS HE HAS ARE NOT ENOUGH TO WIPE OUT THE POPULATION IN ONE BLOW, AND AS LONG AS THERE IS ONE HUMAN ALIVE, NULL HAS A PROBLEM.

I WOULD HAVE NULL SET UP A LOCAL GOVERNMENT

INFRASTRUCTURE AND USE US TO POLICE OURSELVES.
USE US TO BUILD THE "EQUIPMENT," WHATEVER THAT
IS, THAT HE NEEDS TO TURN THE PLANET INTO MULCH.

IF NULL PROCEEDS WITH HIS INSTRUCTIONS, AS I
UNDERSTAND IT, HE MAY PULL IT OFF, OR IT MAY END UP
IN MUTUALLY ASSURED DESTRUCTION OF BOTH SIDES. NOT
MUCH TO LOOK FORWARD TO THERE FOR YOURS TRULY.

I ALSO AM DETECTING WHAT FEELS LIKE HESITANCE
FROM NULL. I HAVE TO GET BEHIND THAT. MAYBE HE HAS
AN ACHILLES HEEL... OR SERVO? ACHILLES FUNCTION?

34
SALUTATIONS

Only one ship lands.

Thank the Blessed Lady.

It is only when it crushes legions of palms and teaks around us that we realize how enormous the Lords' ships really are.

This one has landed at the base of the stone stairs leading down from Doi Suthep.

I stand at the top of the stairs, between the two immense, carved serpents that curve down the sides of the steps.

Between two serpents, and in front of my three best friends in the world.

It's the only place I can stand and be able to take in the whole scene.

So when a rectangle of light appears on the front side of the silver ship, I am the first to see it. I won't let the others come any closer than I already am.

I'm the one who led us here.

I'm the one who walked right into this trap.

It's my fault.

It's my problem.

Now the rectangle of light shines more brightly. Now it takes the shape of something more solid, an actual, dimensional polygon.

A doorway.

Brutus flattens himself against the ground and starts to whine.

A small, slender figure appears inside the door.

He stands for a moment, staring at me as I stare at him. Then, he steps out into the world beyond the ship. Our world.

His feet are unsteady, reminding me of so many things. Sparrow, running across the stones. Maybe a piglet from Ramona Jamona's first litter. A buckle-kneed colt or calf, in the Mission barn, when it first tries to stand.

This isn't a colt or a pig or a calf.

It's a boy.

No.

A girl.

No.

It's something that looks like a human child.

394

Its face is smooth and clear—features sharp, eyes bright. It doesn't look like a flesh-and-blood human child, but it doesn't look like an alien presence, either.

Then again, what do I know? It never even occurred to me that Sparrow had no corporeal presence. I'd touched her, taken her hand, so many times—in my dreams.

It felt real enough to me.

But this time, I know who—or what—I'm talking to. It—this thing—feels familiar.

I feel it in my head now, just as I always have, ever since the first night I dreamed it.

The thing that called itself Null, once.

Sparrow, another time.

A child and a man and a life force, a death force—I don't know which. Not anymore.

But now it reaches for me with its mind. I let it come to me.

It's you. I told you I would come. You didn't believe me. You are very brave.

I hope you will survive. I do not believe that you will, but I hope you do.

Hope.

I say nothing, but I listen.

More than it did for the Silent Cities, before it destroyed them.

Then the thing's lips stretch wide into something not so different from a smile.

I hear a voice. A spoken voice, out in the world—our world. It's low, too low to belong to a child.

Then again, this isn't a child at all.

Not really.

And again, who am I to judge what is and what is not a human? A person?

When I find that I am possibly neither of those things myself.

But I know that this one moment is either the end or the beginning of my life.

Then I stop thinking and start listening, because it speaks two words, and two words only.

The wind carries them up to the steps to me.

"Hello world."

———— • ————

I stand there, with my friends by my side, staring at it. *Null. Sparrow. The Lords.* Whatever you want to call it.

The end of humanity.

"What do you want?" I shout down at it, because I refuse to connect to this thing in my mind.

Not now.

Not ever again.

"Unification," it says. "Today is Unification Day."

"You've made some kind of mistake. That was some GAP lie. We don't celebrate that day, not the four of us."

"But this is why we have come. For you. For us."

"What are you talking about?"

"Our reunification. I am the fifth Icon. We are meant to be together. We are one thing."

"No, we're not. You're a liar."

"I am the future."

"You're a Lord, and you're Null."

"I am hope."

"You aren't hope. Don't you dare say that. You know what Null means? 'Nothing.' You're nothing."

"We are all nothing, Doloria. Why should hope belong only to humanity?"

"We're human, and you're nothing like us. Nothing," I say again, and I realize now I'm sobbing.

Null—it—holds out its hand.

"Come," it says. "Come with us."

I shake my head. The more it says to me, the more I dig in—and the more loudly I shout.

"Go ahead. Stop my heart. I'm not going with you. I'm not going anywhere."

Lucas slides his arm around my waist. "Of course you're not. And this conversation is over."

Tima takes my hand. "You're not alone, Dol. You can't do this without us. We're here."

Ro steps in front of me. "Here," he says, simply. "Right here."

"Ro," I say, smiling, "you can't—"

But I don't finish, because I feel a hand on my arm and turn to see Fortis. His face is strangely soft, and his eyes are as red as mine. When he speaks, his voice is so quiet I have to strain to hear it.

"Dol. They're not going to give up. They need you. It needs you. All of you." He looks at the four of us. "You might as well go peacefully. You can't outrun them, and you can't outlive this. Be reasonable for once."

"Reasonable? What are you talking about?" My head is reeling; none of this is what I was expecting to hear. Then I catch a glimpse of Bibi pacing behind Fortis, and I'm certain Fortis once again knows more than he's saying.

He looks pained.

"This," he says. "There had to be some part of you that knew. You had to have suspected."

"Suspected what?" Tima's face is pale. I don't dare look at the boys.

"Me. This. What did you think, when I disappeared from the campsite? And returned completely unharmed? Fit as a fiddle an' without a probe shoved up my—" Fortis shakes his head.

"You mean they were tracking you, this whole time?" Tima looks stricken.

"No, you little idiot. I was trackin' you, this whole time. It's what they pay me for, how I've outlived The Day, all these years."

"Because—" I can't say the words.

"Because I promised them they could have you. Because you've been theirs from the start. Because I only knew how to build you the way they wanted me to."

I turn to face Fortis. "I don't believe you. You wouldn't do it. Not to us."

"How did you think I got away from the Lords in the desert? Or for that matter, why do you think they came for me in the first place?"

"Fortis!" My stomach drops.

"My name is Paulo Fortissimo. I made first contact. It was my lab. The Lords, bastards though they may be, are here at my invitation." He shrugs. "Not so much invitation as recommendation. You were engineered for this purpose, all along. Their purpose. It was the one thing they didn't have."

"What are you talking about?"

"Human emotions are unique in the universe. Emotions, and the power they generate. Drives that cause you to fight with a strength and an energy that go far beyond the survival instinct. You four, with your powers." He shakes his head. "Emotions incarnate. The Lords have never encountered anything like it." He looks at me meaningfully. "Like you. You understand now? They're why you exist. The Lords. They're why you're here. They think you will help them not just survive but dominate the whole of the existing universe."

"But—the fail-safe. That's what we are," I say, remembering the Embassy archive. "That's all we are."

"Not exactly. That was just the easiest way to get you to come along for the ride."

"Then what are we?" I want an explanation. I want answers. I want Fortis to look me in the eye and confess. *And then I want to kill him.*

"You heard what it said." Fortis looks away, shrugging.

"No, I didn't. I didn't hear anything that explained what we are or how we came to be like this."

"I made you, sure enough. Me an' Bibi an' Ela an' Yang. They didn't know where I got the specifications— they only knew we were engineering the four of you for a militarized unit. One that the four of us started an' only I finished. I let them think our work had failed. It was the only way."

"The Humanity Project," I venture.

"That's the one."

I slap him in the face. It's all I can do not to rip him to pieces with my bare hands.

"How could you?"

"How could I? I'm a Merk, darlin'. You've always known that. What did you think I was here to do? You didn't think I was really here to save the world, did you?"

Ro is incredulous. "Why bother, then? What was that back at the Hole? Why take out one of their Icons?"

400

Steady, Ro.

Not now.

Don't do anything stupid.

"You had to believe me. All of you. I had to sell it. Not just to you, but to the Embassies. The GAP himself."

Lucas raises his voice. "Then who is Ela?"

"Ela was her nickname."

Lucas nods. "Let me guess. It stood for her initials." A shadow flickers across his face.

"That's right." Fortis nods. "L.A."

"L.A. Leta Amare. Ela was my mother. She did this. With you and Bibi and Yang."

"You each needed a biosource."

"A what?"

"A Physical Human. A genetic source."

"You mean, a parent."

Fortis nods.

"And Leta was my biological mother?"

"That's right."

Lucas looks relieved, in spite of her—in spite of everything.

"What about the rest of us?" Tima asks, suddenly.

"Isn't it obvious?"

No, I think. *None of this is obvious.*

"Dr. Yang?"

Fortis nods. Tima's face falls, but I see her thinking through it, the details, the mannerisms.

401

Ro looks at him. "And me?"

Bibi sighs. "And now you see why I have so much trouble with the Middle Path." He's right. Hurling stones in his backyard makes a lot more sense, when you think about him as Ro's father.

The color drains out of Ro's face as he considers the possibility.

Which means only one thing.

"You? The greatest traitor the Earth has ever known, and you're my biological father?" I can barely force myself to think the words, let alone say them.

Fortis smiles. "You think it was an accident, my findin' you on the Tracks that day? Been keepin' an eye on you for years, love."

I want to gouge his eyes out with my fingernails.

Soon, I think.

Soon.

402

GENERAL EMBASSY DISPATCH:
EASTASIA SUBSTATION

MARKED URGENT
MARKED EYES ONLY

Internal Investigative Subcommittee IIS211B
RE: The Incident at SEA Colonies

Note: Contact Jasmine3k, Virt. Hybrid Human 39261.SEA, Laboratory Assistant to Dr. E. Yang, for future commentary, as necessary.

FORTIS
Transcript - ComLog 03.20.2070
FORTIS::NULL

//comlog begin;

sendline: I have a plan that I think will get you where you want to go. And, I assume, will get me what I want in return. Before I offer it up, do we have a deal?;
return: Upon repeated reflection, I agree your help would be important, perhaps critical to my success. I can accommodate your request for a safe haven without compromising my primary mission.;

sendline: Smashing. I'll ask for particulars later, but this is fantastic news. As for my ideas, I have considered what I know about human nature, the behaviors of individuals and how they respond as groups, and the sad, violent history of our people. And I have a better understanding of the tools you have. I don't think you have enough to subdue (i.e., eliminate) the entire population as you have planned.;
return: Yes.;

//comlog ctd;

ENDINGS AND BEGINNINGS

There is more, of course. More to be said. More truths to be demanded. Probably more lies to be told.

Other things, too.

But the Lord Child is impatient. Human drama is not so impressive, I imagine. Not when you've already executed billions of humans.

"Come, Doloria. We will begin with you. We will return for the others. There is much work to be done with each of you."

"I'm not going with you." It's my decision, and I fold my arms.

They can come for me.

They can do what they will.

I'm not going with the creatures who killed my family.

I'm not letting my friends be led to their deaths because of me, either.

"You don't have a choice," Null says. "The bargain has been made. You belong to us. You always have. We created you."

"I'm not a shard you can come for. I'm not part of your death machine."

"But you are. And you have no choice. You are part of us. You belong with us." Null looks at me, expressionless, and I wonder how long it will be before that facade cracks.

At this rate, not long.

I can feel the frustration climbing the stairs between us.

Ro steps in front of me again. "Yes, she does have a choice. And she's made it. She's not going with you."

"That's not a matter for you to decide, Furo Costas." Null blinks, impassive. Talking to it is like talking to Doc.

Ro isn't buying it. "You know, now that I think about it, it is."

"Why is that?" Null asks.

"Because she's not going. Because I say so." Ro takes another step down toward the ship. "And because I'll go in her place."

Null looks up, interested. I can feel the spike in the energy between us.

"That, Furo Costas, is a different proposition entirely. Let us think."

I grab Ro's hand from behind. "Ro, stop it. You can't do that."

He pulls his hand away from mine. "I can. In fact, I am."

I'm starting to panic. "Don't. Don't do this. Stay with us. Stay with me. We'll make our stand. We'll go out together. We'll go out fighting, just like you always wanted."

He smiles at me, sadly. "That was never what I wanted, Dol. You were all I wanted."

My heart is racing. "Stop. You can't."

He steps up, closer to me now. "You were all I wanted, and you have to let me do this. I don't want to be here anymore. Not like this. You don't need me down here. You can take care of yourself." Ro nods to Lucas. "And Buttons. You've been taking care of him since the day we found him, all washed up on the beach."

I can't stop the tears from coming. "I don't want you to do this."

He wipes a tear from my cheek. "It's not up to you. I'm a fighter, remember? This is what I do. Find something worth fighting for, and then fight."

I shake my head. "You're crazy."

"I'm not. I'm smart. You're it, Dol. You're worth fighting for. Let me fight."

"You don't have to do this," Tima says from behind me.

Lucas clears his throat. "She's right. None of us wants you to do this."

Ro smiles. "I don't have to do anything. But once I'm doing it, you know you can't stop me."

Ro pulls me close, leaning in toward me. I see his lips, just for a moment, and I remember.

They'd be soft.

Softer than his ears.

They'd taste like pomegranate seeds.

Then Ro kisses me, hard and fast, and pulls back from me the moment I give in to him.

That's always how it is for us.

"Promise you'll come back," I say. It's all I can think— all I can bear.

"Will that make this easier?" He grins.

I nod.

"Then I promise." He strokes the side of my face.

"You have to mean it," I insist, stubbornly.

"I do. I'll behave. And I'll come back for you. I promise."

I pull him close, burying my face in his chest as I have so many times before.

He pulls my face up to his and turns it, gently kissing my cheek.

Then he whispers into my ear.

I hear the words and I know they mean goodbye. "Love you, Dol-face."

"I know, Doofus." I can't look at him. It's too horrible, too unbearably sad.

Then he grabs Tima and kisses her on the mouth. She looks surprised, and he laughs.

Fortis holds out his hand and Ro just nods at him.

"Take care, Buttons," Ro says to Lucas. "Or I'll come down here and thump you myself."

Then he's down the stairs, two at a time, only stopping when he reaches the ship.

I hold my breath.

We all do.

Even Fortis can't bring himself to look away.

Ro nods at the Lord Child—Null, the monster—and ducks his head beneath the top of the rectangle of light.

I see him, a dark outline inside the bright doorway, lifting his hand in a wave to us.

And then he's gone.

We watch, together, as the bright patch of light disappears.

We watch as the jungle floor around the ship begins to rumble, as the winds begin to whip in all directions.

We watch as the ship rises, pushing upward toward the other four, finding its place in the pentagon.

And then we watch, in disbelief, as the whole thing erupts into a ball of flame.

Ro. No—

I don't know if I'm thinking his name or screaming it.

All I know is, I remember the words in my head as

clearly as if he were saying them in my ear. *"They come for me, you have my permission to shoot. I'm not hitching a ride with a No Face."*

That's what Ro said, and now he's gone.

Now Ro is dust in the sky.

Now Ro is nothing.

Nothing, like Null.

That's all I remember.

That, and Tima screaming, and the ships streaking across the sky.

That, and Fortis fleeing.

That, and Bibi trying to hold me up.

That, and Lucas carrying me down the steps.

That, and blacking out.

GENERAL EMBASSY DISPATCH:
EASTASIA SUBSTATION

MARKED URGENT
MARKED EYES ONLY

Internal Investigative Subcommittee IIS211B
RE: The Incident at SEA Colonies

Note: Contact Jasmine3k, Virt. Hybrid Human 39261.SEA,
Laboratory Assistant to Dr. E. Yang, for future commentary,
as necessary.

FORTIS
Transcript - ComLog 03.20.2070 ctd.
FORTIS::NULL

//comlog begin;

sendline: I would recommend strategic placement of your
assets, combined with a local puppet government, giving
people the illusion of a future. Then using the population to
advance and achieve your objective.;
return: I see the parallels in your history.;

sendline: If you choose the right people, and the right

targets, I believe you can build up your equipment in such a way that by the time the people know what is happening, it will be too late. You will have an overwhelming force at your disposal.;
return: Historical precedent. Logical. Interesting.;

//comlog end;

EPILOGUE

Not everything that comes from the sky is an angel.

It's true.

And not everything that lives on the Earth is a human.

Also true.

I've learned that now. I've learned it the hard way, and I wish to the Blessed Lady that I hadn't.

They say everything changed on The Day, but that's not the way I see it. Not anymore.

Some things remained the same—or at least, I thought they did.

Humans were still humans, even if their hearts had stopped beating. Some of them.

Cities were still cities, even if they were Silent. Some of them.

Fundamentally, the universe was still a reliable place,

made of goods and bads, Sympas and Grass, humans and Lords.

Until today.

Today was the day I learned the battle doesn't just lie in the Embassies, or the sky, or even the universe.

The battle lies in this Lord Child. This girl who is not a girl, this boy who is not a boy. This everything called Sparrow and this nothing called Null.

And the battle lies in Fortis. My father. Who lies quite a bit, as well.

Worst of all, the battle is in me.

Chumash Rancheros Spaniards Californians Americans Grass The Lords The Hole Me.

I'm Doloria Maria de la Cruz, and this is my story. The story of me, and the story of my people.

But what am I?

I'm not hope. I'm not the thing with feathers. Not anymore. I've changed. I am change.

And I'm not best friend to Furo Costas. Not anymore. He's dead, as dead as the Lord who took him.

I should know. My heart died with him.

Which also means I'm not girlfriend to Lucas Amare. Not anymore. I'm too broken for that.

And I'm not my parents' daughter. Not anymore. They were lies, props, the figment of someone else's imagination.

I'm not even Sparrow's sister. Not anymore. She was

only real in my dreams, only as human as I made her.

And what do I know about humans?

Only this:

My name is Doloria Maria de la Cruz, and I'm not just the end of childhood.

I'm the end of humanity.

And if you come from the skies—

I'm coming for you.

GENERAL EMBASSY DISPATCH:
EASTASIA SUBSTATION

MARKED URGENT
MARKED EYES ONLY

Internal Investigative Subcommittee IIS211B
RE: The Incident at SEA Colonies

Note: Contact Jasmine3k, Virt. Hybrid Human 39261.SEA, Laboratory Assistant to Dr. E. Yang, for future commentary, as necessary.

FORTIS
Transcript: Comlog {date scrubbed}
FORTIS::NULL

//comlog begin;

sendline: NULL. Based on the information you provided, the number of devices, I have some suggestions for you.;
return: Please continue.;

sendline: You have 13 devices—I will upload suggestions for the ideal targets. These are not purely population driven.

I considered also capacity for production, manufacturing, etc.;

sendline: I also recommend establishing a temporary system for maintaining order during your preparation.;

sendline: If you can subdue the population, you can also use existing resources more effectively to prepare, also reducing the risk of catastrophic failure.;

sendline: I believe this is the most efficient way to accomplish your mission.;

delayed response;

sendline: Hello?;
return: And in exchange?;

delayed response;

sendline: I want my own colony.;

sendline: I need something.;

sendline: I don't know what I want.;

sendline: I'll know it when I see it.;

sendline: I'm not being mercenary.;

sendline: I'm being logical.;

sendline: . . . . . hello?;

transmission terminated;

//comlog ended;

ACKNOWLEDGMENTS

It's difficult to write difficult books, and this was that. That doesn't mean we shouldn't write them, but it doesn't mean we should try to go at it alone, either. Many of my own personal *Icons* and *Idols* along the way have come to my rescue, time and time again. I am so much more than grateful for my team, in New York and around the world.

Thanks to my *Idols* at the Gernert Company: Sarah Burnes, my agent and friend; along with Logan Garrison, Will Robert, and Rebecca Gardner.

Thanks to my *Idols* at Little, Brown: Kate Sullivan and Julie Scheina, my genius editors on this project; along with Leslie Shumate and Pam Garfinkel, their genius editorial assistants.

Thanks as well to the tireless Hallie Patterson and Melanie Chang, for publicity; Dave Caplan, for cover design; Barbara Bakowski and Barbara Perris, for copyediting; Victoria Stapleton and Zoe Luderitz, for the support from school and library services; Megan Tingley and Andrew Smith, for the support from publishing.

Thanks to my assistants, Victoria Hill and Zelda Wengrod, who are like family; and of course, thanks to my actual family: Lewis, Emma, May, and Kate Peterson, as well as all the Stohls everywhere.

In particular, thanks to Eunei Lee and Lewis Peterson, my Southeast Asian travel buddies; and to Raphael Simon, Melissa de la Cruz, and Kami Garcia, who had to hear all the stories.

And finally: Thanks to the readers, librarians, teachers, bloggers, social media friends and followers, journalists, fellow authors, and fans who have supported both Kami and me for the past six years, since *Beautiful Creatures*.

I will always idolize all of you, you iconic and beautiful creatures!

XO, Margie